Murder in Vancouver 1886

Marion Crook

Epicenter Press Inc.
Alaska Book Adventures™

Seattle, WA

published by Epicenter Press

Epicenter Press
6524 NE 181st St. Suite 2
Kenmore, WA 98028.
For more information go to:
www.Camelpress.com
www.Coffeetownpress.com
www.Epicenterpress.com

Author website: marioncrookauthor.com

This is a work of fiction. Names, characters, places,
brands, media, and incidents are the product of the
author's imagination or are used fictitiously with the
exception of some well-known places and people who
lived in Vancouver 1886.

ISBN: 9781684921614 (trade paper)
ISBN: 9781684921621 (ebook)

LOC: 2023945719

DEDICATION

To the many readers who enjoy living
vicariously in another era.

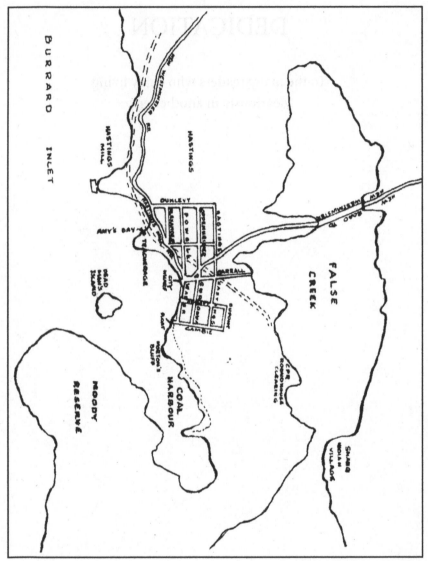

Map courtesy of Glen Crook

AUTHOR'S NOTE

My thanks to the staff of the Vancouver City Archives and my local library who made their material on Vancouver's early life available to me. My thanks to Glen Crook who drew the map of Vancouver 1886.

The main characters of the story are fictitious but minor characters such as the mayor, Superintendent Roycroft and Mr. Alexander lived at that time. The methods of logging, the state of the streets, the newspaper stories, and the everyday small facts of life in Vancouver are reported as they were.

The plot of rebellion, Amy's home on the spit of land and her position as school teacher are creations of the author. A Mr. Palmer was the school teacher at Hastings Mill in 1886. The anti-Chinese riots occurred on Feb. 24th, 1887, not June, 1886. The North-west Rebellion took place in 1885 and in 1886 people were fearful there would be another uprising. The mood of the new city of Vancouver: the business dealings, the advance of the railroad, the possibility of amalgamation with the United States and the promise of trade with China are accurate reflections of the life in the city at that time. Many of the details of the fire are as reported in old newspaper accounts. The Indigenous people in Kitsilano and the North Shore rescued many who fled the fire. There was no need to create those incidents as they actually occurred. Vancouverites rebounded quickly and in five weeks had constructed buildings and homes.

MURDER IN VANCOUVER 1886

Vancouver, 1886, is a bustling city with a growing population and tantalizing opportunities. Some of those opportunities are illegal. When Amy MacDonald, the school teacher at Hastings Mill, discovers new Winchester '86 rifles are being smuggled through the city, she tries to enlist the aid of the earnest but slow-witted provincial policeman. She involves a curious local newspaperman, a businessman, a knowledgeable woman of the street, and her irrepressible younger brother in her efforts to prevent the contraband from flowing to the Métis re¬bels in the North West.

Vancouver life is complicated by the murder of a Métis man, the persecution of the Chinese people living in the city and the intent of the mob to oust the Chinese onto boats and out of the new city. Amy manages to move between different the levels of society but not without risk of being dismissed from her teaching position. She tries to do what she believe is morally right without being discovered. All her plans and careful stratagems are disrupted suddenly and dramatically by the devastating, overwhelming fire.

MISS MACDONALD OF VANCOUVER -1886

In June of 1886, the new city of Vancouver bustles with a growing population and increasing opportunities for business and trade. When Amy MacDonald, the school teacher at Hastings Mill, discovers new Winchester '86 rifles are being smuggled through the city, she tries to enlist the aid of the earnest but slow-witted provincial policeman. She involves a curious local newspaperman, a businessman, a knowledgeable woman of the street, and her irrepressible younger brother in her efforts to prevent the contraband from flowing to the Métis rebels in the North West.

Vancouver life is complicated by the murder of a Métis and the persecution of the Chinese living in the city and the intent of the mob to oust the Chinese onto boats and out of the new city. Amy's teaching life is tinged with tragedy as childhood diseases cause deaths in the community, no more than is usual for a small city, but hard to accept. Amy manages to move between different levels of society but not without risk of being dismissed from her position. She tries to do what she believes is morally right, even imperative, without being discovered. All her plans and careful stratagems are abruptly disrupted.

CHAPTER ONE

The path from the teacherage to the Hastings Mill School followed the road for most of the way and then turned onto the wide plank boardwalk to the school door. The air was fresh this morning—only a little smoke hanging in the air as usual. A light breeze blowing toward the inlet ruffled my skirt and sent tiny dust devils scurrying in circles in front of me.

"Ain't usual, Miss MacDonald," the lamplighter told me last week. "We always get rain and some miserable weather every month, especially in June."

I hadn't seen rain since April.

The salt from the ocean and the heavy sweet scent of blackberries blossoms mingled with the dust of the road. Closer to the school the smells of the mill prevailed: the grease from the machinery, wood-smoke from the cook shack, the sharp odor of sawdust and fresh wood shavings.

It was early in the day but the whine of the saws and the thump of heavy machinery in the low building near the wharf told me the men were already busy. A man shouted at a horse, winches creaked and groaned as logs bumped against each other and fell over the edge of the embankment in a sudden crescendo of sound to crash in the water below.

Smoke from the burner billowed over the houses near the mill. I was high enough to see past the rough board homes to the trees beyond. This was very different from Ontario. There, the houses had tidy gardens of flowers and shrubs and well-pruned trees of apple and cherry and, occasionally, trimmed evergreens. Here the trees, the reason for all this industry, had been cleared from the settled area and kept back as though they were a menace. There were boards, bark, and debris on the streets and in the water but, except for a few deciduous behind the school, no trees until the far edge of the clearing. There, they stood thick and tall. The forest stretched away from the cabins and cottages of Hastings, marching into the wilderness for miles. The mill had only cut timber on this piece of land between Burrard Inlet and False Creek. Soon they were going to move south and east into the trees between Hastings and New Westminster to supply the great world market for masts and spars. The mill had been operating since 1869—seventeen years—and yet the surrounding settlement still looked like a temporary town, ready to be abandoned the minute the mill shut down.

Ten sailing ships in the harbour waited for the long spars to be transported to San Francisco, Australia, and Europe. Holes had been cut into the ships' sterns to fit the 30-to-60-foot spars. Hastings Mill had orders for all the spars they could make and, by the looks of the forests around us and across the inlet to the north; the mill will be operating for hundreds of years yet.

I paused for a moment as I neared the mill yard and watched the oxen skid logs to the top of the embankment. The driver halted the big beasts and pulled a chain free, standing back as the huge logs tumbled down the greased cross poles into the water below. Spray rose into the air and the logs in the boom heaved on the ensuing waves until they settled again into a quiet pattern of brown and yellow lines.

My school day would start soon. I tucked my hair into its roll above my ears and at the back of my head and prayed it would stay there. It took a great deal of effort to keep tidy, but I was determined to be a good example of respectability to the children. I was Amy MacDonald, school teacher of Hastings Mills, and I had position to maintain. I turned toward the school.

There was no real division between school and mill. The mill yard melded into the school yard without demarcation with hedge or fence. The children were used to the men and the noise and managed to keep out of the way of the equipment. The mill managers very kindly supplied most of our wants and allowed us to use the old empty store for play time during the winter when the weather was inclement. The warm, dry room prevented many cases of ague and fever, at least in me. I supervised the play time and much I preferred to do that out of the cold and wet.

Most of the children walked to school but John Exton was riding that fidgety mare again.

"John, put her down by the trees behind the school. It's too hot here in the sun anyway." That would keep the horse away from most of the children. I was afraid it would kick.

He nodded and led his horse away. Felicity Grant gave me a shy "Good morning, Teacher." She looked pale today—not her usual colour. I hoped she wasn't ill.

Eager students like Felicity make me wish I was a better teacher. I try, but I can't keep order the way good teachers can. The five-year-olds don't stay quiet and some days all seventy children whisper and mumble at once. It doesn't matter if they come from the mill cabins in Hastings or the fine railroad managers' homes in Vancouver. They all talk. Some days this uncontrollable drone sings in my mind like a monotonous melody and I find myself almost hypnotized. It's an effort to shake it off, especially on a hot afternoon.

I looked over the water of the inlet and back toward the spit of land that was my present home. A faint haze of smoke hung on the tall pine trees. This morning, Lydia had used the stove in the summer kitchen, a few yards away from the main house, to boil the water for tea and for dishes. The stove would be cooling now, leaving only a trace of smoke in the air. We lit it as seldom as possible when the air was this hot and dry. I turned back to the school. It was in the shade of the old mill store until noon and was reasonably comfortable.

I taught arithmetic as the first subject in the morning. For one thing, I have an aversion to it, and teaching it first thing eliminates it for the rest of the day. For another, many of the older children had to help their parents in the afternoon and needed their basic curriculum before noon. Some of the girls worked as domestics and some of the boys ran errands for businessmen in the city. They left school about eleven-thirty, so I tried to give them reading, spelling and arithmetic in the morning. Nature studies and history took up our afternoon.

I sent the ten and eleven-year-olds in my fourth form to the shore near the mill wharf to collect seashells. They had fifteen minutes to collect enough shells for their arithmetic lesson. They were learning division today and could divide seashells into piles. A few shells would break during the morning and that would change their calculations, so they would argue and recalculate and come to a group answer at which point, theoretically, they would all understand the process. I gave the babies (I would have to stop calling those five-year-olds babies) buttons. They could try to discover the difference between three and four. Everyone was busy and I sat at my desk trying to get the spelling bee ready for later in the morning when Ruth Grant came to my desk.

"Please, Teacher. Felicity is sick."

I looked up at her sister. Felicity pushed buttons around on her table, but she was flushed now and her eyes looked red.

"You'd better take her home, Ruth, and come back when you can."

Ruth, a self-sufficient eight-year-old, took her sister by the hand and left.

Ruth wasn't back by lunch time, but I thought her mother might need her help at home. There were other little Grants younger than Felicity and Mrs. Grant would be reluctant to send such competent help as Ruth back to school.

We were down to fifty pupils by two that afternoon. The weather had been unseasonably warm and it was difficult for anyone to concentrate in the stuffy confines of the classroom. The afternoon desertion of the older children happened every year towards the end of the school term but not usually as early as the second of June.

I was supposed to teach history this afternoon. I gave an art project to the babies (I must stop that) and tried to interest the older children in English history as it pertained to Canada.

I have trouble explaining Canada to the children. I argued with my Aunt Lydia about it last night after the supper dishes were cleared away.

"Canada will be a Dominion from sea to sea," Lydia said quoting from the Parliamentary report in the last issue of the *Vancouver News*. She dumped the crumbs from the table into the stove and continued talking. "It's natural to be one country—one country and British."

I picked up my cue. "It's not natural at all. I think we were tricked into this Confederation by that drunken Tory back east. We should get out before the easterners bleed us of our property, our taxes, and our young people."

I try to take the opposite side of any political argument Lydia offered. When she was enthused, Lydia could talk for hours, quoting bits from newspapers and history books and giving pithy comments on politicians.

I nursed a warm cup of tea and sipped slowly trying to make the evening last a little longer. "I don't want to belong to the same organization as Toronto and Kingston. I think we should get out of it."

"Why? Toronto and Kingston were good enough for your parents."

"But my father and his friends and everyone back there in Ontario think they are the centre of the universe. They have no idea of our problems out west. Anyway, the practical problems of keeping in touch are beyond our abilities. The Rocky Mountains will always keep British Columbia separate from Central Canada."

"The railroad's been at Port Moody since November and you're still talking about being separate from Canada? We're getting closer all the time."

"It's at Port Moody but it's not going east. There is a big section around Kamloops Lake that isn't finished yet. Anyway, I'd rather have a fast link with San Francisco."

"Those rebels!" Lydia sniffed. The American Revolution was almost a hundred years ago but Lydia still maintained the British disdain for the colonists. You'd think she'd understand the Americans' rebellion; her Scottish ancestors fought the English at Culloden.

"You'll have to come to terms with the Americans sometime, Lydia. Vancouver is full of them."

"I suppose." She smiled and the hard lines around her eyes softened. She's my aunt—my mother's younger sister, but she's only ten years older than me. We don't look alike. She has brown hair parted in the middle and pulled straight back into a bun and snapping black eyes in a heart-shaped face. She looks like an elegant cat. I look more like a mouse. I'm shorter than Lydia, and slimmer. Her nose is straight and patrician. Mine turns up at the end—just a little. Lydia says she's a black MacGillivray and I'm a green-eyed MacDonald and that we have hundreds of prototypes from generations back.

I still have my maiden name because at twenty-four I'm not married and don't plan on it. I came west at the request of the Mill manager who knew my father in Ontario. I had taught four years in a small town near my home and I was ready for a change. At the same time, Hastings Mill needed a schoolteacher. So here I was, Amy MacDonald, spinster of Vancouver.

Lydia is a Smith. She was born a MacGillivray but married Alistair Angus Smith when she was twenty-eight. He left home one day when Lydia was thirty and she hasn't seen him since. She is Mrs. Smith and I'm Miss MacDonald and we are happy with our settlement here in Vancouver.

"It's good to live without men," Lydia said suddenly.

"You don't count Stanley?" My brother lives with us.

"Stanley is fifteen and still manageable."

I had some doubt about that but he, Stanley, was usually amiable. "Why this particular evening is it good to live without men?" I had my own list of reasons, but I wanted to hear hers.

"Because if there was a man in the house we'd never get to talk about politics. For some reason men think they own the subject."

"Well, they own the vote." I knew I'd provoked her but, as usual, it was irresistible. We both ardently wished for the vote, but it didn't seem probable that the men of this country would loosen their hold on the government, and I didn't see how we could force them.

She snorted and banged a wooden spoon around the wash pan but didn't begin any discourse on women's right to the vote.

"You'd better tackle that arithmetic lesson. It doesn't get easier for the leaving."

She was right and it was a good thing I had prepared, as the next day the arithmetic lesson went better than usual.

Despite what I had told Lydia last night, I think a Dominion of Canada may work. There are many problems that must be solved first. I find it difficult to explain our peculiar confederation. The Prime Minister of the country accepts graft, drinks, and makes frivolous promises. Some people in this area and in the Port Moody area lost their savings because Van Home, the Canadian Pacific Railway General Manager, and a friend of the Prime Minister, manipulated the terminal site. The railroad is coming here at monumental cost to the taxpayers and for the benefit of a few eastern financiers. Even our banking system is peculiar. If I put my savings into a bank in San Francisco I can borrow three times as much from that same bank. If I put my money in a bank in British Columbia I can't borrow from that bank because my money goes back to Ontario. The savings of the people of British Columbia are used to develop the east. I'm supposed to teach the children that British Columbia is in Canada and has been part of the Dominion for fifteen years. It will be a long time before anyone here feels a part of the East. Perhaps we would have been better off with the United States.

I decided to teach about ancient Greece. Afternoon sun beat down on the board walls and baked us as if we were sitting in a wooden oven. The children and I had tried to grasp the world of ancient history, but the air was close—no breeze now—and the room was stifling. We abandoned school about two.

Outside the afternoon air was warm, but at least it was fresh. I had a cup of tea with Lydia, washed my face and then returned to Hastings to visit Mrs. Grant. I had a few buttons in a jar for Felicity and a bag of biscuits for the rest of the children.

The saws were noisier now as more men were working. A sailing ship was loading and there was much shouting and banging of timbers on the wharf and against the ship.

The Grant cabin was past the Caufield cottage and on the mill side of Dunlevy Street. I knocked and heard Mrs. Grant shout, "Don't answer the door. None of you children answer the door. Just a moment." The last, I assumed, was to me so I waited.

She opened the door herself. She was short, a solid sphere dressed in a plain brown dress, straight without bustle or crinoline and covered with a stained apron. Her brown hair escaped its pins into untidy wisps around her face. Her eyes were almost black and large, fringed with dark lashes and quite beautiful.

"Miss MacDonald. Don't come in. It's the measles."

We stared at each other. Measles! It would kill some of the children. It always did.

"So late in the year?"

She nodded.

"I've had them." I moved forward. It wouldn't kill me.

She opened the door wide, and I followed her inside.

We sat at her kitchen table in silence for a few moments. Measles can kill. Measles can leave children blind and stupid. There was always some disease waiting for children—consumption, fever, smallpox.

"Are you sure it's the hard kind?" German measles wasn't as serious.

"It's the red measles all right," she said. "I've seen both kinds. Felicity's real sick."

I pushed the buttons and the biscuits across the table to her.

"I'm sorry, Mrs. Grant." I tried to stay calm. I wanted to scream at her to keep Felicity's fever down and feed her water often, but Mrs. Grant knew better than I did how to keep death away.

She nodded. "You'd best warn the mothers, although they'll know fast enough. Measles don't hit just one."

"But most children survive measles without injury," I suggested tentatively.

"Yes," Mrs. Grant agreed. She was not suffering imaginary horrors. "Yes, I know. But I've got eight children. I hope they all come through it all right. It's going to be hard nursing for the next month."

I looked around the cabin. In these crowded conditions, all the children were going to be exposed to measles.

"I hope Felicity has a mild case."

"I gave her a draught of vinegar and I'll try a broth of honey vinegar and onion. The doctor will be out this afternoon but there's naught he can do." She shrugged her shoulders and I rose to go. There was nothing I could do either. I could feel my throat closing, my shoulders tighten. I took a deep breath and swallowed my worry.

"Thank you kindly for coming, Miss MacDonald. Felicity likes you real well. and Ruth too." She walked to the door with me.

"They're good children."

She smiled then. I left her at the cabin door, standing straight, watching me leave, marshalling her courage for the month ahead.

Stanley was home when I arrived. He worked loading and unloading supplies for the hotels in Vancouver and at any odd jobs that came his way. He had a delivery at Hastings Mill and had stopped off for a snack. Stanley ate at every opportunity. I grabbed him as he flew past me.

"Hey! I need you."

"What for?" He paused good-naturedly. He was taller than me, very thin and strong. His body is still a boy's, but his mind is growing more adult every day. There was little opportunity for work in our hometown in Ontario so he'd joined me here in Vancouver last fall. It was called Granville then and had a population of about six hundred. There are one thousand here now and it's growing steadily. When the railroad arrives, the city will blossom and Stanley will have opportunity for more work. At the moment, he's busy and useful to us.

"I need you to organize about six older boys to go house to house and tell everyone the Grants have the measles and anyone who has not had the measles cannot come to school."

"The what?"

"The measles."

"Have I had the measles?"

"Lydia?" Dear God. I hoped he'd had the measles.

"Yes, the spring you were away at teacher's college, Amy, and we almost lost him too." She turned to Stanley. "You were eight-years-old and you were so sick I thought the Grim Reaper had your name picked out."

Lydia spoke as though frustrating the Grim Reaper had been a disappointment to her.

Stanley grinned. "Good. Can I get them twice?"

"No, not the red measles."

"Can you go to the homes of the children tonight?" I wanted him back on task.

"Sure, if I can find some help. It'll be late though before we get it all done—maybe midnight."

"All right. Be careful and watch for the men coming out of the hotel at ten-thirty. Some of them get quite....quite...."

"Drunk?"

"Urn, yes. I need that message to go around."

It was all I could do. We had epidemics of something every few years. Sometimes the children survived and sometimes they didn't.

I dragged *Dr. Wilkins: The Family Advisor* from the shelf and read what I could on fevers and illnesses. Lydia mended another hole in Stanley's long pants. I pulled out another book published in Ontario called *A Manuscript Notebook*.

"Listen, Lydia. 'Take 14 ounces of Sarsaparilla root, add 8 ounces of Burdock Root, 8 ounces of White Ash Bark, 8 ounces of Alder Bark, 6 ounces of Moose Wood Bark'" I looked up "'Moose Wood Bark'?"

Lydia raised her eyebrows; but couldn't enlighten me.

"8 ounces of Throughwort, 2 ounces of Lobelia, if green, 1 ounce if dry, 2 Tablespoons of Balm of Gilead buds, 2 ounces of Butternut Bark. Use green barks and root if to be had. Cover with water. Boil six hours. Strain and boil to one gallon. Add two pounds loaf sugar, one part rum. Dose: 2 Tablespoons before eating three times a day. Boil in a brass kettle.'"

"What's that for?" Lydia turned the pants over and attacked a tear in the back.

"It's for fever. It's called 'Indian Blood Pacifier.'"

"Does it work?"

"I don't know." I passed on to read other remedies. There were many cures that sounded worse than the disease. If Stanley were sick, I wouldn't know which one to choose.

"How many children will you have in school tomorrow?" Lydia snapped off a thread.

"The younger ones will stay home to avoid the measles and the older ones will stay home to help their mothers." I shifted in my chair. "I have no idea."

I let the book slide onto my lap and thought about the children who would stay home in an effort to escape disease. I listed them in my mind and pictured them at their tables: Judith, Percy, Andrew, Jean, Mary, Theodore, Isaac, Alistair, George. Their faces came to mind, their smiles, and their frowns of concentration. How many would escape the effects of the measles? Would any of them die? Then I scolded myself for a fool. Measles didn't always kill; it didn't always cripple, but I sighed and closed the recipe book.

At that moment, I was fiercely glad I had no children of my own.

CHAPTER TWO

Lydia cleared the supper dishes and put a plate aside for Stanley. He was still trying to get word to all the parents. I spread my classroom work on the table and trimmed the lamp. I didn't need it now, but I would before I finished getting that arithmetic lesson organized for tomorrow.

The air was still tonight. I could hear the frogs trilling in the low damp areas across Hastings Road. The smoke from the clearing fires diffused the evening light creating a warm amber glow. I sat for a moment with my chin in my hands, looking out the window to the clump of pines at the edge of the clearing.

What was I doing in Vancouver in this year of our Lord 1886? Should I have stayed in Ontario? Taught at the local school? Been a good daughter in my father's house and an aunt to my sister's children?

A nighthawk whistled outside the house and I blinked, more alert now, and ready to face lesson preparations. I sharpened my pencils and was struggling heroically with long division when Lydia announced a caller.

"Mr. Hartman," she said with a sniff. Lydia doesn't like Frank Hartman. I'm not sure if it's the general disapproval she accords all men or whether she thinks he's too handsome to be honest. She admits he is respectable, though, and even went so far as to say he "was as good as most men" though in such a way as to leave me in some doubt as to the intent of her remark. She's pleased enough to hear him speak of San Francisco where his father and family run a business and she likes to hear about some of the places he's visited—London, Italy, Hong Kong. I looked at the work I still had to do—bother arithmetic!

"Ask Mr. Hartman if he minds coming into the dining room to visit while I finish my work."

"Ask him yourself." Lydia stomped back to the kitchen.

I pushed back my chair and started toward the front hall, but stopped at the kitchen door. "Come out and sit with us, Lydia. You know you should be chaperoning me."

Lydia looked at me without smiling. "Don't be so particular. I'm close enough for respectability, but not close enough for boredom."

I left her. She wouldn't be bored by Frank Hartman. In fact, I had a good idea she'd have her ear to the kitchen wall for the duration of his visit.

If Lydia didn't live with me, I wouldn't accept calls at this time in the evening. Her chaperonage, perfunctory as it sometimes was, certainly gave me more freedom than most unmarried women.

Frank Hartman always looked distinguished. His smooth white collar set off his tanned face. His dark hair was brushed back carefully and his dark beard was neatly trimmed. I liked the loose dark tie and black suit. He looked like a successful man.

"I have faith in my future because I plan well and I'm, therefore, always secure," he'd told me once.

I'd spoken before I thought. "I wish you a month of poverty."

That amused him and embarrassed me. It says a good deal for his tolerance that we are still friends.

"I have to finish working, Frank, but come into the dining room and talk to me while I write. Have you heard any more about the railroad?"

Everyone talked about the railroad. The tracks were being laid to Granville—Vancouver, I suppose I should call it now. There was a lot of work going on down at Coal Harbour with double tracks, buildings, and wharves. The Canadian Pacific Railway Company had pushed the railroad through to Port Moody last November. We had all thought the railroad would stop there. Then Van Home had been given huge sections of land in Granville by the government of Canada and decided to track the railroad this way. The people of Port Moody were furious. They had the C.P.R. and its General Manager Cornelius Van Home in court now trying to stop him.

"I have a newspaper from Oregon that might interest you. It's an old paper but my father discovered it and sent it to me. See, I've marked the paragraph."

I glanced at the paper. I like Frank but I sometimes found his knowledge and cosmopolitan interests a little overwhelming. I'm not interested in everything Frank is.

"This one?" Frank pointed.

I read. "'Coal Harbour, the western terminus of the Canadian Pacific Railway in British Columbia ... First class openings for businessmen of all classes ...We would therefore advise those looking for first class investments in real estate to come here and see for themselves.'"

I looked up at him, a little puzzled.

"Check the date."

"Frank! This paper is two years old!"

"I know. It looks as though someone knew the terminus would be Coal Harbour, Vancouver."

"Or someone made an accurate guess."

"The people of Port Moody are going to court on the fact that the C.P.R had agreed to have Port Moody as a terminus. If this paper is any indication of their intentions, they had already made plans two years ago to have the tracks come on to Vancouver."

"Do other people know of this?"

Frank shrugged. "Not many. The paper doesn't have a wide circulation."

We talked for a half hour or so. I made desultory marks on a couple of my preparatory papers, trying with one part of my brain to plan tomorrow's lesson—without success. At nine Frank was ready to leave when Lydia announced Robert Carr. This time she brought him right in and pulled up a chair, electing to stay. Robert is as untidy as Frank is neat. Robert's red beard bobs as he talks making him look excited even when he is calm. His clothes fit his short, stocky frame but without distinction.

"Good evening, Miss MacDonald. Hello, Frank. I came to find out about the measles." Robert pulled out his notebook and pencil and directed his bright blue eyes at me.

Robert owns and reports for the Granville Star. He'll have to change the name soon since the city was officially named Vancouver last April. He says the people aren't ready for it yet and, in the meantime, he publishes and does much of the writing, hustling around town finding information. He's interesting in a different way from Frank. Frank's company is almost always relaxing. Robert's leaves me feeling as though I've been whirled halfway across a river and left to find the rest of the way myself. I knew he was serious about the information he wanted, so I concentrated on what should appear in the paper.

"As far as I know one case of measles has occurred in the Hastings area. Anyone who has not had the measles should not come to school for three weeks and should talk to Dr. Reynolds if they are worried. How's that?" I looked up.

"That'll do for a quote. Know anything more? How's the child?"

I felt a sudden resurgence of fear. "I don't know. She had a fever this afternoon. She's such a little thing."

Robert nodded. "Hope it's a mild case."

I accepted his sympathy and said no more. Disease and accidents are the whims of fate. It is fruitless to bewail their occurrence.

"What's that drunkard back east going to do with this railroad?" Lydia, despite her conviction that the railroad was necessary to Canadian unity, did not like John A. Macdonald.

"Well, the Tories have promised the railroad to Vancouver this year or early next year. We may get it. Port Moody should be running trains next week." Frank sounded doubtful. "It certainly would help commerce, but I don't see how it can ever pay for itself." Frank's interests were commercial. The railroad should help businesses.

"I heard Macdonald bribed the C.P.R. by giving Van Home most of Vancouver so he could be a land developer as well as a railroad builder. What with the land grants on the prairies and those throughout the west Van Home will end up owning half of Canada." Lydia moved closer to the table.

Robert nodded. "They're clearing the C.P.R. lands near False Creek. I hear they plan to build the roundhouse on it."

"And those poor people in Port Moody expected to be able to sell their land at a good profit. The C.P.R. wouldn't terminate at Port Moody as they planned because Van Horne couldn't get enough money in land deals to line his pockets."

While Lydia might be right. I didn't see the morality of a few private speculators like Frank lining their pockets was any different from a few private financiers lining theirs.

"You know, we have a better deep-sea dock for ships here in Vancouver, Mrs. Smith, and the railroad can service Hastings Mill." Robert offered some sense.

"Those politicians in eastern Canada are only looking for ways to stay in power. Look at the scandalous John Macdonald. He's taken bribes from the people who are building the railroad. Three hundred and fifty thousand dollars his Tory party took from them in '72. In spite of that, the voters put him back in. Who are the voters? Any man who makes more than four hundred dollars a year. In this room how many vote? Just Mr. Hartman. That's how many."

Robert's eyes twinkled. He was amused that Lydia considered him so poor. "Actually, Lydia, I vote."

"You?" Lydia's eyes crinkled at the edges, and she smiled. She had led Robert into admitting his income.

"And, actually, Mrs. Smith, I don't have citizenship here." Frank was apologetic. "So, I can't vote."

The twilight had deepened and shadows filled the corners of the room. I reached over and lit the lamp and moved it to the centre of the table.

Lydia rose and lit the sconces on the wall near the mirror. Her petticoats rustled as she settled back in her chair. "But Amy and I don't get to vote; nor do the workers in this country." Lydia returned to her argument. 'The Tories wouldn't get elected if the vote represented the population and not the wealth of a few."

"The Tories won't get the next election anyway," Frank said.

"Why not?" I asked. Frank may not be British, but he understands politics and I liked to hear opinions of future events. I might have been Greek in a previous life for I am sure I would have consulted an oracle if oracles were part of community life. Even a tea-leaf reader interests me.

"Because they hung Louis Riel and the people of Lower Canada and the prairies consider Louis Riel some kind of a saint. So, the Tories, who up to now have been strong in Lower Canada, will fall off in that territory."

Lydia looked thoughtful. "You know, I've always thought Louis Riel was a good man, but a little unbalanced."

"Most of the saints are a little crazy," Robert offered. "I mean why hang around your enemies to be murdered. It isn't a sensible plan."

I had a sudden mental picture of Robert advising St. Peter to give Rome a miss and I laughed.

Lydia looked disapprovingly at me.

Frank continued. "The government of Canada should have asked the States to take Louis Riel back when he caused so much trouble here."

"Take him back? Wasn't he a British subject?" Lydia forgot her prejudice against Frank and leaned forward.

"No. He was a citizen of the U.S. He took out citizenship there a few years ago and you could have dumped the whole problem on us Americans. Instead, the Government of Canada made a martyr of him and now you have a dissension in your North West, and Manitoba ready to revolt."

"And the Chinese question will put the Tories out of office too." Frank had continued while the rest of us sat in the lamplight thinking about his prophecies. "Allowing all those Chinamen into this country was foolish. Business is now used to cheap labour. What will happen when the railroad is finished? We don't have work for white men in this country. Some people think we should start deporting them now."

"A boatload left for China last autumn," Lydia said.

'Then you agree with the anti-Chinese laws proposed by the Attorney-General?" Robert leaned back and waited.

"What's that?" Lydia said sharply.

"Mr. Davie proposed an anti-Chinese clause be inserted in a private bill. This would mean no one could hire Chinese labour."

"And the government wouldn't have to take responsibility for the bill either if they introduce it as a private members bill." Lydia was cynical. "But what are the Chinese supposed to do if they aren't allowed to work?"

"I suppose," I said slowly, "they would go back to China."

"A deportation law has its problems," Frank said. "We have Chinese labour. It's not easy to get rid of it."

We all looked at him.

'The city of Vancouver wants to put in a water system and street lights. They can do it if they can use cheap labour. Cheap labour means Chinamen."

"If the Chinese stay, here they'll want schools and doctors and services and work and food and property. Is that possible?" Lydia looked at Robert, but it was Frank who answered.

"They won't get schools with white men. Maybe they'll start their own. They have their own medicine. No, the biggest problem is the jobs they'll take."

I disagreed. "That's the problem right now, but they must be allowed to go to school. Perhaps their own schools but the children should be able to better themselves."

Frank smiled at me. "You have a kind heart."

For some reason that made me angry. I bit my lip and lowered my eyes for a moment. I don't know why I was angry and hoped Frank would think I was blushing.

Robert laughed. "Not a kind heart so much as a clear head. If Canada is supposed to give opportunity to people, we are going to have to give it to all people."

"Newspapermen are always radicals," Frank said.

"And not just give opportunity to men who earn more than four hundred dollars a year." If being convinced and determined was radical, then Lydia qualified also.

'Well, I don't want to see Miss MacDonald here teaching a group of little Chinamen."

"How do you feel about it, Miss MacDonald?" I thought Robert really wanted to know so I took some time about my answer.

"I can't get around the fact Chinese people are people. The children are still children. Given that, the children have the same right to an education as anyone else. So, I suppose, I feel they ought to be able to go to school."

"You can take that too far," Frank said slowly. "I just can't see a Royal Northwest Mounted Policeman with a pigtail down his back."

I didn't laugh although it seemed improbable. What if the Chinese men had the same freedoms as every other man here? Then a Chinese North West Mounted policeman might become possible and even advisable. We were a long way from that kind of freedom.

"I should have the vote." Certainly, Lydia could organize a better country.

While Frank had been talking Robert had taken my arithmetic lesson and read it, listened to Frank but added information to my lesson at the same time. When the Bristol clock on the cupboard chimed ten both men stood to leave. Robert handed me the paper, the lesson completed. I scanned it for a moment to be sure I understood it and then thanked him. I felt I had been very efficient: enjoyed my company and completed my work at the same time.

Stanley arrived just as the men were leaving. His soft cap sat at the back of his head; his sandy hair stood around it in untidy clumps like dry winter grass. He had another hole in his pants at the knees and a button missing on his white shirt. His wrists showed bones and angles below his cuffs. Why hadn't I noticed before that his shirt was too small?

Stanley shook hands with Frank and Robert and reported he had talked to the mill owner who would tell the workers about the measles in the morning. Six boys were taking the measles alarm to most of the houses in the district and, if I told the children at school in the morning, by tomorrow evening the whole community would be aware. Robert's report would appear in next Wednesday's paper.

"How's the job, Stanley?" Robert asked at the door.

"Which one?"

"Oh? Busy, are you? I meant the one at the Granville Hotel unloading supplies."

"Not too bad. I work there from one to six. Sometimes I work at the livery stable and sometimes at the Deighton Hotel. The work's pretty steady, but I guess I won't get rich at it."

"If you ever want to come around and see how the presses work, we usually set up for the Wednesday paper on Tuesday."

Stanley was tired, but he brightened at the invitation.

"Yeah? I will if I can get the time one day." He nodded politely and moved toward the stairs. He attended his last year of school in the morning and loaded wagons in the afternoon and he'd had a full day. He must be tired indeed if he wasn't going to visit the kitchen before bed.

Lydia and Frank continued a discussion politics—this time American politics.

Robert turned to me and spoke softly. "I have a friend, a Chinese boy who wants to learn. Would you teach him?"

I was startled. "The trustees wouldn't let me."

"Would you teach him?"

"Are you going to get me into trouble?"

"After school?"

My shoulders drooped with the thought of teaching more hours.

"You won't?" Robert sounded disappointed and a little angry.

"I didn't say I wouldn't," I snapped at him. "At the end of the day, I'm tired. Of course, I'll teach your Chinese boy, but I'm not looking forward to putting in any more teaching hours, that's all."

Robert's frown lifted. "Oh, is that all?"

"Yes! That's all." Robert has boundless energy and thinks the rest of the world ought to keep his pace. "What do you think I do all day? Sit in that stuffy classroom daydreaming? How would you like to spend as much time as I do?"

"Shh!"

I suppose I was loud. Frank and Lydia likely wondered what subject caused such acrimony but turned back to their conversation when I stopped talking.

"Good. Look. His name is Sung Wick. He lives near False Creek with his mother and father and two sisters. He delivers laundry so if you could just arrange to have him deliver your laundry at 4:30?" He raised his eyebrows and waited.

I nodded. "You arrange it."

"Then he could stay for half an hour and you could teach him how to read and write English."

I felt as though a tidal wave had washed over me and left me alone on an island. I'm sure I would be the only teacher in Canada teaching a Chinese student. Would I lose my teaching certificate?

"For heaven's sake, don't tell anyone."

"What's the matter? Can't you defend your principles?"

"I just don't want to borrow trouble. I have no intention of being a crusader, so don't set me up as one."

I knew my eyes were snapping and my colour was high but there is something about Robert Carr that brings out the worst in me.

CHAPTER THREE

I woke earlier than usual the next morning with little Felicity Grant on my mind. I could see her bright face on the first morning of school, her eyes lighting with the excitement of new ideas. Superimposed on that face was the vacant stare of the grocer's daughter who had suffered measles when she was a tiny child and never developed normally. The twin visions faded and reappeared like persistent ghosts.

I threw back the bedclothes and moved to the window. The sun had just risen and flocks of crows glided and dipped over the waters of the bay stretching their wings to the first warmth of the morning. The sea was calm. No mist over the water today. There was little movement on the sailing ships and only the occasional bang of ropes against a hull. The saws were silent at the mill; no sounds came from the city. I could smell salt and seaweed and the sharp, pungent odour of tidal sand. The clearing fires of yesterday had died and there was little smoke at this hour of the morning. I would slip quietly down to the bay and swim.

Lydia disapproved of my surreptitious morning swims. Most people in this city would disapprove. School teachers are not supposed to indulge in anything so risqué and dangerous. Swimming encourages typhoid fever, pneumonia and other ills guaranteed to wreak vengeance on a reckless nature. As well, it was a bad example to the young, but there was no one to see me and I was determined to learn.

I dressed in the bathing costume I'd brought from Ontario: striped knickers and a long middy blouse with a big sailor collar. One day I'm going to cut off that collar because when it is wet, it's heavy and flaps against my back. The knickers fit tightly under a knee-length skirt. The yard and a half of wet skirt weighs me down, but it is the wide collar that irritates me. I put my traveling coat over the costume, pinned my hair on the top of my head, buttoned my shoes only to the ankles and crept from the house.

The sun lit the cedars near the bay with bright patches of green. Long shadows of night still covered the shoreline. Cedars draped their branches into the water, curtaining the banks of this almost circular small bay. An opening to Burrard Inlet was wide enough to admit the passage of a rowboat but at such an angle to the Inlet that no one from the anchored ships or from Hastings Mill could see into the bay without coming right up to the entrance. It was a perfect place for secluded bathing. I discovered it the day after I arrived last year and have been determinedly teaching myself to swim there ever since. I have progressed to the point where I can move my arms and legs and keep myself afloat for some time. I still am not comfortable when my feet are off the bottom, but I know I could swim cross the bay if I had to. I have seen men swimming at picnics and watched the way they brought their hands over their heads and turned their heads to breathe. They must blow air into the water. I tried that, but my hair gets wet that way and takes a long time to dry. Also, I catch water in my air passages and do a lot of sputtering and coughing. I think I am afraid to put my face right down into the water. I know I'll never be a proficient swimmer until I master the face-in-the-water trick.

I left my boots and coat and bath blanket on the rocks near the shore and walked out on the old raft beached there. I sat for a moment with my feet in the cool water relishing the peace and tranquillity of the undisturbed bay. At five in the morning this part of the world is still and silent just as it must have been a hundred years ago, before iron and the white settlers.

I scooped a handful of clear water and let it drop back in little rivulets through my fingers. This is a wonderful country. I savoured my well-being for a few minutes and then pushed off from the raft and allowed my feet to drop to the sand bottom. The cold water shocked me for an instant but I moved my hands and started my sedate swimming and soon became accustomed to the temperature. By now I knew the limits of my height, depending on the position of the tide. Low tide took me to the entrance of the bay. At high tide, as it was now, I could only swim to an imaginary line between the big cedar to the south and the old stump to the north. After that, I would be in water past my nose. I swam pushing the water away from me and kicking my feet. That combination of strokes seems to move me in the direction I want to go without soaking my hair.

I would never be a good swimmer if I persisted in keeping my head above the water. I paddled in the bay until I convinced myself I should at least try to blow air out into the water. If I didn't have to swim at the same time perhaps I could manage it. I planted my feet on the sandy bottom, held my hair securely on the top of my head, took a deep breath and lowered my face to the water. I was fascinated by my reflection coming closer and closer. My green eyes looked dark this morning and the high cheekbones sharper and more angular than usual. I started to laugh when I was just about to put my head in the water and had to start all over again. This time I screwed my eyes shut so I wouldn't see myself and lowered my head. I had misjudged the distance, so when I did touch the water, I wasn't expecting it quite then and my eyes and mouth flew open. For a split second before my mouth filled with water, I saw my foreshortened legs in the water below me. Then I coughed and choked, clearing my mouth and nose of the salt water. My feet were still on the sand, so I wasn't frightened. A few ringlets slipped from the hair pins when I jerked back so I stopped and secured them again. This wasn't going to be easy. I gave up the face immersion and returned to the smooth, uneventful motions of my regular, head-above-water strokes. The sailor collar pulled at my neck and flapped on my back. I ignored it.

The sun had not yet moved high enough in the sky to light the centre of the bay. I could see a dark log floating about six feet past my height limit. Some days I swam out to a log and rested on it, then kicked my way back pushing the log. I could manage the short swim to this one. My mind was not really alert. I had relaxed into the rhythmic strokes of my swim and I was unaware of the log as a particular log until I reached out to touch it. Then I only reacted in slow stages.

First, I thought: *That log has some old clothes hanging over it.* Then: *The clothes seem to be full of air.* Then: *This is not a log.*

When I got that far in my reasoning my mind froze. I could not make myself reach the obvious conclusion. I stopped swimming toward it. I looked at the body of man without really understanding with the top level of my mind that it was a body. All I thought was *I will not touch that. I will swim back and I will not be afraid. If I am afraid, I may never get to shore; so, I will slowly and steadily swim back to shore. I will not be afraid.* I couldn't turn my back on the thing. It seemed to me if I turned my back, it might reach out and grab me. So, I kicked my feet forward and kicked myself backwards, half on my back facing the body. When I could touch bottom, I waded out and sat on the raft. Only then did I let my mind grasp the fact there was a dead man in the bay. I shook with cold and fright. I took some deep breaths. This was silly. There was nothing a dead man could do to me. There was nothing I could do for a dead man.

Amy MacDonald, behave yourself. I reached for the bath blanket and vigorously scrubbed myself dry. I put on my travel coat and my boots. I couldn't fasten the buttons on my boots. My fingers felt clumsy. I wanted to run up the path screaming my discovery to the world but that was impossible. I wasn't supposed to be swimming here. Staid school teachers did not swim.

I crept back to the house; changed to a dark skirt and white blouse. I hung my wet bathing costume at the back of the summer kitchen where it could dry unobtrusively. I lit the fire and boiled some water. By the time I had a hot cup of tea, my hands had stopped shaking so I could fasten my boots. When Stanley appeared, I handed him a cup of tea and some bread and butter and told him to go and fetch the constable.

"There is a dead man floating in the bay. I discovered it while I on my early morning walk."

"Been swimming again, have you?"

Not a lot gets past Stanley. "No one is to know that."

"All right. You went out for walk. Was it creepy?"

I shuddered. "Yes, of course, it was creepy."

Stanley swallowed the last of his bread. "Can I go look?"

"May I," I corrected automatically. "No, you most certainly may not. You may go to fetch the constable or whoever is at the jail."

"It'll be the constable. Ever since they sent him over from Victoria he's been living at the jail. The mayor's still mad that Victoria sent him. He figures Vancouver can handle the Chinese without help from any Provincial policeman."

"The mayor doesn't seem to understand the problems that the white men can cause. I don't think the problem of violence rests with the Chinese. Anyway, go fetch him."

"I don't know what that constable could do anyway."

Stanley always seems to know a lot about what goes on in town. As he unloads supplies at the hotel he must listen to gossip. Men forget that the youngsters scurrying around them can hear and understand. Stanley told me once that if he's careful not to speak the men forget he's there.

He was back by the time Lydia was up and making breakfast. I had spread my hair down my back to dry and was pinning it when Constable Richard Parkinson arrived at the front door with Robert Carr behind him.

"What are you doing here?"

Robert correctly interpreted this question as being directed to him.

"I cover all the stories for the paper. You ought to know that."

"Miss MacDonald," the constable interrupted, "your brother tells us you discovered a body in the bay."

"Yes," I invited them in. "I was out for an early morning walk. You know we have measles in the school and I was worried and couldn't sleep..." I knew I was talking too fast and too much, but I'm not a good liar.

Robert looked at me sharply.

I ignored him. " I saw what I thought at first was a log in the bay." My speech slowed. This, after all, was true. "I realized it wasn't a log and must be a man. He wasn't moving, just turning with the movement of the water..." My voice died away. I could see that red and black shirt and the dead hand trailing pale and distorted in the bend of light below the water.

"Could you show us?"

"Couldn't it wait until after breakfast?" Lydia demanded.

The constable looked affronted.

Robert spoke quickly. "If we could get Miss MacDonald to show us the spot she could come right back."

"You'd better have your breakfast here, Mr. Carr," Lydia peered at the policeman. "And I suppose you haven't had yours either, Mr. Parkinson."

"Constable" he corrected.

Lydia ignored his amendment. "If you want breakfast, you come back to the house."

The constable hesitated, his dignity warring with the smell of scones and maple syrup.

"Thank you, Ma'am I will be back."

We trekked down to the bay: Robert, the constable and me with Stanley following, munching a scone and excited by the prospect of something ghoulish.

The body was still in the bay, a little closer to the shore now and easier to see.

The constable licked the end of his pencil and made some entries in a small notebook. Robert made some notes in his. Stanley and I stood in silence and waited.

Then the constable said, "I suppose we'd better bring the body up on to land. Young man, why don't you..?"

"No," I said flatly. "That's your job. Why don't you?"

The constable looked at me with some disapproval. "I only thought that since the young man is barefoot and would only have to roll up his trousers."

"He is not going out there to bring in any dead body. It might fall apart for heaven's sake."

A look of distinct loathing passed across the constable's face. His mustache quivered, but he didn't persist in his request. He was a big man, almost six feet tall, broad across the shoulders and strong. He could bring the body in.

Robert offered advice. "I tell you what, Richard. I'll hold your boots, socks and trousers and you wade in for your body. Miss MacDonald will retire discreetly, I'm sure."

I nodded.

The constable accepted his fate and Stanley moved closer the better to get a look at the body and the constable sans his trousers. It is a waste of time trying to protect Stanley's sensibilities. I didn't think I needed a closer look and certainly I had to leave while the constable undressed, so I returned to the house.

Lydia had breakfast almost ready and I had another cup of tea.

The three returned and reported. "Looks like a Métis," the constable said. "Haven't seen any Métis around here, have you?" He asked the question of Robert, but it was Stanley who answered.

"He came on the stage from New Westminster a couple of days ago. I thought he was an Indian but I never heard him speak 'cause he sloped off as soon as the stage stopped."

A Métis would probably speak with a French accent.

"I'll look into it." The constable wrote in his book again.

"Well," Lydia demanded. 'How did he die? Drown?"

"Don't know. I'll have Doc Reynolds look at him. Hard to tell. He's been in the water a while."

"Hey, young man," Constable Parkinson said, "you go off and get the doctor."

"After breakfast," Robert said firmly. "The doctor won't come to a dead body until after his breakfast anyway."

"Oh, all right, after breakfast."

Stanley's view of his first dead body didn't seem to upset him too much. He packed away five scones with maple syrup and three cups of tea.

The doctor arrived and disappeared with Robert and the constable and, of course, Stanley.

I met Robert later, on the walkway to school.

"Poison," Robert said. "Doc Reynolds says it's poison. The man's face is black."

I hadn't noticed that when I swam close to the body. Perhaps I didn't look at his face.

"Someone didn't like him." Robert fingered the pencil behind his ear and looked thoughtful.

"So, they poisoned him?"

"Seems like it. Do you go out for a 'walk' very often?"

I looked up quickly.

Robert reached over and lifted a brown ringlet. The end was still damp and dark. I twitched if out of his hand.

"Did the constable notice?"

"He only notices what someone points out to him. Your secret's safe."

I wasn't sure what was safe and what was a good newspaper story, but I couldn't see anything to be gained by admitting I had been swimming. "Can you get the body out of the water before the children come?"

Robert checked the timepiece in his pocket. "We could take it away after they are all inside."

I nodded. "All right. I don't know how many I'll have with the measles scare,"

Robert put his hand on my arm. "I asked Doc Reynolds how the little Grant girl was."

"And?" I looked up hopefully but was dismayed by the steady look I received.

"She isn't very well. Two of her sisters and her brother have the measles now as well."

The pebbles on the path seemed to merge and blur with my tears. I blinked, took a deep breath, and straightened my shoulders. "Thanks for telling me. I suppose I should go to the school. The children will be arriving.

Robert's hand was still on my arm and he patted it comfortingly. "You go give them the devil in arithmetic," he said absently.

For some reason that amused me, and I managed to enter the schoolroom tolerably composed.

CHAPTER FOUR

There were twenty children at school—most of them older girls. Many of these would have to leave at noon to help with chores at home. None of the Grants were there.

Mrs. Best arrived about nine-thirty. She has five children in the school and is a great help to me on concert and picnic days. Although she had little schooling herself, she was determined her five children will do well and managed her children, her husband, her husband's father, and the Ladies Auxiliary to St. James Anglican Church without depletion of her remarkable energy.

She swished her dress past the tables and advanced on me at the centre of the room. I stood, and we talked in low voices in front of the children.

"You might as well close, Amy," she said. "None of the mothers will send the little ones—even the ones who have had the measles— because they are afraid they'll get it again."

"Can that happen?"

"I don't think so, but I'm not a doctor and I don't know, not that doctors do either—by guess and by golly most of the time, I think. Charge for it too, taking as much as they think a body can pay. Anyway, it's almost the end of the year and most of us think there isn't much use sending the children back now. We'd rather let them be outside playing in the sun. Maybe that will keep the sickness away."

"It's late for measles, isn't it?" Maybe the children would be better outside in the fresh air.

Anna Best nodded. "It is, but I guess it can come any time. I mind a spate of it when I was a girl. We had four deaths in our Concession that year. Mostly the little ones but one was a girl sixteen years old. Friend of mine she was. Had one eye funny colour. I remember that."

"From the measles?" I had trouble as usual following Anna's thoughts.

"No. She was born that way. Measles is funny. Sometimes it does no harm at all, just aches and fever and that. Sometimes it makes kids blind and silly." She paused for a moment and we stood silent.

For all her volubility Anna was a shrewd woman, given to common sense and good works. She felt the danger of this threatened measles epidemic as much as I.

"Thanks for coming and telling me, Anna. I'll send Stanley to the mill and ask if I can close."

"All right, but they won't mind."

"Maybe not, but I rely on the mill as well as the government, so I'd better do them the courtesy of asking."

"You don't want to ruffle any feathers if you don't have to," she agreed.

"How are your children?"

"Fine. They've had the measles—all five of them."

I sent Stanley off to the mill office after Anna left. He was back in half an hour with permission to close, and I dismissed the students. Technically, I didn't have to ask the mill owners for permission; I was employed by the provincial government. They paid my salary regularly each month, the amount dependent on the number of pupils I had. The mill owners acted as the local school board and it only made sense to consult them. We had planned a big picnic at the Naval Reserve for the last day of school and I knew the children would be disappointed to miss that. There would be no gathering of children until the measles scare was over: no picnics, no races, and no parties. It was impossible to prevent the healthy children from fraternizing at play, but the adults would not organize any gatherings. I sent everyone home. Stanley helped me tidy the classroom, clearing off the slates, and putting the chalk in the drawer. We walked home together.

"Do we have time to go target shooting?" Stanley asked me.

I looked around quickly. No one had heard him. Target shooting was another of my nefarious activities known only to Stanley and Lydia. I nodded. It was just what I needed, an hour or two in the fresh air.

Stanley called out our intentions to Lydia as we left the house. He picked up his Henry and ammunition and we walked up Dunlevy Street and around the south end of the mill to the trees and thick woods beyond.

We spent a happy hour there. Stanley had improved. Since I was responsible for him, I thought he should know how to shoot well. He may move north into the Interior at some time and up there he would have to be able to provide his own meat. Target practice also gave me a good excuse to improve my own shooting. Stanley was sworn to secrecy.

The cartridges were expensive but, I think, worth it to improve our shooting. They traveled about fifty yards with accuracy.

We picked up our empty shells—the Henry ejected them when they were spent—and I put them in the pocket of my long skirt. Thank God the styles had decreed shorter skirts, so I could walk without dragging material on the ground.

"Want to walk through Chinatown?"

I shook my head. "Not carrying a gun, I don't. We'd probably spark a riot."

"Things are pretty touchy with the Chinese, aren't they?" Stanley's strides were getting longer as his body grew.

"Slow down, Stanley. You'll have me running."

He shifted the rifle to his opposite shoulder and slowed his pace.

"So many Chinese came here to work on the railroad. Now many of them are without jobs." I didn't like the situation. The government wanted them to come and now abandoned them.

"I hear guys at the hotel complaining the Chinese take the jobs for less money."

"And so, they do. That's why Onderdonk and Van Horne imported them. Because the railroad wouldn't have to pay them much. Now the Chinese are here, of course they're going to work for less money. That's all they're offered."

"Do you think they should leave now?"

"It would help the immediate racial problem, but nothing's simple. What can we do? Some of the Chinese have been here for ten years. They want to live here the same way your grandfather wanted to live here when he left Scotland."

Stanley nodded. "Big difference though. Grandpa was white."

"That seems to be the problem," I agreed.

We turned north down Carrall Street. The day was warmer and I was glad of my hat. I recognized Frank Hartman's horse in front of the Sunnyside Hotel, and then Frank himself walked onto the street just as we approached. He tipped his hat, said hello to Stanley, and walked beside us leading the mare.

"I hear you closed the school."

"An hour ago, I closed the school," I said. "It doesn't take long for the news to travel."

"Mick Best was in the hotel." His children were my pupils.

I don't know why Vancouver bothers with a newspaper. Information passes so quickly by word of mouth.

We could see the smoke from the mill puffing up in fat clouds. The whine of the saws was so constant I hardly noticed it any more. Sometimes we could hear the clang of heavy machinery and sometimes a whistle, but usually just the background high-pitched scream of the saws.

"So, you're free now for a month?"

"Yes." I brightened, "until the end of July." Suddenly I *felt* free, a woman of a leisured class.

Frank smiled. "Would you like to go for a drive to Colonel Moody's Reserve on Sunday?"

The land is a thousand acres of land set aside by Colonel Moody as a military reserve at the time the Americans were occupying the San Juan Island. It isn't used by the military and the new city council of Vancouver are hoping they can get it into the city as a grant of park land from the Dominion government. They are fighting the C.P.R. for it. They even have a name picked out for it, Stanley Park, after Lord Stanley, not after my brother Stanley MacDonald.

"I'd like that very much," I said sincerely. It would be wonderful to take a drive on Sunday in Frank's phaeton. His horse has a smooth gait and, if the weather was still good, I would enjoy it. "Thanks very much."

We walked in companionable silence for a while, Frank's horse following docilely.

Then Stanley said. "Are you in the lumber business, Mr. Hartman?"

Frank looked at him. "No. Why do you ask?"

"I unloaded some barrels from the Moodyville barge for you. They had a label that said they were machine parts. I thought maybe you had a lumber mill somewhere."

"No, I buy and sell goods, Stanley. That was a consignment I had for a town up in the Interior, a place called Soda Creek. They wanted some machine parts for haying equipment. You'll probably find I have quite a lot of goods coming in. I buy and sell, you see. That's my living."

I thought it kind of Frank to take such time to explain things to Stanley. Stanley's curiosity didn't always sit well with adults. They were inclined to call him nosey.

"Will you use the railroad when it's running freight?"

Frank snorted. "That railroad! It took all kinds of money to build it and it'll take all kinds of money to operate it. I doubt if we'll ever get good service from the C.P.R." He paused and looked over at Hastings Mill. "No one here is going to profit from the railroad, not the mill owners, the flour merchants, the farmers. No one is going to ship their goods on the C.P.R. Not when we have such a good market south of us in the States. The States has an operating railroad west to east. We're going to find it a lot cheaper and more reliable to ship south and then east—if we need to ship east. We'll probably find all the markets we want between Seattle and San Francisco."

"But the people in Ontario will want our gold and our lumber." Stanley's roots were in Ontario and he wasn't about to ignore them.

"The C.P.R. will make it impossible to ship to Ontario. They only built the railroad so they could cash in on free land. Maintaining a good service is not on their books."

I wondered how Frank could know all that. He sounded so sure and he definitely sounded pro American. "Frank, are you advocating secession?"

He nodded.

"But that's rebellion!"

"Oh, no." Frank jerked his horse's head as he brought his hands together in an effort to explain himself. "Not at all, Amy. Not rebellion. I'm talking about a political separation. Even the Premier of B.C. is talking about a new country from Manitoba to Mexico." He patted his horse and continued to walk with us. "And in spite of what Amor de Cosmos said way back in '72, I don't want fighting."

"What did he say?"

Frank could match Lydia in his ability to remember snippets from newspapers.

"I guess you were just a little girl back in Ontario at that time. I was a young man when I read his speech in the San Francisco papers. He advocated union with Canada but said," Frank paused while he searched his memory for the exact words. Stanley and I waited. "He said 'I would not object to a little revolution now and again, if, after Confederation, we were treated unfairly.'"

"What an idiot." This was from Stanley.

Frank smiled. "Well, he was an eccentric and those remarks certainly caused a stir in San Francisco. I don't think you'll have rebellion here. It isn't necessary. I think you can develop trade routes, establish them well and then apply for secession. You're only a confederation, not a union. You could get out of it without bloodshed."

"We'd have to leave Victoria behind." I thought of the English in Victoria determined to be a bastion of the English empire.

"I suppose," Frank agreed. "Mind you, if the railroad actually operates, I might reconsider my ideas."

"Lots of people would rather stay with England than be independent or go with the States." Stanley was ready to argue.

I had had enough of the whole question. "Look at the lupines. I haven't seen such a fine field of them since I left the East."

We stopped for a moment at the corner of Carrall and Hastings where an empty lot bloomed with blue, mauve, and pale lavender lupines.

Frank mounted his horse and waved. "I'll call on you tonight."

I nodded.

"He calls on you all the time," Stanley complained.

"There aren't many young women in town to call on. Perhaps he doesn't have anything better to do."

"He does a lot of business. I'm always shoving his heavy barrels around."

"Speaking business. You'd better get your lunch and get to work."

We hurried the last few yards and caught up with Jack Bullman. He is the millwright of Hastings Mill, about forty-five, medium build with big shoulders and big hands, kind blue eyes and a sandy beard. He attends to any problems at the school and the teacherage. I nodded to Stanley to go ahead and he ran for his lunch. Jack touched his cap.

"Heard you'd closed the school, ma'am."

I nodded.

"Thought I might make a start on that cloak room you wanted."

"Oh, good, Jack. Did you take the measurements?"

"I'm on my way there."

I looked down at the bouquet of yellow daisies he carried in his hand. "Thought Mrs. Smith might like these to brighten up her room."

I hid a smile. Jack Bullman had been quietly pursuing Lydia for months. Lydia ignored him most of the time. She was a married lady she had informed him at the beginning of the school year.

She wasn't interested in men. He agreed with everything she said and continued to drop off a roast of venison, a dozen fresh eggs, some blackberry wine. This was the first time he'd brought flowers, however, and I wondered what Lydia would do with them. I like Jack. He is an accomplished machinist, apparently keeping the mill machinery working and supervising all the operating machines. Early in the year he took it upon himself to personally supervise all the work at the teacherage making it a comfortable home.

"You'll find Lydia in the kitchen giving Stanley his lunch."

I let myself in the front door and allowed Jack to present his bouquet at the kitchen door in privacy. Stanley would be too intent on eating to pay much attention to him.

I slipped into the kitchen about fifteen minutes later and saw the daisies were in a vase on the shelf almost hidden by the winter stove. I said nothing. At least, she hadn't thrown them out.

I told Lydia about closing the school and we talked about our plans for the summer. We hoped to get started on the preserves. I would be able to help now, and Lydia looked forward to getting out of the house to pick berries.

Lydia and I had a tendency to walk more than most women. We sometimes removed a petticoat—no one could see it after all—and freed our legs for large steps. We wore the modified bustle, now bustles were back in style, when we went to church or to house parties. I had adopted a loose plain skirt and white blouse for school and had managed to reduce my underclothing to a chemise, an outer corset and one petticoat. I couldn't bear to carry all the material so many women draped on themselves. I had to be careful, though, to maintain respectability, but no one was counting my undergarments.

"This afternoon I'll visit the Grants again." I outlined my plans to Lydia.

She frowned. "You take a dozen buns now. I spent the morning in the summer kitchen so that poor woman would have some fresh baking."

"Lydia, you're a dear."

"Don't be silly. Everyone has to help. I'm sure she'd do the same for me if my family was ill."

Mrs. Grant probably would. All the same, Lydia was thoughtful.

I saw Dr. Reynold's horse and buggy at the Grant's house and hesitated before going in. I had to deliver the buns, so I knocked at the kitchen door. Mrs. Grant opened it.

"Ah, come in, Teacher," she said and turned back to the doctor. He washed his hands in the wash basin and turned to nod at me.

"It's all I can do for her, Mrs. Grant. The others don't seem to be as ill. But I'm not keeping it from you. Little Felicity is having a tough time of it."

Mrs. Grant's eyes were dry and she stared at the doctor a little vacantly.

"I hear you closed the school," the doctor said to me.

"It seemed wisest."

"A case of closing the barn door after the horse has bolted."

"What do you mean? I thought the children shouldn't congregate. I thought measles spreads when children get together."

"Measles spreads before anyone gets sick. Most of the damage is already done."

I felt a little of Mrs. Grant's despair.

"However, you might have saved one or two from picking it up. Who knows? I'll call tomorrow." He dropped the towel on the wash stand and picked up his hat and bag. "You're doing all the right things. Try to get as much water down her as you can."

Mrs. Grant saw the doctor to the door and then returned to the kitchen.

I handed her Lydia's buns.

"Oh, thank you. That's kind of her, Miss MacDonald. Very kind of her." Then that formidable lady started to shake.

I watched in a kind of helpless immobility as her bulk heaved and shook. Finally, tears squeezed from her eyes and trickled down her face. She took great breathes trying to control her sobs. I covered her hand with mine and then stroked it. She turned her hand over and squeezed mine letting the tears pour down her cheeks. Then she wiped her face with her apron and put her hands in her lap.

"I'm going to lose her, Miss," she said quietly. "She's such a tiny thing and she's getting worse. She doesn't know me now, Miss. She keeps tossing and fretting. Sometimes she's calmer and I can hold her and feed her a little water and some gruel broth, but she's getting weaker and there's naught anyone can do. I cannot stand it, Miss. I cannot stand it!" Her voice rose to a wail.

I was appalled. If only the doctor hadn't left. What could I do? There were other children here. I had jumped to my feet when she screamed. Now I grabbed her shoulders.

"Mrs. Grant!" I shook her. "Be quiet! Be quiet!"

I put my arms around her and hugged her close. She put her head on my shoulder and cried great heaving sobs.

"My little one. My little Felicity. I named her that, you know, because it was a light and pretty name and she was like that— all light and pretty and dainty looks and pretty sounds. What kind of an evil God is there, Miss, that takes such a pretty thing away?"

I took a deep breath. "She isn't dead yet. You'll have her buried and mourned and she isn't dead yet."

One of the older girls put her head around the corner of the kitchen door, her eyes wide and frightened. I motioned her to leave us alone and smiled to reassure her. She ducked out of sight.

"I don't think you need to give up yet. I'm going to make you a cup of tea and you'll have one of Lydia's buns. She put some apple conserve in there too, so you'll have some of that. I don't suppose you've had anything to eat for days."

I busied myself with the tea and chattered about silly inconsequential things until Mrs. Grant had drunk two cups of tea and eaten a bun.

"Will you be all right?" I asked her as I got up to leave.

"Yes, Miss. Thank you."

"You give my love to Felicity...if she can understand..." My voice trailed away.

"I'll give her your love. That's all we can give her, I'm thinking."

She shut the door behind me and I was left with a frustrating anger at the cruelty of the gods. Children died all the time. Almost every year someone in my class had died. It was just as bad in Ontario. Why couldn't I get used to it? Every year I was angry—angry at a careless accident, at a drowning, at diphtheria, at consumption, at a weak chest and measles and influenza. I walked briskly along the plank walk to Hastings Road, trying to diffuse my boiling emotions.

CHAPTER FIVE

By four o'clock I was calmer and ready for Robert's Chinese boy. He was punctual. Lydia had a package of laundry ready for him to take when he left and I had a slate and chalk. Now school was closed it would be easy to supply him with equipment and I would not be tired after a full day of teaching.

I had seen Chinese people in the streets here in Vancouver, never in Ontario, but I had not spoken to one. He was interesting to look at. He wore a dark blue tunic coat that seems to be the uniform of the Chinese men here and the usual dark, baggy pants. His skin was almost translucent. I wouldn't have called it yellow—more a pale brown with a light, shining quality to it. His eyes, of course, slanted up and his black hair was pulled back and braided into a long queue.

He bowed. "My name is Sung Wick."

I bowed. "My name is Miss MacDonald. This is Mrs. Smith."

He bowed to Lydia. "Mrs. Smith," he repeated.

Lydia stopped stirring the pie plant jelly and gave him a half bow in return.

I showed him the kitchen table and the slate. His English was good—stilted but correct. He had no understanding of the letters at all. I started teaching the alphabet.

After half an hour Sung Wick rose, picked up the slate and the laundry, bowed and slipped out the door.

"'Well," Lydia said, "he's quiet enough."

"I think he'll learn quickly. He's certainly attentive."

Robert knocked on the kitchen knocked and poked his head in.

"How did it go?"

I shrugged- "Fine, I think." Then I remembered the last time I had seen Robert. "Did the constable tell you anything about that man in the bay?"

Robert grimaced. "More than he should have. Come for a little walk with me."

I followed him out the door. "What did he say?"

"He said the man was a Métis."

"You said he looked like one."

"Right. But he was a Métis from the North West Territories and he'd been working for the North West Mounted Police."

"Doing what?"

"Spying on the remnants of last year's rebellion."

"I thought that was all over with Riel's execution last November."

"All that did was make Riel a martyr. There's plenty of rebellion left out there in the North West."

"And this fellow was bringing information to the constable?"

"The constable doesn't know why he was here, but the man had a letter on him that was still readable authorizing him to travel on the railroad on government business. The constable is telegraphing the man's name to Battleford and expects to hear he was some kind of informant."

"This is ridiculous. Why would the constable tell you all that?"

"Because the constable is neither bright and nor discreet. Also, because he was afraid I'd publish the fact that a Métis was found murdered in the bay and that would start anti-white feeling in the North West. The government doesn't want any more rebellion or any more martyrs."

I started to smile. "Forgive me, Robert, but is your paper influential in the North West?"

"I'm not even influential in Vancouver," he said glumly, 'but Constable Parkinson seemed to think there might be a link between Vancouver and Battleford. I have a suspicion he has some information from the police in the North West—perhaps some instructions to look for troublemakers here."

"I don't think Parkinson, our great sleuth, would be able to uncover any kind of plot."

"Unlikely," Robert agreed.

"So, what are you going to report in your paper?"

"The fact that a resident of the North West, a Mr. Joseph Anthony Dubrant was found dead in the bay. Any persons who had any knowledge of the man will be asked to inform Constable Parkinson so he may notify the next of kin."

We had walked down to the bay and back to the house Robert setting a brisk pace. I enjoyed stretching my muscles to keep up with him.

"All the same, Robert, who did kill him?"

"I don't think Constable Parkinson will ever find that out."

He left me at the kitchen door.

Stanley was quiet tonight and took himself to bed immediately following supper. He uses his energy loading supplies at the hotels, handling horses at the livery stable and growing. I'm sure must make his body tired.

Frank arrived about eight o'clock carrying a huge bouquet of lupines. He had a few daisies for Lydia. She thanked him and retired to the kitchen to find some vases. It was thoughtful of him to bring me the flowers I had admired in the afternoon. We sat in the front parlour and talked about the warm weather and about the lumbering taking place in the area south of False Creek. Lydia worked on some embroidery and made a few random comments. She sometimes took her status as chaperone seriously. I don't think she thought Robert needed a chaperone. He was usually in a hurry and she probably thought he would not stay long enough for dalliance. Frank was a man of substance, a serious potential suitor, someone who needed the restraining influence of a chaperone— when it suited her to act like one.

Frank inquired after the severity of the measles in the community. I could only report on Felicity. Lydia had talked with Mrs. Best when she dropped in this morning, and reported the measles was quite severe in the younger children and would probably last three weeks.

Frank then offered scenes of disasters he had known and worked his way to the cholera epidemic in San Francisco years before. "It was bad for the young children but just as bad for some of the adults. People were dying in the streets. The hospitals couldn't take them all and they didn't want them either, for the doctors thought the cholera victims were going to die anyway and they didn't want them cluttering up beds that could be used for the sick who might recover."

"Were you there at the time?"

"No, I read about it in the paper. That same paper I left with you last night. It has a whole page of San Francisco news. The back page has a list of all the dead. You'd think San Francisco had been fighting the Métis. The names look like casualty lists."

Lydia looked around her and found the San Francisco news. I'd left the paper by the chair. She scanned the front page and turned to the back; her embroidery ignored on her lap.

Frank continued to talk, now about the new ship the Spreckles Company was building to increase trade in the Pacific. We speculated on the plans of this shipping company and left Lydia to peruse the lists of cholera casualties until her sudden exclamation drew our attention.

"If that isn't just like him!" She crushed the newspaper and stood, her face flushed, her eyes blinking rapidly and her fists clenched on the paper.

I stood beside her bewildered by her sudden show of temper.

"Like whom? Like what?"

She thrust the paper at me. I opened my hands in a reflex action and took it.

"If that isn't just like a man! Alistair in particular! Just why couldn't he have let me know?"

She started to leave the room.

"Lydia!" I wailed. "What are you talking about?"

"Alistair Angus Bruce Smith died in the cholera epidemic of '84 and never let me know."

"Are you sure it's your Alistair?" I was beginning to understand.

"How many men would have a string of names so distinctive? Alistair's mother insisted on naming him all those Scottish names after her side of the family. That family always did quarrel," she said more to herself than to me, and swept from the room.

Frank stood now, looking confused. 'What the devil?"

I processed what Lydia had just said. It was a little shocking.

"It's all right, Frank. It's not your fault. You just brought news of Lydia's husband—at least, the paper did. She never did know if he deserted her permanently, or died, or changed his name and married again. She had no idea of his whereabouts until she read his name in the paper. Naturally, it's a shock."

"It must be." He lowered himself to his chair. I continued to stand, holding the paper. I stared at Frank for a moment and then, 'Would you mind leaving now, Frank? I'm not sure how Lydia is and I think I should go to her."

He stood quickly. 'Not at all. Good idea."

"I'm looking forward to our drive on Sunday." I smiled at him as I escorted him to the door.

He tipped his hat. "I am also. I hope Mrs. Smith likes the news the paper brought her after she gets used to it."

I didn't know if that was an insensitive remark or the simple truth. Lydia might feel relieved to know what happened to Alistair, but Frank's remarks seemed hard.

"Thanks for the flowers. I'll see you Sunday." I shut the door behind him.

I found Lydia in the kitchen standing over the table absently stirring the jam cooling in a bowl.

"All right?" I asked.

"I suppose so." She watched the fruit move slowly down through the gelatinous syrup.

"Do you think that was your Alistair?"

"Surely to God there couldn't be two of them." She stirred a little more vigorously and then slowed her rhythm. "So, I'm a widow."

"Does it bother you so much?"

"I much prefer being a widow to being a wife. Especially Alistair Angus Bruce Smith's wife."

"Was it so bad?" I didn't want to pry into her affairs, but I'd been curious for years.

"It wasn't so bad. He didn't beat me or yell at me or kick me or anything like that. He just took me for granted—like his horse."

I sat down suddenly and stared at her. "He took you for granted," I said. "Is that all?"

"You don't think that's hard to live with?" She strode up and down the kitchen now gesturing with her hands, then wiping them on her skirt as if they were moist. "He expected me to have his meals ready whenever he wanted them. He expected me to mend his clothes, wash his socks and on the same level be a wife to him when he wanted me. He was kind to me in the same way people are kind to old people or crazy people—kind and tolerant. I don't think he ever really knew what I was like, what I thought, or what I felt. I was a thing, a 'wife', someone to look after him and keep him comfortable. Do you know what that does to your soul, Amy?"

I shook my head. I couldn't have gotten a word in in any case.

"It makes you two people. One person stirs the porridge and mops the floor and mends the clothes. The other person is in your mind. That person thinks and feels and questions and gets angry and weeps and shouts and argues. That person never gets out." Her voice calmed a little. "When we were first married, I tried to change things. I tried to tell him how I felt. Sometimes I even let him see how angry I was." She looked out the kitchen window at a distant point and stood quietly for a moment. Then she sighed and turned back to me. "And he agreed with me and petted me and told me I'd feel better in the morning. And in the morning, it was all the same as it had been. I was like one of the horses in the barn. Occasionally, for no reason at all, I would 'act up'. If a man was patient everything would go back to normal soon, and it did. How could I fight that? He wanted someone to make him comfortable. If I didn't make him comfortable, he didn't want me. I tried, Amy. I really tried. Other women lived that kind of a life. Why couldn't I?" She sat across from me at the kitchen table looking straight into my eyes trying to explain.

"I don't know, Lydia."

She sat back. "Anyway, it got worse. I kept trying to be true to myself and he kept trying to make me his comfort. I wanted a child, Amy, but I didn't want to be married to one!"

She stood and started pacing again. "He wanted me to look after him and feed him just like a child. It was ridiculous."

"And so, he left you?"

She nodded. "I felt so sorry for him too. He didn't understand and he felt like a failure. I felt like a failure and we were unhappy. So, he took the easiest way out for him and left me. I never blamed him, but he could have told me where he was. As an old friend, at least I cared how he was."

She stopped by the setting jam and stirred in the fruit. "So now he's dead, poor soul, and I'm a widow. I have no protection against men now."

"What in the world are you talking about?"

She waved the sticky wooden spoon. "You know how many men are out there in Vancouver, to say nothing of Hastings. All those men and very few women. It doesn't matter how long in the tooth you are, there are men out there who will want you. Up to now, as a married lady no one could expect to be encouraged by me. I was protected from fatigue, overwork, from infection, death in childbirth—all the ills and diseases that come with married life. I was protected from subservience to some man. I was protected from ridicule as a spinster and I was protected from ever giving time and attention to anyone but myself and you and Stanley."

"So, what's different now?"

"So now, I'm a widow. I have to make decisions about things and give reasons."

Her brown hair stood in tiny electric wisps above her braided coronet until she looked like a wild woman in an illustrated *Paradise Lost*.

"Nothing's simple anymore." She stopped walking and looked around the kitchen as if she was looking for an escape. She caught sight of the yellow daisies and reached over, grabbed them out of the vase, lifted the lid of the stove with one hand and prepared to thrust them down inside. I grabbed her arm and took the flowers away.

"They'll smell if you put them in there. We aren't using that stove."

"Ah. Ugh." She shuddered and sank into a chair staring straight ahead. I put the flowers back into the vase.

"Are you all right?" It was a silly question. Obviously, she was upset. I was trying to reassure myself.

Lydia jumped to her feet- "Blast!" she said and took three cups from the shelf. They were remnants of life with Alistair Smith, keepsakes of his mother's. She strode over to the stove and deliberately smashed them on the lid. Then she swept them into the ash box. "They won't smell," she said.

"Would you like a cup of tea?" My panacea for overwrought nerves.

"I'll make it," she said with decision.

I didn't object. By the time she brought the tea pot to the table she seemed calmer.

"Are you all right now?"

"Yes, I am. Don't you tell anyone I'm widowed?"

I was silent.

Lydia said. "I suppose Frank will."

"It doesn't usually take long for information to get around Hastings and Vancouver."

"Blast!" she said again, but she didn't break any more cups.

CHAPTER SIX

On Saturday morning we sent Stanley for the horse and dog cart. We have a standing arrangement with the proprietors of the livery stable behind the Granville Hotel to lease a horse and dog cart every week. This morning as Stanley drove us to Vancouver, I was determined to see Robert. What did he learn about Mr. Dubrant? Perhaps I was only curious and not altruistically motivated. If so, Robert should have great sympathy for my failing as it is part and parcel of his talent as a newspaperman. Curiosity, Lydia has often reminded me, is not necessarily a virtue but the staple of all gossip-bearing tattle-mongers in the country—which is close to telling me to mind my own business.

I had looked at the map of North America on the school room wall this morning when I was gathering books there and rediscovered the great North West, a vast land between Ontario and B.C. If it was controlled by the Métis it would separate B.C. from Ontario and me from my family.

I found I disagreed with Frank. I don't wish to be an American. If the North West rebelled again and founded an independent country would the Americans feel bound to defend British Columbia against invasion? I don't think so, unless they plan to make B.C. a battlefield from which they could conquer the territories all the way to Manitoba. As foolish as Constable Parkinson undoubtedly was, I had more faith in the Provincial police and the new Royal North West Mounted than I did in the rather loose law organizations and vigilante committees of the United States. There should be no more rebellion in Canada.

In spite of all that marvelous reasoning I knew my strongest motivation was curiosity. I wanted to know what Mr. Dubrant had been doing in British Columbia, in Vancouver. Was he connected with last year's North West Rebellion? Had he been working for the rebels and trying to start a rebellion here?

I confided nothing of this to Lydia as we drove along Hastings Road. She had enough on her mind this morning. She would only tell me I had an inflated opinion of my own abilities and importance and probably comment on my vulgar curiosity. I kept a sharp eye out for Robert.

The drive was a short one. Stanley walked the horse sedately around the curve of the road and onto Water Street.

I saw Robert on the verandah of the Sunnyside Hotel. I tapped Stanley on the shoulder, asked to be put down and arranged to meet Lydia later at the dry goods store on Cordova Street.

Robert raised his hat as I approached.

"I want to talk to you." I flicked the dust from my skirts.

He looked mildly interested. "Now?"

"Have tea with me inside," I said. "You can put your notebook on the table and people will think you are interviewing me about the measles."

"No." He followed me into the tea room. "Let them think I'm enjoying your company."

Was he sarcastic? I thought over his remark for a moment, and then grinned. "Are you paying me a compliment?"

'I'm trying, but it's difficult. I wish you wouldn't look so surprised. It takes the joy out of the exercise."

"I'll try harder to be gracious next time."

We ordered tea. I removed my gloves and leaned forward. "Robert, I want to talk seriously."

"So do I, but I can see that now is not the time. Proceed."

"It's about the Métis, Mr. Dubrant."

Robert sat back in his chair and waited for me to continue.

"I looked at the map this morning..." and I told him my thoughts on the importance of tracing Mr. Dubrant's activities.

Robert nodded and listened without interrupting.

"Well, what do you think?" I said when I had finished.

"I think you are a crusader. A born newspaperman."

"Robert," I spoke more sharply than I had intended. "Stop making personal remarks and comment on the substance of my conversation."

He raised his eyebrows. "Yes, Teacher," he said and drummed his fingers on the table. Then he spoke slowly. "You may be right. I might as well tell you. I have already started nosing into where Mr. Dubrant came from and why he was traveling. I sent a few telegrams to Battleford. No one seems to have seen him here after he arrived except Stanley. I have learned the Royal North West Mounted found some of the new Winchester .86 rifles near the fort at Qu'Appelle and are very interested in knowing how they got there. Those rifles are repeaters and they can fire quickly. The police are issued with Winchester Carbines, a Model 76, good guns but not as good as the Winchester .86. And we don't sell Winchester .86s in Canada."

"I suppose they could have come up through the American mid-west, or from the east."

"Or from the west."

"Or across the frozen wastelands from Russia! Be serious, Robert!

"From the southwest. San Francisco."

"Oh." That was possible. "What have the gun discoveries have to do with Mr. Dubrant?"

"He may have had information on where the guns were coming from, and whether there was an organized supply or just a few individual guns trickling into the area. Constable Parkinson doesn't seem to know any other information that might be relevant at this time."

I sipped my tea for a moment, thinking about what Robert had told me. "You know, Robert. If I was Constable Parkinson's superior, I wouldn't tell him the time of day." Imagine a constable confiding in a newspaperman!

Robert's grin was wide. "How wise."

I continued, ignoring him, "There may be all kinds of information that's significant. There may be political meetings in Winnipeg that look ominous; there may be societies forming whose purpose is to overthrow local governments; there may be money coming in from the east, perhaps even from the opposition party, to finance the procurement of guns. Or Mr. Dubrant may have come to Vancouver to arrange to sell guns. There may be many activities occurring that Constable Parkinson doesn't know about."

Robert nodded. "And we have only a slight indication—if a body is slight—that the problems of the Métis or the problem of the guns, or both, are linked to Vancouver."

"Did the constable file a report to his superior?"

"Oh, yes. One thing the constable knows well is how to report. He sent the information on to Superintendent Roycroft in Victoria."

"So, we can hope someone in a higher position is assimilating all this information."

"We can hope," Robert said.

"And in the meantime?"

"In the meantime, I'll see if I can find any information from anyone who might have seen Mr. Dubrant with another person from Vancouver or Hastings. I may even go to New Westminster and see if I can pick up his trail there."

"Frank Hartman does a lot of traveling," I said. "He might be able to help." I turned to leave but Robert caught my arm.

"Listen, Amy. You mustn't tell anyone what we're doing. You could endanger yourself and you could endanger me."

I stared at him for a moment. I had exhorted him to be serious but it was I who had ignored the seriousness of an investigation into murder. "Frank wouldn't..."

"It isn't Frank I'm warning you against. It's telling anyone. A secret is only a secret between two people. After that, it starts leaking."

He was right, of course. It annoyed me that I hadn't realized it. "All right. I'll be silent." I was able to avoid snapping at him, but only just. I would have enjoyed talking to Lydia about the problem, but Robert was right. Silence was protection. If more than two of us were looking into Mr. Dubrant's death, the murderer would soon be aware of it.

We shook hands and I walked up Carrall to Cordova Street and joined Lydia at the dry goods store. Stanley loaded sugar, oatmeal, and some flour into the lockers below the seats on the dog cart. Then we called at the shoemaker's for my repaired boot. By twelve, we were trotting into the lane beside the teacherage. I didn't notice the little girl sitting on our back step until Stanley had tied the horse and was unloading the parcels. It was Ruth Grant. Her fair hair hung in untidy ribbons and her eyes were red, her face streaked with tears. I jumped off the cart and went to her.

"Felicity?" I asked.

She nodded. "Mother said to tell you Felicity's all laid out if you wanted to come and say goodbye." She caught her breath on a sob but stood solidly before me.

I put my arms around her and held her close while she buried her face in my skirt. "When did she die, darling?"

"Last night."

"I see. I'll come right now." I squatted down keeping my hands on her shoulders and hugged her. "We'll get Stanley to drive us in the cart."

A flicker of interest sparked for a moment in Ruth's eyes and then died.

"Come in, Ruth. Have some bread and jam."

Ruth followed docilely and sat at the kitchen table while Stanley inhaled his lunch, washed it down with milk cool from the well and hurried out. I sipped tea and Lydia offered milk to Ruth, but she chose tea.

"Mother says we aren't to drink milk anywhere but at home where she knows it's been boiled."

Lydia repressed her first annoyed reaction to aspersions cast on her housekeeping abilities. "Very sensible," she said. "Have some tea.'"

I looked at Ruth surreptitiously for signs of the measles but could see none. I suppose poor Mrs. Grant watched each child in the same way.

Ruth sat quietly as we rode in the dog cart to her house. I had Frank's bouquet of lupines in my hand and a plate of Lydia's biscuits. I thought about Mrs. Grant's strictures on drinking milk. It was part of her plan to try to keep her children well. Most mothers try to buy milk taken from a particular cow they are assured doesn't cause fevers. They keep the milk cool in wells or ice holes and then, when fever does strike, they boil it before serving. All because they think that somehow bad milk causes fever. I sometimes think the old witch's charms above the kitchen door were just as effective as some of our health practices.

There was a white wreath on the front door of the Grant house. "My father's at work," Ruth said.

I suppose there was nothing he could do here and the family needed the three dollars he would earn today. I recognized the two children in the kitchen and assumed the other four were in bed with the measles. Mrs. Grant was quiet today, almost dignified.

Her apron was clean, white, and starched, standing stiffly in front of her like a uniform. Her hair was caught by numerous hairpins in a tidy bun at the nape of her neck. She wore her best black dress that rustled as she walked. We shook hands and I offered her my condolences. She thanked me and invited me into the parlour. Felicity lay on a board on a table. She looked as though she was sleeping, her eyes closed and her hands across her chest. Someone, her mother probably, had brushed her pale hair and laid it in a fan on her shoulders. She wore a white muslin shift and held two lavender blue lupines in her hands. The lupines were wilting from lack of water and suddenly seemed symbolic of Felicity's fragility and innocence. I had to blink and swallow to keep from crying.

"She looks nice, don't she?" Mrs. Grant said.

I nodded. Mrs. Grant walked over to Felicity's body and twitched the blond hair into a perfect position. Then she absently caressed the cold cheek.

I trembled a little but managed to approach Felicity and lay my bouquet of lupines at her feet. Her mother picked up the flowers and arranged them around Felicity until she looked to be sleeping in a bed of blue.

"This is nice, Teacher. Thanks for bringing them. Come and have a cup of tea with me."

We returned to the kitchen and I sat near the table.

"We'll bury her on Sunday after church services. You'll be there?"

I nodded again. Somehow, I was more ill at ease with Mrs. Grant today when she was calm and resigned than I had been when she screamed at God. "You're all right now?"

She carried the kettle to the counter top and poured hot water into the teapot. She watched carefully and didn't speak until she had the pot full. Then she returned the kettle to its position at the back of the stove and joined me at the table. "I'm all right and you're wondering why I'm not crying, aren't you?"

"Yes."

"It's like this, Miss MacDonald. There ain't nothing I can do now. Do you understand? When I could try to help Felicity, when there might be something I could do to help her, well then, I tried real hard. Now I can't help her. Now, God is looking after her."

"You'll miss her."

"I'll never be whole again Miss," she said simply. "Mothers feel like that. There aren't many of us who don't lose a child, or two, or three." She stared at her teacup, absently turning it around in her hands. 'When I'm an old lady, if I ever get to be an old lady, I might have four of my eight children around me. That's life. Everyone knows it will happen. You just keep hoping it won't happen to you."

We were silent. Then I ventured the question that had been worrying me. "Are the other children all right?"

"I have four in bed with the measles. The doctor says they aren't as bad as Felicity. Little Joe isn't too strong, but the doctor says he's stronger than he looks and he's not too worried about him. I've got garlic wrapped on Little Joe's feet and the windows all closed and the curtains drawn so he won't suffer in his eyes, and I'm praying."

We sipped our tea. She'd survived childbirth eight times. She'd lost her figure and any hope of a life of her own. Now she'd lost her child. Yet she sat there with more dignity and courage than I could hope for. I felt shallow and inadequate.

"People will come today to see Felicity," she continued. "Not children. I won't let any children in there. Felicity might still be able to pass them the measles even though that red faded right away when she died. The doctor says no children, but their parents will be here and I'm glad Felicity looks so nice."

"Yes, she does."

"And, she'll keep good. The cook at the mill is sending over some ice tonight. He keeps some in the sawdust out behind the cook shack so Felicity will stay real nice for the funeral."

Oh, dear God. I couldn't stand this. If I wanted to leave with dignity, I realized I'd better go now.

"When your other children are a little better I'll bring some slates and some stories over for them. It will give them something to do." I managed to stammer that out.

She escorted me to the door. "You're a good woman, Miss MacDonald. Generous."

We shook hands and I offered my condolences again. By the time I had walked down the Mill Road and down the path below the teacherage to my bay I realized I was angry, not just sad that Felicity had died, but very angry. The Bible says death is a punishment for the sins of mankind. Little Felicity hadn't been old enough to understand sin much less commit any. I pictured her, a helpless child stretched out in death and her mother resigned to it. Why do mothers love children so much when they know they are going to lose them? The tears started then, tears of anger, frustration, and sorrow. I would miss Felicity; and how many more would I miss before the summer was over? If it wasn't the year for measles it would be typhoid or infection or fever. I kicked a rock out of my way and leaned against a pine tree. The tears were coursing down my cheeks and I muttered to myself.

"Why have children? It's too much caring. It's too risky. I will *not* have any children. I will *never* have children. Why have children to see them die?"

I was so upset I didn't hear anyone approach and almost fell into the bay when a firm voice said, "Young woman, don't fret yourself into a knot. There are ways to prevent having children."

I whirled around to see a modish older woman leaning on her parasol watching me. I fumbled for my handkerchief but accepted hers.

"So sorry," I said. "My friend's little girl just died, and I'm upset."

"And so, you should be. No one should be so hard they could accept the death of a child."

She had an interesting face, long and narrow with wide dark eyes. Crow's feet fanned away from her eyes, but the rest of her face was smooth and clear. Her lips were narrow and tight making me think she could be strong and even hard.

"I couldn't help but overhear you. You sounded frightened of getting pregnant. Now look," she said before I could explain the theoretical nature of the problem, "don't you listen to a lot of silly talk. If you don't want to have children, don't have any."

She started then to give me practical advice on effective ways to prevent conception. No one had ever told me such things before. I didn't know people did such things.

"You may feel differently about children after a time, but it doesn't hurt to have a few years of loving attention from a husband without children." She paused and straightened her back, then tapped the point of her parasol into the ground.

"Not that I've ever had a husband, but I know what they're like." She adjusted the ribbons of her hat to fix the net and straw creation a little more firmly on her head. She looked down at me coolly. "You really must learn to deal with life. Everyone must."

This tall, arrogant woman was well into her advice before I realized what she was talking about. My mind went from grief and anger to frozen incredulity to embarrassment to amusement in the space of about fifty seconds.

"Thank you very much, Mrs...?"

"Miss Porter. Maude Porter. I work at the Granville Hotel most often. Not that I expect to meet you again, you understand. I come out for walk to keep my figure and my sanity, but I usually go toward the Moody Reserve This is the first time I've come this way."

"Oh."

She was respectably dressed in a dark walking skirt and a navy hat that must have come from San Francisco. She wore dark gloves and carried a parasol with a blue and white polka dotted flounce. Her clothes were not elaborate but were of good quality and I would never have known she was as a prostitute if she hadn't just told me. Her arrogant air was worthy of a San Francisco society matron, but she had the look of someone used to hard work. Her hair was red, a dark mahogany red. I wondered what she did to keep it that way.

I realized I hadn't said anything, and I was staring. "Uh, MacDonald. My name Amy MacDonald and I'm the schoolteacher for the Hastings Mills School."

"Oh, no!" She backed away. Then her face closed into a bitter look. "You're not married! Why didn't you stop me from making a fool of myself? Was that your idea of grand fun?" She whipped around to leave me, and I caught her arm.

"Stop, Miss Porter. Wait. Thank you very much. You don't know how much you helped me. Don't apologize for your kindness. I appreciate it."

She turned back and stood for a moment looking down. Her hands gripped the parasol tightly. Then she let it swing down and sway like a pendulum while she looked at me.

"I must have embarrassed you. I'm sorry."

"Well...." I didn't know what to say. In fact, she had embarrassed me, but she had meant it kindly.

She bowed and again started to leave.

"Wait! Don't go away." I spoke awkwardly, but I didn't know what to do or say. "It was kind of you to care about me. Besides, I might need that information you gave me someday and where else would I learn it? Don't worry. You've distracted me from my anger and my sorrow and I'm grateful for that also. Thank you."

I walked beside her. "Do you come this way often? Oh, no, you said you didn't."

Miss Porter settled her light shawl with a twitch of her shoulders. "As I said, Miss MacDonald, I usually go to the Reserve. The women generally don't know who I am, and the men won't recognize me, so I can have a pleasant stroll by myself. Business is usually slow about five in the evening, so I try to get some exercise and some solitude. This is as far as I've come this way. Not that it's very far."

"You come again," I said. "We must get to know each other."

Miss Porter smiled. "That's very nice of you—foolish though. Mind you don't know me in town. I won't have that. If you don't snub me on the street, I'll snub you. So don't try to be friendly with me in public."

I took a deep breath. I knew this would cost me something. "Miss Porter. I wouldn't snub you in public."

She looked amused.

"I know the world better than you do and you must promise you won't recognize me in public. You see," she continued setting a brisk pace back toward the teacherage and the town. "If folks saw we were friendly they would wonder about you. They'd wonder how a maiden lady got to know me, and that wouldn't be good for you."

I started to protest, but she didn't pause.

"And if the men of Vancouver saw you were friendly with me, they would be suspicious I was trying to become respectable. They would think that meant marriage to a respectable man and that would scare them, and I'd lose business."

The business ramifications of this social intercourse hadn't occurred to me. "I see. Have you any inclination to be respectable?" I was curious.

"Are you going to promise to ignore me in public?"

"Yes. All right."

She adjusted her parasol, so it shaded her face more completely. "Yes, I do have plans to be respectable. I have always valued my independence, so my respectability isn't going to begin or end in marriage. I am saving my money and as soon as I have enough, I'll start my own bakery shop."

"You like to bake?" I blurted out the question. It seemed such a mundane activity.

"Yes, I like to bake and I am looking forward to letting my hair go gray, getting fat and living on the other side of the clock."

I stared at her.

"I will have to rise at five in the morning and work until about two in the afternoon. Right now, I rise at two in the afternoon and work until five in the morning. I thought it would be a change to live in the morning hours."

I nodded. There were many things in life that had never crossed my path before.

"Will a bakery shop make you respectable?"

"I think so. People will tolerate a good deal for their stomachs, and I intend to be very good. I'm very good at my present job." She looked at me speculatively. "If you ever need advice."

"Thank you very much," I said hurriedly. "I'm afraid I couldn't listen to it right now. I think I would be shocked."

"You don't seem to shock easily. Comes of being a schoolteacher, I suppose."

It was my turn to be amused. "How's that?"

"Teachers are always curious. Always looking up things in books. I have a customer who was a teacher once. He even brings his books with him. Odd stories of a man trapping his wife and her lover in a net and another of hitting an old man over the head with an axe so he could give birth to a daughter. Horrible stories about men eating their children." She shuddered. "After reading things like that I don't suppose anything shocks him."

"Cronus!" I said in sudden understanding "Greek Mythology! Zeus giving birth to Athena." Suddenly it was all too much for me.

I threw back my head and laughed and laughed. I finally leaned against a stump and held my hand to the stitch in my side. "Oh, Miss Porter. You must have some wonderful stories of your own."

This time the smile touched her eyes "Well, it's not all roses, my dear, but it's not all briars either. Are you feeling better?"

I shook her hand and smiled at her "You are a pleasure to know. Thanks for stopping to help."

She flicked my hands with her gloves. "It's a pleasure to talk to another woman. I work as an independent and find it lonely at times." Then she sailed down the road, parasol high, head erect.

I walked to the teacherage still with the aching sadness of Felicity's death bruising my mind but no long in despair over the injustice of death. Life was hard for everyone in some way or other. I suppose Maude Porter had to put up with a lot of unhappiness to make her way in life. I'm glad I met her just when I needed someone or something to help me with my distress over Felicity. Maude Porter must know a lot about people. It was only then I wondered if she might have information about Mr. Dubrant.

CHAPTER SEVEN

I slept late on Sunday morning. There was no time for a swim if I planned to be at church on time. We warmed the irons on the stove while we boiled our morning tea. I pressed my jabot and Lydia's collar and cuffs while she brushed off Stanley's trousers. Stanley polished everyone's shoes and we managed to be dressed and walking along the road with a little time to spare. I wore my good navy-blue dress, white jabot and carried a black lace shawl. The dress was appropriate for Felicity's funeral and still suitable for my drive to the Reserve. I took a quick sideways look at my family. Lydia was quite handsome in her good brown bombazine and Stanley looked like a neat and tidy scarecrow. He would fill out into muscled shoulders and a sturdy body like our older brother back home, but right now he was all angles and bone and loose joints.

My mother would have been pleased. She died in childbirth when Stanley was seven having spent much of her young life ill from miscarriages and difficult pregnancies. If she had rest and leisure now, wherever she was, I hoped she enjoyed the sight of Stanley at his best.

The air was hazy. Slash burned south of the city and long streaks of the smoke drifted back toward the inlet. All the trees had been cleared from that section of the peninsula and the brush left on the ground was dry and flammable.

The C.P.R. expected to sell many of the lots south of town and they were bringing in men and oxen to do the job quickly. Lydia and I wondered if we should try to obtain a lot before more speculators than the railroad company increased the prices. Robert told me he had bought a lot near Moody's Reserve so he could fish and hunt when he felt the urge. That would be a pleasant section of town but quite a walk from the school. I would have to buy a horse. Perhaps Lydia and I should buy the lot now and wait until Stanley was settled in some kind of occupation before we spent our savings on a house.

The sun glinted off the water of Coal Harbour. I stood on the church steps for a few minutes looking out over the C.P.R. roadbed and the docks and wharves under construction near the water. Today everything was quiet. Most days the hammering and sawing and banging, the hooting of whistles and the shouting of men rang in the air demanding attention to the bustle and progress of the city. Today, we could enjoy the peace of the blue water and the towering green mountains across the inlet. There was tranquility in this scene. The dead should be able to enjoy it: Felicity and my mother. Maybe even Alistair Angus Bruce Smith.

I walked into the church and sat with Lydia. Stanley deserted us for the back row and the young people. Felicity's rough coffin lay on some planks as front of the church heaped with the blue, lavender, and pink of fresh lupines. Two blue flowers had spilled over and lay on the floor. Mr. Grant sat with his wife and two of the children. He was a grizzled man, twenty years older than his wife, tall and almost gaunt. Hard work and poverty combined to give that look of suffering I had seen many times. Hard work and poverty also gave that tough spirit to generations of his Scottish ancestors. I could see them in my mind standing behind him, wresting food from the barren islands of the Hebrides, fighting for Prince Charles and dying at Culloden.

I closed my eyes and prayed for the future of his children.

"May You grant them health and prosperity, Oh Lord. Health and prosperity."

Mrs. Grant sat dry-eyed throughout the ceremony.

I spoke to her on the way out. "A sunny day for Felicity."

"She'd like that," Mrs. Grant was clam. "I'm sorry we can't have folks back for a collation but there is still measles in the house and folks don't want to come to the measles. Don't seem right to send her off without a neighbourly meal, but people wouldn't come with the measles there and all."

"Best not to have people in," I agreed.

"And little Joe is still sick," she continued.

"How sick?" I looked at her in alarm.

"The doctor thinks he'll make it, but Mr. Grant is that worried about him."

I looked quickly at her husband moving his feet back and forth impatiently at the church door.

"I'll let you go then."

She nodded "We're burying her on Deadman's Island. I can see it from the mill site and that will be a comfort."

Deadman's Island is a small island near the Moody Reserve in Coal Harbour.

"It's right pretty there and Felicity will have a view of the mill yard and the ocean and all the boats and things. Angus MacKay is buried there too. You mind he fell off the dock a month or two ago and drowned?"

I nodded again. Vancouver did not yet have a cemetery. We had only a few births. Little Margaret MacNeil was the first white child born here in April, and we hadn't organized our deaths yet.

"I hope the children improve quickly."

She thanked me and joined her husband. Men from the mill would help Mr. Grant load the coffin into a boat and row it over to Deadman's Island to the new grave I had seen open this morning. We left the Grant family to lay Felicity in the ground and returned to our own lives.

It was too hot to eat a big dinner, so Lydia and I picked at a few cold meats and buns. Stanley ate everything he could see. There was no waste of food with him in the house.

Frank was prompt at one o'clock and good-naturedly took Lydia and Stanley up in the phaeton with us. Stanley stood on the step and held on as there was no room for him to sit. We joined many others who gravitated toward Moody's Reserve on Sunday afternoon.

The path to the Reserve wound through tall Douglas fir. It was rough but Frank set a comfortably slow pace and I thoroughly enjoyed the cool woods. We tied the horse to a rail near the Reserve because, as yet, there was no bridge across the narrow channel. Frank and I stopped to talk to a couple we knew, and Lydia and Stanley wandered off to join groups of their choice. Frank crossed the log to the Reserve first and I gingerly picked my way after him. This is the only entry to the Reserve and while it is a little nerve-wracking and not to be attempted in the rain, it is worth some initial trepidation to spend the afternoon promenading in the Reserve.

As we walked on the paths, I carried my blue and brown parasol to protect my face from the sun. The tallest trees had been removed for ship spars but there was still some shade from the remaining pines. The air was free of smoke here and I enjoyed the tang of the pine pitch and seaweed and the feel of the slight breeze on my face. I had taken some pains with my hair today, so it didn't hang around my shoulders in untidy wisps the way it usually does. Today it was in place in a cluster of fat, disciplined ringlets on the top of my head.

Frank was fashionable. His dark green suit made him look distinguished, and with his bright white shirt and wide loose tie, even elegant. I thought we were quite a modish couple. We talked and stopped and exchanged pleasantries with others who were walking with equal pleasure in the afternoon.

We halted near the beach and looked back over Vancouver. The shoreline disappeared under the pilings. Piles of trees and debris littered the land between Vancouver and the mill site, remnants of the domino-style logging the C.P.R. had conducted. The spit of land and trees hid the teacherage, and beyond that, the cluster of buildings of the settlement of Hastings spilled down the slope into the wharves and docks at Hastings Mill. Beyond the shores everywhere we looked was the timber country. I wondered where Robert's lot was.

"If I were going to buy a lot from the C.P.R. Frank, which one should I buy?"

He looked surprised. "Why would you want a lot?"

"For the same reasons you want one, investment. Which part of the city do you think would make the best investment?"

"Oh, I see." He thought for a few moments. "I have a few lots on Carrall Street myself. I think when the Chinamen go back to China that section of the town will build up. The lots are cheap there. I'll hold onto them for about ten years and then I should do well on sales."

"What makes you think the Chinese will leave?"

"There should be some legislation to get them out by then. The government might expropriate their property adjacent to mine. I should be able to pick up bargains then. In the meantime, I'll rent to the Chinamen who want to live there. It's a good investment. And then he pointed to the area behind the road to the Reserve and further up the hill." I have a lot about six up from the water in the middle of the trees. The plans call for Burrard Street to be located there. I have another lot. I think it's fourteen up from the water, on the same street. When that section is cleared, I'll build a house right there overlooking Coal Harbour."

I turned and looked at him speculatively. This was the first I had heard he planned to remain in Vancouver. I had always thought of Frank as an American who would return to San Francisco. "You're staying here?"

"It's starting to look good to me," he said and smiled.

It is the habit of most men to pay women compliments when they are together socially, but I thought Frank might mean it. Of course, he could be talking about Vancouver's financial climate.

I smiled at him. "I thought you would return to the States."

"Who knows? Vancouver's a lot like San Francisco. Maybe it will be in the States someday. I like the mountains. I can't stand the plains—flat miles and miles of nothing with the wind blowing all the time."

I thought of the flat land I'd crossed on the train from New York to San Francisco before I took the ship to Victoria. "It is miles and miles of nothing."

"It's not so bad in the north country—some hills and some green trees. But the south," he shook his head, "they should leave it to Big Bear and Poundmaker."

I tried to fit that description into my map of the American plains and then found that the rolling hills in the north and Poundmaker in the south fit the Canadian plains. Frank must have come across the Canadian plains.

We were interrupted then by a tall, thin man in a dark suit. He tipped his hat to me and spoke to Frank. Frank introduced us. "Miss Macdonald, this is Joseph Sanders. He is a visitor here from the east."

Mr. Sanders removed his hat exposing a bald head. His eyes were sharp and black, his skin so tight on his face he looked as though it was drawn back into his scalp. I thought of the caricatures of death I used to see in the eastern papers.

"How do you do." He nodded at me.

"Mr. Sanders came out to see what the C.P.R. is doing with their money."

"With your money, Mr. Hartman. I represent the riding of York West in opposition to the government as I'm sure you know, and I decided to take a trip out west to see what Van Horne is doing with all that money he borrowed from us; the taxpayer's money."

He repeated his motives to be sure the ignorant like myself would understand how conscientious he was.

"Have you been here long, Mr. Sanders?"

"I arrived in Victoria last week, Miss MacDonald, and have been availing myself of your wonderful weather and interesting sights in Vancouver for three days now. Mr. Hartman has kindly shown me a few of the local industries and introduced me to some entrepreneurs."

They exchanged a quick look.

The last entrepreneur I'd met was Maude Porter. I wondered if either of them or both of them, knew her. Two days ago, I would not have thought such a thing.

"I hope you like it here," I said conventionally.

"I'm sure I shall. It was pleasant to meet Mr. Hartman again. He and I had some interesting discussions at Battleford this spring and I enjoyed my exposure to his opinions."

"Mr. Hartman is well travelled," I said. Battleford! That was in the North West. What was Frank doing in Battleford? What had Mr. death-like Sanders been doing there?

"So pleasant to meet you, Miss MacDonald." Compliments flowed easily from him.

I nodded. "Goodbye."

He walked away at a quick pace. We walked on more slowly.

"He, uh, never did see me in Battleford," Frank said. "He mixes me up with someone else, but it didn't seem polite to correct him."

That might be true, and it might not. Frank was very polite, and the man was an obnoxious soul who would be hard to snub. We watched a few bathers in the Coal Harbour bay. Usually there were many children but today the measles kept the young children away and only a few older boys waded in the shallows.

"Hello, Miss MacDonald." Constable Parkinson had come from one of the side trails. He escorted a pale, frail looking girl, one of the Kingley-Smiths from Dunlevy Street.

"Hello, Constable. Hello, Miss Kingley-Smith. Do you know Mr. Hartman?"

She nodded shyly and shook hands.

The constable fell in step beside me and forced Frank to escort the young lady.

"I wanted to ask you something." He stepped out briskly and left Frank and the slower walking Miss Kingley-Smith out of earshot.

"Indeed?"

"Yes." He ignored my annoyance or, more probably, didn't even recognize it.

"Why is this Robert Carr so interested in the Métis who died here? He's a friend of yours and I thought you could help the government by telling us what Mr. Carr is up to."

Robert's credibility was suffering from his curiosity. I almost laughed but then realized that Constable Parkinson, dear thick Constable Parkinson, was serious and in a position to do Robert harm.

"He doesn't know much about Mr. Dubrant, Constable, but he is very curious. You see Robert is much like a child who is insatiably curious—all the time," I added in the likely event that words of more than two syllables were unfamiliar to the constable.

He nodded.

"And Mr. Carr is curious about almost anything. He is a newspaper man, you know. They're very nosey."

"Yes, I suppose," the constable said. "But he telegraphed Regina asking for a background on Mr. Dubrant and that's my job."

I now understood the constable's annoyance with Robert.

"I suppose he thought you would be too busy to manage to do that. Had you already telegraphed?"

"Well, no. I hadn't gotten around to it yet. I was busy."

"I'm sure Mr. Carr was only trying to save you time, but he certainly should have consulted you." I made my voice sound censorious. "Most rude of him to strike out on his own without supervision like that. He could ruin your plans."

The constable looked at me quickly and I wondered if I had exaggerated beyond the point of belief. I tried to control the tone in my voice." Has he done anything else to bother you?"

"He telephoned New Westminster from the book store."

"What did he hope to learn from that?"

"I guess he wanted to know how the Métis got from the North West to New Westminster and then on the stage to Vancouver."

"Did he find out?" I asked with real curiosity.

The constable drew himself up. "I haven't asked him yet."

I put a placating hand on his arm. "Why don't you give Robert a job to do such as collecting information about Mr. Dubrant? That way you'll know what he's doing, and he won't get in your way. You'll have good control of the situation."

The constable stroked his blonde mustache. "I'd thought of that. The only thing I'm worried about is perhaps he already knows everything."

I looked at him questioningly.

"Maybe he's a spy for the Red River Métis."

"Robert!" I swallowed a laugh. "I suppose someone in your position has to consider all possibilities, but I would think with Robert's conservative Halifax background he's more likely to have the curious printer's ink in his veins than the French-Indians fire of rebellion."

"Halifax?" the constable said slowly.

"Yes," I prevaricated. His father owns the Halifax News."

"Oh." The constable let the wheels of analytical thought rotate slowly.

As far as I could remember Robert said his father grew potatoes in Nova Scotia, but I didn't think that would impress the good constable.

He touched his hat. "Thanks for talking to me, Miss MacDonald."

"Not at all," I said gravely. "I wish you well on your investigations."

The constable smiled and returned to his young lady.

Frank was not pleased. "What did he have to say?"

"Oh, Frank. He is such a ridiculous soul." I would like to have told Frank about the constable's suspicions just to laugh with him about it, but that might harm Robert and I didn't want to repeat such a slanderous story. "He asked me more about the body I found in the bay."

Frank leaned closer, interested. I would have to practice if I wanted to become a good liar.

"The Métis?"

"Yes. I don't know any more than I've already told him. It really isn't my business anyway. It was only a coincidence I found him." I was uncomfortable and hoped Frank wouldn't notice.

"He didn't try to accuse you of poisoning the man, did he?"

"Oh, no. Why would he? He only wanted more details. I hardly looked at the body I suppose he didn't either and now has to fill in a report." I turned to Frank. "Does everyone know what happened to the man? That he was poisoned?"

Frank looked startled for a moment and then smiled. "It's Vancouver, isn't it? There aren't any secrets here."

I returned his smile. He really is a charming man. "Well, I admit Vancouver passes news around faster than any other place I've ever lived but someone's keeping a secret. After all, someone poisoned the Métis."

I looked over the bay at the calm blue inlet and let out a deep breath. "Let's forget the constable."

"Agreed. If he bothers you, you let me know. I don't want you disturbed."

I smiled at him. If Frank was serious about me, wanted to marry me at some time, he would be a good protector. I speculated on his admirable qualities. He was intelligent and an interesting businessman. I might enjoy being married to Frank. He'd be safe, give me a reasonably sedate, respectable life. I suppose I will have to consider marriage at some time. There isn't much else I can do. As long as Lydia lives with me, and I or Stanley are working, I could continue to live unmarried. If Stanley wants a home of his own and if Lydia leaves me, I could not continue to live alone. I just didn't want to embrace the married state yet. I looked at Frank out of the corner of my eye. Handsome too. The children would be good-looking, but then I didn't want children. I wonder if he would prevent conception if I asked him to. I blushed at my own wayward thoughts. Frank saw that blush. I hope he interpreted it as a reaction to his declaration of protection.

We walked to Brockton Point and looked toward the Indian village of Ho-mul-che-sun. There were more people living there than in Vancouver. Luckily, they were peaceful. Lydia and Stanley met us at the phaeton, and we had a slow and easy trip back to the teacherage.

CHAPTER EIGHT

Frank had just disappeared down Hastings Road when Sung Wick presented himself at the back door. I hadn't expected him on Sunday, but I was willing to teach. Lydia made the evening meal, and I spent an hour teaching the alphabet and beginning sounds. Lydia got involved with this lesson because I used household nouns like "water", "dish" and "cup" and spelling the words on the slate while showing Sung Wick what they were. Lydia even became gay and popped a cup onto the table when we weren't expecting it and demanded,

"What?'

At first Sung Wick was alarmed, but after a few times he enjoyed it and grinned and grabbed the chalk and tried to write the word. He left before our supper hour.

After the meal Stanley drifted off to visit friends. Lydia said she had letters to write. I suppose she had people in the east to inform of Alistair Angus Bruce Smith's death. I washed up the dishes, hung the tea towel on the outside line and looked at the fading sunset. It would be dark in a few minutes. The air was still, humid, and warm. My dress clung to my shoulders and hips. I would love a swim.

Why not? It was unlikely a body would again appear in the bay. Vancouver people were not in the habit of killing each other. No one would be down that way at this time of night. All I needed was a little resolution. The cool water would feel delicious.

I hurried into my room, changed to my bathing costume, and traveling coat and picked up a bath blanket.

It was dark when I let myself out the back door. No moon lit the sky; no lights of any kind penetrated the fields and woods between me and the bay. I felt my way slowly down the path. When I was within fifty yards of the bay, I could see the bobbing lanterns on the ships out in the harbour. That gave me a sense of direction and I was able to walk more quickly.

The water was silky, warm, and refreshing. I had never swum in the evening before and hadn't realized how much warmer it felt—almost like water warmed for a bath. I left my white blanket well up on the shore with my shoes and cloak near it so I could find everything when I finished. I could have left my bathing costume there too but lacked the nerve to bathe, even in the pitch dark, without any clothes.

I didn't go over my head in the water because I was afraid, I would become disoriented and not be able to find the shore. I paddled happily back and forth in the shallow part of the bay, putting my feet down on the sand and reassuring myself I was safe. I hummed a little to myself and stretched out my arms and legs doing slow waltz steps.

After I'd been splashing and swimming for about ten minutes, I decided I should continue my swimming lessons and force myself to put my head under the water. There was no one at the house to care if my hair was wet, and it would dry in the warm air tonight. I planted my feet securely on the sand, took a deep breath and slowly lowered my chin, mouth, nose, eyes, and hair under the water and then shot up. I was elated! I had actually put my head right under. True, I hadn't mastered blowing the air out, but I had gone under. If I had to hold my breath under the water, then I'd do that for a while. I tried it again. This time I sank a little more quickly and stayed under just a fraction of a second longer. Then I swam back and forth parallel to the shore well pleased with myself. Since my hair was soaking wet anyway, I lay on my back and floated for a time, looking up at the stars and speculating on the universe. The collar of my bathing costume was heavy and hung straight down when I floated on my back. I would cut it off. No one ever saw me bathe so what difference did it make if my costume was fashionable?

I had just come to that conclusion when I saw a star glow and diminish. I stared at the edge of the bay. I must have seen it through the trees. There it was again. A star that pulsated? I stood with my feet on the sand and concentrated. Then faintly, over the scent of seaweed, and salt, over the pungent scent of cedar came the unmistakable sharp smell of tobacco.

I froze where I was. Someone was sitting on the rocks at the edge of the bay, smoking.

If I tried to creep out of the bay into the woods and home, I'm sure he could catch me. He would hear me move out of the water. All the material of my bathing costume held water and streamed off me when I emerged. I could take the suit off and slip out of the water but that meant risking capture when I was naked. The man on the rock knew I was there. I'd been humming and singing. He'd have to be deaf not to know I was there. Presumably, he didn't want to get wet, so I was better off in the water. Lydia would wonder where I was in an hour or so. Perhaps Stanley would come home and look for me. Nothing would be gained by pretending I hadn't seen him. He didn't seem to mind if I knew he was there. If he had wanted to stay concealed, he wouldn't have smoked. Unless it was Constable Parkinson who might not know how to stay concealed.

I gathered my spinning thoughts into some kind of order, swallowed, coughed, swallowed again and then said, "Who's there?"

There was silence for a moment and then, "Neptune waiting for the water nymph."

"Robert Carr!" I was angry with relief. "You, ignorant, meddlesome, bothersome gnat! You scared me badly. What are you doing here?"

"I came to talk to you and reached your home just as you snuck out the back door. I thought you might be up to something interesting."

I breathed more normally now. "Didn't it occur to you I might want privacy?"

"Oh, yes."

"And you followed anyway?"

"Assuredly."

I gave up. "What did you want to talk about?"

"Can you talk from the water?"

"I don't see why I should curtail my swim to suit your convenience."

Unexpectedly, Robert chuckled. "Come a little closer then, so I can talk a little more softly."

I swam toward the rocks.

"The Constable has been giving me the cold shoulder. Do you know anything about that? I saw him talking to you today in the Reserve and wondered if he told you anything."

I laughed. "He thinks you are a Métis spy."

"Oh, for God's sake!" Robert was disgusted.

"I told him that you were born meddlesome but that you were harmless. I don't know if he believed me."

"Thanks." Robert's tone was dry. I still couldn't see him, but I could see the end of his cigar glow and dim.

I moved my hands and feet in circles then allowed the waves to wash me up on the small rocks. "Robert, do you think Frank may be a government spy? I mean sent here by the Government of Canada to find out about the Métis?"

"What brings you to that conclusion?"

I told Robert about meeting Mr. Sanders, the politician, and how Mr. Sanders had said he met Frank before in Battleford.

"It's possible," Robert mused. "I hadn't thought of that. I can't see why the Dominion government would use an American citizen, though but it might explain why Frank's so interested in the movement of freight to the North West."

The cigar grew bright for a moment then Robert continued. "On the other hand, Frank is truly a businessman, and it would be unusual if he wasn't interested in the movement of freight."

"Is he?"

"So, Stanley says."

"Oh, does he?"

"There's not much Stanley misses around the hotel and a lot of supplies come and go on the stage. The roadbed's completed for the railroad, but right now everything comes and goes by stage and Stanley helps load and unload it. He gets to know a lot."

"I hope Stanley doesn't know everything that goes on at the hotel?"

"Why?"

"I met Maude Porter yesterday."

"How did you meet Maude Porter?"

My feet drifted with the tiny waves while I held onto the rocks and moved slowly like seaweed in the gentle action. I told Robert about Maude. "I liked her," I said defiantly. "She's genuinely good-hearted, and a little sad," I added.

"Oh, Maude's good-hearted," Robert agreed and I wondered how well he knew her. "She's right though. You ought not to be seen with her."

I moved my fingers through the soft water. It seemed a little cooler now. "I suppose not. I wouldn't have a teaching job next year if the townspeople thought I was friendly with her. All the same, she would be a great source of information. I wonder what she could tell us about Mr. Sanders."

"She probably wouldn't tell us anything. She has her own standards," Robert said. "Are you going to stay in the water all night?"

"I'll come out now." I swam back to the middle of the bay, waded out and dried myself with my bath blanket. I could hear Robert walking through the trees but didn't see him until he was beside me.

"I could ask Maude if she'd get specific information for us and tell her why. We need help now and I think we could risk letting Maude know what we know." He settled my traveling coat around my shoulders as he talked.

We walked back toward the teacherage, Robert holding my elbow and guiding me past the stumps and low branches. "She would help us if she thought she was trying to catch a murderer. Maude's heart's all right."

"Good. Perhaps we'll learn something." We were in the field behind the house when I asked suddenly and irrelevantly. "Can you swim?"

"Yes." 'Robert said. "But I didn't have a costume and I thought even the intrepid Miss MacDonald might be embarrassed by a nude swimming companion."

I was grateful for the dark for I blushed at the thought.

"And I meant to tell you," 'Robert said, "I think your bathing costume is very fetching."

"You can't even see it. It's too dark."

"I'm a journalist. I have eyes like a cat and can see everything."

"And you have a vivid imagination."

Robert leaned toward me and laid his hand on my warm cheek. "I think your imagination is active also."

I put my hand up to snatch his away and found once I had his hand in mine, I didn't want to move it. We stood there for a moment. Robert turned my hand in his and kissed it softly.

"Good night, Amy."

"Good night," I said quietly and left him at the gate.

CHAPTER NINE

The smoke was so thick the next morning that Lydia complained she would be asphyxiated if the mill didn't control their slash fires. We were up early. No school this Monday morning but the salmonberries were ripe, and we planned to pick as many as we could before the sun was hot in the sky. Stanley disappeared after breakfast to join some friends bathing and playing on the log booms. I worried he would get caught and drown underneath the acres of floating logs, but Lydia encouraged Stanley to use his common sense and be independent.

"Worry can cripple a boy, you know."

"And drowning can kill him."

"He won't drown."

Since Stanley had already left, the whole conversation was academic.

I tied an old apron over my cotton skirt and carried two big lard pails up the Hastings Mill Road to a spot where loggers had missed a low-lying glen with a small creek, dry now, that gave fertile soil. Ripe, red berries hung under the broad leaves of the bushes. Red juice stained my hands, but the resulting jam and preserves would be worth my efforts. The sun warmed my back while I picked industriously for an hour. Lydia joined me and picked quickly.

She complained again about the smoke. It originated near the wharf at the mill. We could see the thick column rise and then spread and drift toward us. Fire had been burning in a hollow near the wharf for some time. Perhaps it was a pile of slash or sawdust. A knot of men peered down at it. Usually, the men stoked the steam engines that ran the saws with debris from the mill but occasionally they burned the wood and slash on the ground. Certainly, fire was always a hazard in this country, but this particular fire was very close to the water and shouldn't be dangerous. Jack Bullman told us they had hoses ready for emergencies.

The fire must have caught at a dry pile of wood or grass for the smoke increased suddenly and billowed into the air. I stopped picking to watch. Men ran to the water and into a shed on the wharf. I saw them tossing around gray strips of canvas. Then there were so many men scurrying around I could not make out what they were doing. I heard a horse clattering up the road behind me and turned in time to see Robert gallop by bare headed, his coat unbuttoned and flapping around him. He must keep that mare saddled and ready to dash.

Onlookers came from the bay too, as some boys on logs in the water paddled around the point to the side of the wharf where they could watch the action. Two mill workers manned a pump at the water's edge alternately pushing and straightening. Above them on the bank, six or seven men held the end of the grey canvas hose. The hose writhed, straightened in sections, then a jet of water burst from the end. When the water hit the fire, the smoke billowed in a squat puff close to the ground before disintegrating to a small column and then to wisps and after a half an hour to nothing at all.

The men had been quick and efficient. Of course, there was so much water around us that fire could be easily controlled. Water was never far from any of the settlements here.

I redoubled my efforts to fill my pails and by nine had them brimming. Lydia's pails had been full long since as she hadn't stopped to gawk at the fire. We carried our fruit home to wash and preserve.

Stanley arrived, hair slicked back and wet. He ate two buns and talked with his mouth full.

"They have a fire-fighting team at the mill Jim Best told me. They practice putting out fires so they can do it real fast. Everyone knows what to do and they do it so quick that the fire doesn't have no chance at all."

"Any," I corrected automatically. When Stanley gets excited his grammar slips.

"Do you think we could buy some of those hoses and sell them to the businessmen in Vancouver?" He turned to me.

"Why?"

"Well, they might want to have the same kind of fire protection as the mill?"

I thought for a moment. "Some of those buildings on Water Street are built over Coal Harbour so the owners would just use a bucket and dip into the sea. I don't think the merchants would be interested in paying for a hose, but you could ask."

"The minute I ask around the city someone else will bring the hoses in." Stanley's business sense was more finely honed than mine. I had other areas of interest.

"Stanley, could you swim if you fell off the log boom?"

Lydia raised her eyebrows in disapproval of my question.

"Naturally." Stanley considered it a foolish question, but I wasn't sure he could manage by himself that far from shore. Their combined disapproval kept me silent. Perhaps I was "fussing".

"Can you take an hour to go hunting?" Stanley changed the subject. "I'll have to work all the time from now on so I'd like to get some hunting in while I can."

Lydia nodded permission "It won't take two of us to start the jam. Take a couple of pails with you and fill them on your way home."

The sun was hotter now, so I took a bonnet from the peg by the door and some ammunition from the shelf. Stanley picked up the Remington shotgun and we walked quickly over the Hastings Mill Road, up Dunlevy Street and into the scrub bush behind the mill. The ground dipped into this brush so we couldn't be seen from the city. This was our favourite grouse-hunting spot. The birds hid in the long grasses and didn't emerge until we were almost on them; then they burst into the air with an explosion of feathers.

Stanley shot two grouse within ten minutes with a clean head shot to each. Then it was his turn to carry the grouse and pails while I stalked the birds. It took me a half an hour to bag my two grouse; it is difficult to get an accurate shot with that Remington Aubrey. It's double-barrelled gun and fairly light, but old and not particularly easy to use.

We walked back to the salmonberry bushes and laid the grouse in the shade while we picked more berries.

"Are you getting enough work to make money, Stanley?"

Stanley ate every second berry and soon had a faint red rim around his mouth. "Yes. Frank Hartman gives me jobs loading and unloading his supplies and Robert asks for me when he gets a load of nails or materials for the new house he's building."

"That's good."

"It's okay. Both those guys help me out when they can, and the livery stable gives me work with the horses whenever there is any. Things are getting busier every day, so I guess I'll be making more money soon. I'm doing okay. Saving money, anyway."

"For what? What are your plans?"

"I'm not sure. Frank Hartman says I can work as a shipping clerk in his operation in San Francisco if I want to move down there. I'd like that."

I kept my dismay from my face. If Stanley wanted to move to San Francisco, I wouldn't stop him, but it is a wild city and I hate the thought of Stanley growing up there. Still, it was kind of Frank to make a place for him in his business.

"And then I thought I might try my luck in the gold runs near Yale. They've been getting some paying stuff out of there."

Again, I held the dismay I felt inside. Stanley was far too young to be let loose in the gold camps.

"And then," he said putting four salmonberries in his mouth at once, "Robert Carr told me he'd lend me money if I wanted to buy a lot in Vancouver. The price of lots will go up once the railroad is here."

I really didn't know if that was any better. One of my friends advocated Stanley move away from me and the other introduced him to speculation.

"Both those men are nice to me. I suppose because of you. Are you going to marry one of them?"

I ate one of the berries and savoured the sweet flavour. "I don't know. I'm a little afraid of getting married. You know Mother was always so weak and so tired and she died so young. I don't know if I want to risk all that."

Stanley nodded. "I think if you really like someone you will probably risk it."

"What makes you think so?"

"Other people do," he said simply. "Anyway, don't stay a maiden lady just because of me. I might not stay around here."

"Thanks. The responsibility was chaining me to my spinsterhood. You've given me great relief."

He grinned and lifted the full pails of berries.

Lydia was pleased to see the grouse and the berries. I cleaned the birds while Stanley changed for work. Lydia started another batch of jam while the first batch simmered on the summer stove. We had opened the windows in the summer addition to allow the breeze from the water to cool the house. It was pleasant.

We finished two batches of jam and then had a light lunch. In the summer it seemed silly to have our big meal at noon and we usually waited until seven or eight in the evening to sit down to a full dinner—except on Sunday. On Sunday we had a formal noon meal.

Lydia and I tidied the kitchen, scrubbed our hands with vinegar, then walked down Hastings Road to the post office on Carrall Street. Lydia wanted to mail her letters. I noticed one was to a Miss H.R. Smith, perhaps Alistair's sister. I don't remember many of his relatives, but I know they live on the same county road as Lydia's family in Ontario.

It took us some time to get to the post office for we stopped and talked to many people. The tide was on the ebb and the smell of sewer and decayed vegetation was strong. It was something I had trouble accepting. Vancouver residents dropped their waste into the sea and hoped the ocean movement would take it away. I tried to ignore it.

The measles epidemic had not claimed any lives other than Felicity's, but I was afraid someone would tell me about another child. Luckily, there were many other topics of conversation. The railroad was coming. The court action taken by the city of Port Moody to prevent Vancouver becoming the terminus for the railroad had failed and the tracks from Port Moody were being laid this month.

This caused much speculation in land and buildings in Vancouver and hammering and sawing went on all around us. Perhaps Stanley should buy a lot. Perhaps Lydia and I should also. We have no proper sidewalks on Hastings Road. Water Street was planked and railed where necessary, but our shoes and skirts got quite dusty on the other streets. There is room for many more improvements in this city. Improvements meant increasing values.

We met Robert in the post office collecting a series of telegrams. He held them in his hand, folded them, then placed them in his pocket when he saw us.

"Where are they from?" I asked quietly. I was curious and willing to appear rude to satisfy myself.

"Battleford," he had time to tell me quickly before we were interrupted.

The post office was in a corner of Mr. Tilly's bookstore. With more than three people standing and conversing the area was crowded. Mr. Tilly searched through the letters to assure himself he had not missed anything. We moved toward the door. Jack Bullman came to collect his mail and stopped to talk. Frank arrived also and collected a telegram. He read it and joined us. At this point we had to move outside for we had completely filled the store.

Once on the street Frank touched Lydia on the arm. "Mrs. Smith?" he said.

We were silent. Frank seemed so serious and so formal.

"I have just received confirmation from the courthouse in San Francisco. The man who died of cholera, the one in the paper?"

Lydia nodded.

"It was Alistair Angus Bruce Smith, aged 34, height," he consulted his telegram again, "five foot ten, brown eyes, brown hair."

"Yes," Lydia said quietly, "I did believe it was my husband when you first told me but thank you for confirming it."

"I'm sorry," he said.

Lydia seemed more embarrassed than sad.

I glanced at Jack Bullman. He stared fixedly at Lydia.

"Ah, do you know Jack Bullman?" I said quickly and touched Frank's arm.

He turned to me and nodded at Jack.

"Mr. Bullman's with the mill."

Jack offered his hand and Frank shook it.

"Frank Hartman," I said.

"Had a little fire at the mill, did you?" Frank offered some conversation.

Jack nodded. "Got it out all right, though. Lots of water handy." The men nodded.

"You've been in the salmonberries." Robert reached over and touched a stain just showing above Lydia's summer gloves.

She smiled. "Yes, we're trying to get some preserves up. We're looking for crab-apples too if you know anyone who has some?

"I could get you some from New Westminster," Frank said. "I have a shipment of supplies coming in on the New Westminster stage next week. I'll ask around and see if someone can pick a couple of baskets for you."

Frank was generous and kind to Lydia as he was to all the people he liked. Perhaps that was enough. Perhaps it was unrealistic to expect a man to be kind to all. Frank didn't see people as equal. Some, such as the Chinese or the local Salish Indians, he didn't see as people at all. But he grew up in San Francisco where that kind of prejudice was normal and accepted. It was hard to fault a generous man for his upbringing. I reminded myself I needed to be more tolerant.

Jack Bullman turned east onto the Hastings Mill Road and Robert escorted Lydia to the Sunnyside Hotel tea room. Frank walked with me. I thanked him for his efforts on Lydia's behalf, but he wasn't attending to me and responded absently.

"Are you with me, Frank?"

He smiled, looking suddenly younger. Then surprised me with his next question. "Did Robert Carr pick up any telegrams in the bookstore?"

"Were you following him?"

Now Frank looked surprised. "No. I happened to see him go in the bookstore as I walked up Carrall. I did go into the store to see if he received any telegrams but I didn't follow him there. Why?"

"I wondered." I liked Frank. I liked Robert. Somehow I didn't think they liked each other. Robert would not appreciate me telling Frank anything at all. Frank would never consider I would report anything he told me. On the other hand, Mr. Tilly probably would admit Robert received telegrams if he was asked.

I took a deep breath. "Yes, he had some telegrams but he didn't offer any explanation of them." That was true. He hadn't offered any. I'd asked.

"I wonder if he knows anything about that Métis who was killed?"

I thought quickly. What could I tell him that wasn't an outright lie? "I suppose he knows about the discovery of the body since he was there with the constable. Is that what you mean?"

"Not exactly. I wonder if he's been trying to discover who poisoned the Frenchie."

"Do you think it's important to know?"

He looked at me quickly. "Not really. Lots more where he came from. I guess. I'm just curious." He smiled "I'd like to keep this city clean and the problems like this one well away from you."

I was shocked by his attitude toward the Métis, and then gratified by his concern for me. I took his arm impulsively, "You are kind, Frank. Nevertheless, I like to be involved—not in murder, naturally, but in some excitement. I spend so much time in the classroom I miss all the interesting activities in the city."

He patted my hand. "Well, don't get involved in this murder. I don't see how you could, of course. I'll tell you anything I think you should know about it."

"Too kind," I said sedately.

Frank looked at me sharply, suspecting sarcasm—as well he might.

He left me with Lydia at the tearoom for a business appointment. Lydia and I drank our tea and watched the bustle of activities at the hotel and livery stable across the street.

I caught a glimpse of Stanley occasionally, lifting and pulling barrels and baskets. The New Westminster stage arrived in a flurry of dust that settled as the horses were taken to the barns. A respectably dressed matron with a young child disembarked. The stage remained in front of the hotel for Stanley and several other young men to unload.

Maude Porter came down the main staircase of the hotel and walked toward the kitchen. I caught her eye and smiled. She looked past me as if she'd never seen me before. Lydia turned to see who attracted my attention but, as Maude had disappeared into the kitchen and one of the young men dropped a basket on the road just then, she was distracted from asking me any questions.

We walked home about four in the afternoon in time to meet Sung Wick as he entered our yard. He bowed and we bowed, and all went into the kitchen. Lydia took her pails and went for more berries while I taught Sung Wick the similarity between cat, mat, bat and sat. Usually, I teach children to read by teaching them to recognize the individual words. But Sung Wick understood the principle behind the sounds, and he was able, very quickly, to guess at words by reasoning, reaching into his mind for the logic of the sound. Of course, English has many exceptions, so he wasn't perfect, but he was so quick it was exciting to teach him.

He talked to me a little more this time and told me he had two sisters at home, and his mother and father. His father was a farmer and cultivated a garden near False Creek. His mother did laundry. He considered his family lucky to be together. So many Chinese here left their families at home in China and made money to send to them. Sung Wick's family tried to make a living together and he felt privileged.

After he left, clutching his slate, and bowing his way out the kitchen door, I lit the summer stove, sliced the breasts from the grouse and lay them with vegetables in a pie for supper. Lydia returned and minded the fire while I walked back to the inexhaustible bushes of salmonberries. I had filled one pail and began on the second when I heard a call from down the road, "Coo."

It was a hard, quick bid for attention. I scrambled back to the road from the ditch and met Maude Porter as she drew up alongside me in the dog cart driving our mutual livery stable horse.

"I'd shake your hand," I said, "but I'm stained with juice."

"You'd better not shake hands with me on a public road. I'll not get down." She was dressed in black today—a very elegant black afternoon suit with a smart black hat swooping over one eye, a feather drifting back over her shoulder. It looked to me as if the wages of sin were good clothes.

"You didn't come out this way again only to remonstrate with me."

"No," she began seriously, "Mr. Carr asked for my help in your plans to discover the murderer of the Métis."

How did Robert see her so quickly? He must know her daily routine.

"I have some information for you. You understand I will only repeat information to you that pertains to murder, or treason," she added.

I nodded.

"And I will give only as much information as I think you need to know."

Again, I nodded.

"I have a reputation and a business to maintain. I cannot be known to betray confidences."

"I can understand that."

Maude continued. "A customer of mine is on business here from the east. He is planning to meet with a local resident to advance him money with which to finance something illegal."

"What is he financing?"

"I don't know, but it sounds to me as though it is going to involve a lot of money, thousands of dollars. The figure mentioned was one hundred thousand dollars. The customer would like me to think he is going to set up his own kingdom where he will be the future emperor or king or something powerful. I wasn't clear on that part of it. About the money I'm very sure. I saw it. And," she added as an afterthought, "I got some of it."

"What could he want to buy, Maude? We don't make guns and ammunition here. It's hard enough to get the makings to load your own shells. The closest place to buy guns would be the eastern United States."

"It might be opium. We do have opium factories here that produce good quality opium for reasonable prices—about fifteen dollars a pound. That wouldn't be illegal, of course, but perhaps exporting it to some parts of Canada or the States would be illegal. I don't know."

I didn't know either.

"Some people will sell anything," Maude said. "A slave girl can fetch four thousand dollars from a miner in the Cariboo. She's kept half-starved and perhaps on opium for the transport and then sold as a slave into the gold fields. A seller can make a profit of about three thousand dollars on each girl."

"You're making me ill, Maude." I couldn't stand the idea of selling girls.

She nodded. "It makes me sick too. I've never been able to stop any of that traffic, but I'm always alert for it. If a girl wants to start an independent business in prostitution—that is one thing. But if she's forced into slavery—that's another." Maude sat in the dog cart straight and stiff delivering her philosophy crisply, almost without emotion.

"Do you think your customer is trafficking in girls?"

She thought for a moment. "If he is, I'll kill him."

I believed her.

Finally, she said, "I don't think so. Not in women—perhaps guns, something illegal. Perhaps he's going to bring in an army of mercenaries. I'll watch him."

The horse stamped his foot to dislodge the flies that were buzzing around his forelegs. Maude sat even straighter and gathered her reins. "I must go. For some reason, it's busy today."

"Thanks very much for taking the time to come and tell me. I'll tell Robert as soon as I can. And Maude," I wanted her opinion on a question that had been bothering me, "where would a murderer get poison?"

"There's lots of poison around, Miss MacDonald. There's arsenic for the rats, solvent for cleaning, and there are the poisons the doctors hand out. There are many plants that can be boiled and prepared to make poison—pie plant leaves for one, lady slippers for another. Anyone could pick up poison. The Métis wasn't in town long though. It is the Métis you're thinking of? Not planning on doing away with any of your pupils?"

I shook my head. "Yes, it's the Métis I'm thinking of. No, I'm not planning on poisoning anyone."

Maude continued. "He wouldn't have had time for a meal. I don't think so anyway. Most probably he got the poison in a drink. Some of the liquor that is made in this town is so bad it would disguise the taste of lye." She shrugged. "It's easy to kill with poison. It's a wonder more people don't do it."

She flicked the whip over the horse's head and started back to the city.

I filled the other lard pail and carried the berries back to Lydia. The man from east could be Mr. Sanders. As far as I knew there were no other visitors in town. Robert would know for sure. I wondered if Frank exported opium. There wasn't anything illegal about it. It just seemed wrong to spread that kind of debilitating habit to other parts of the country. I suppose I could feel that way about whiskey too. If there was no opium some people would have to live in terrible pain. It might not be Frank Mr. Sanders dealt with. It might be Robert, or anyone of the many men who were trying to buy and sell and make money in this city.

CHAPTER TEN

I heard Jack Bullman's heavy boots on our kitchen step about eight o'clock that night. He had driven a buckboard full of lumber for the new cloak room to the school, unloaded it there and continued on to pay us a visit.

Lydia and I were starting the last batch of preserves and had the empty jars and canning kettles in the summer kitchen and the preserves simmering on the stove.

"Nice night," Jack said.

"Is there a moon?" I asked as I stirred the preserves. If I don't watch the pot carefully, the sugar can stick to the bottom of the kettle, burn, then taint the taste of the jam.

"A slice of moon—enough to see logs and things in the water."

"Are you going on the water?" Lydia made Jack a cup of tea and pushed a tin of oatmeal biscuits close to his hand.

"Thought I'd take a canoe ride. I have a canoe from the Indian village across the inlet. A nice little craft, well-balanced, rides a little low in the water, but it's stable."

"Where do you keep it?" I watched the preserves. The fire was a little too hot and I didn't want the berries scorched.

"I have it on the wagon now. Would you like to go for a ride?'

I looked up quickly, but Jack was looking at Lydia.

"I can't swim," Lydia snapped.

Jack smiled. "Don't have to swim—just sit."

"I don't want to get wet."

"Won't get wet if you sit still."

"If I'm going to ride in a canoe, I want to do some of the paddling."

"Got two paddles," Jack said.

"Jack Bullman, you can't think of everything."

Jack looked at her over the rim of his tea mug and said nothing. She stood in the centre of the room wiping her hands on the tea towel and staring at him.

"Lydia," I said *sotto voce*, "it's not a marriage proposal."

She ignored me while she turned and spread the tea towel on the rope line behind the wood stove. "You mind we're only going for a short canoe ride," she said.

"For sure," Jack said quietly. "It's pretty out there tonight with the lights on the sailing vessels and the lanterns on the shore. I think you'll like it."

Lydia looked unconvinced, but she allowed herself to be escorted out the back door. She popped her head back in. "Don't go off reading or something and forget the preserves."

I shook my head at her. "Have a good time."

She raised her eyebrows in doubt, but she did go.

I was still stirring the kettle when I heard a knock on our front door. I gave the mixture a vigorous swirl and ran to answer it.

Frank stood outside, his hat in his hand and a smile on his face.

"Quickly. Come into the kitchen. I'm preserving." I whirled around and ran back, plunged the long wooden spoon into the berries and stirred. I felt the bottom of the kettle cautiously with the spoon. Thankfully, that few seconds of neglect hadn't caused any calamity. I moved the kettle on the stove trying to find a cooler spot.

Frank stooped at the low kitchen door and put his hat on the china cupboard. "Where's Lydia?"

I didn't think Lydia would appreciate complete honesty. "Just gone out for a few minutes. She's been in the kitchen most of the day. The salmonberries are ripe."

Frank looked at the rows of jars on the table and the china cupboard. They seemed like a bank of flowers against the wall—

red with flashes of carmine where the lantern light reached into the depths of the jam.

"You shouldn't have to do this kind of work."

I looked up in surprise. "I like it. I wouldn't like to do it all summer, but I like packing away the berries and apples and peaches. Berries are easier because we don't have to peel them or pit them. Have a chair, Frank."

He sat down, still with a disapproving frown on his face.

I looked down at my Mother Hubbard apron stained by berry juice and soiled by the pots from the stove. I admit it wasn't glamorous. I posed dramatically with the dripping spoon in one hand and my other arm out flung. "Small is the worth of beauty from the light retired."

Frank rubbed the side of his cheek. "Well, I like seeing you dressed up in something a little more ...well... "

"Feminine." I supplied and moved the kettle to the edge of the stove.

"Yes. I'd like to see you in lace and feathers and that pretty, blue dress you had on Sunday. I guess I don't like to see you work so hard."

I smiled at him. It was pleasant to have someone care about me. I felt a little reckless. "Do you like delicate women, Frank?"

He shifted uncomfortably, as though he suspected me of teasing him and continued to rub his cheek.

I ladled the preserves into the jars with great concentration.

"You're delicate."

"I think you just paid me a compliment. Not accurate, though. I'm not delicate, thank you."

Frank smiled. "And I think you're playing with me."

He reached over and took my wrist in his hand.

I held my body immobile, the ladle in my hand, and looked at him.

"I'm not sure what you mean. I hope it's encouragement."

"Sorry, Frank. I was being a little frivolous. I don't want to encourage you too much. Not right now." I know I'll have to consider marriage eventually but not right now, not with Frank, not with anyone.

He nodded and released my arm.

I continued my work with the jam.

"Tell me about San Francisco, Frank. Stanley got quite excited about it the other day. What's it like?"

That diverted him and, while I worked, he talked about the culture in San Francisco, about the plays and the musical presentations and the boating expeditions and the horse racing. He painted a picture of ease and elegance and a society that had worked hard and knew how to live well.

"Do you see Vancouver ever achieving that kind of culture?"

Frank shook his head. "Not for years. Vancouver is a wonderful place to invest and make money. After ten years of investing here, I'll be very wealthy. There is still lots of gold in this country and lots of investing opportunities for staking mining companies and selling shares. Most of the money is in freighting supplies, though. I'm in the way of getting a monopoly on the freight lines. When I have that, I'll print money."

"And will you stay here?"

He toyed with the spoons on the table.

"Perhaps. I don't know," he said. "San Francisco is a better place to live." He smiled at me, apologizing for his preference. "I might keep a house here for the summer months and return to San Francisco for the winter. Perhaps I could do something like that. I'd still have many interests here, so I'd need a permanent base—a house with a staff of permanent servants—something like that."

I thought Frank might do it, too. He was astute. Most men liked him and would do business with him. If Vancouver grows the way he thinks it will, Frank's business will grow with it. "How far do you plan to extend your freight lines?"

I took the empty kettle to the pump and pumped water into it.

Frank got up and helped me carry it over to the stove.

"I have a line going to New Westminster now. I see one going to Fort Langley and another to Yale. I should get a ship from Victoria and another bigger one from San Francisco to Vancouver and then I would be able to move goods up and down the west coast and into the Interior."

"What about the Orient?"

He nodded. "If I could move lumber to the Orient and tea or silk back, I could get myself a slice of the trade between England and the Orient. It would be cheaper for English merchants to use the railroad and my ships for trade with the Orient than to go all the way by ship as they are doing now. That's only if the C.P.R. works out and isn't washed away in the Rocky Mountains every winter. I have to establish my local business solidly, then I have to get a couple of lucrative hauls to obtain the capital I need to buy the ships."

I was almost overwhelmed by the scope of Frank's ambitions. They sounded so plausible. I added a stick to the fire so I could warm the dish water. I wanted to have all the equipment clean when Lydia returned.

"If I could haul something into the Cariboo that the miners want and then take gold back to Vancouver, I'd make money. If I could buy some product cheaply and sell it miles away, preferably hundreds of miles away for a big price and do that many times then I might make the purchase price of a ship."

"What kind of goods?" I'd asked the question idly in general interest, but I saw his eyes flash for a moment, and I thought of my conversation with Maude. "Opium?"

"You know, Amy, I could transport and sell opium. There isn't any law that prohibits me from doing that."

"I realize that. It just seems to be such an immoral thing."

Frank looked at his hands. "I've given that some thought too. I don't know how I could guarantee the opium I transported would only be used medicinally—I mean, there isn't any way I could ensure that. So, do I deny the medicinal use of it because I can't control the addictive use of it?"

"I suppose freighting opium isn't the same thing as setting up opium dens. It just seems a little sordid."

Frank nodded. "I appreciate that," he said. "But it would be lucrative."

I looked at him steadily for a moment. "Tempting, is it?"

He nodded. "It's tempting to transport the Chinamen too."

"To where?" I hadn't heard of any plans to deport the Chinese.

"Back to China. If the government passes a law that kicks them out of the country, then they'd have to go back to China. If they can't afford the passage, then the government will have to pay it. Could be a lot of money in transporting them back and bringing a load of tea east."

"I don't suppose they'd transport them in style. I suppose they'd transport them like cattle at so much a head."

"In any case, I hope they stay."

I was surprised. "Why?"

"Because I have a contract to clear three hundred and fifty acres for the C.P.R. If I use Chinese labour, I can clear it for $90 an acre. I'll get $150 an acre for it from the C.P.R. and make $21,000 on the project. If I have to use white men, I won't make any money."

I should have known Frank's reasons would be concrete ones.

"And the new city of Vancouver won't get any of those new electric streetlamps or any water system if they can't use Chinese labour either."

"But the people are getting so bigoted, I don't think they'll tolerate Chinese people in the streets. There was some edict, put out by the Knights of Labour that promised a boycott on anyone who dealt with the Chinese. They even objected to a merchant selling them food."

Frank shrugged. "It's not a good situation. So many of them are without work now and hungry."

"Robert told me it's worse in Victoria."

"When I was there last, the city of Victoria had set up a soup kitchen for them but there was still a lot of disease and hunger."

The water in the kettle wasn't quite hot enough. I continued to talk to Frank. "So, you think the answer is to deport them back to China?"

"Many of them only came here to work and they want to go back to China. I think it will be cheaper to use the labour we need and send the rest back, even if we have to pay their way."

"What are they going back to?"

"How do I know?" Frank's head jerked. He was probably checking his temper.

I suppose I was foolish. There wasn't any way I could solve the whole problem of the Orient today.

The water bubbled in the kettle now and I was in the middle of moving it to the sink when the front door knocker banged. "Get that, will you, Frank?"

He returned to the kitchen with Robert.

"Hello. Hello. Hello. What is this? The kitchen maid?" He turned a chair around, straddled it and observed me with a critical eye.

I turned from my washing and curtsied. "Small is the worth of beauty from the light retired," I repeated.

Robert's eyes lit. "Bid her come forth, suffer herself to be desired, and not blush so to be admired". He completed the quotation and grinned.

I felt a bubble of laughter rise, struggled with decorum, and surrendered. "I'd call you wicked, Robert," I said weakly when I could, "but I have an uncomfortable suspicion I asked for that."

He chuckled, got off the chair and started wandering around the kitchen. "Are you looking for a tea mug?"

"Are you hiding them?"

"Here." I handed him a cup. "The tea's on the edge of the stove."

He helped himself to the pot then returned his cup to the table. "Nothing to eat?"

I turned back. "There's oatmeal biscuits on the table near Frank. Help yourself."

Robert munched a couple, then turned to Frank. "How's business?"

I could feel Frank's frustration and was a little amused by it. Robert certainly had interrupted a pleasant evening's conversation, but I didn't see any reason to deny Robert.

Frank shifted in his chair and answered civilly. "Quite good. I have the contract with the supplier in New Westminster, so I should be running a wagonload into Vancouver every day now."

"There's a lot of building going on. You should do well."

"Yes, I will."

"Could you get me some supplies for my house?" Robert reached for another biscuit then turned his attention back to Frank.

"Where are you building?"

I dried my hands on the tea towel, poured myself a cup of tea and joined the men at the table.

"Up near Moody's Reserve on the higher ground."

"A good spot. Certainly, if you want to give me an order, I'll try to fill it as soon as I can." He paused for a moment. Then, "Are you building for speculation or are you thinking of settling down?"

Robert helped himself to two more biscuits. His appetite rivaled Stanley's.

"I'm always thinking of it." He turned to me and winked.

I saw Frank's fingers tighten on the teacup.

"Robert," I said sharply. "Don't be vulgar."

"Who's being vulgar? I'm being perfectly proper. I haven't made any vulgar suggestions yet. You're going to have to curb your imagination, Amy."

"'You have such a facility with words you lay a trap for those of us who haven't. That's pretentious."

"You're right," he said, "but that's no reason for you to be in such a taking over it. As far as that goes, it isn't good manners to read morality lessons over your guests."

He was right and it made me so angry I banged my cup on the table and broke the handle.

Robert laughed and suddenly, I laughed. Frank looked a little shocked by my childish display of temper.

"Tell us about the fire today, Robert, and perhaps we can enjoy a civil conversation."

Robert agreed and reported the mill fire was started by one of the men who had been careless with a match after lighting his pipe.

Frank suggested the escape route he would take if a fire ever swept through Vancouver.

They argued the merits of driving a wagon down the New Westminster Road or boarding a ship in the harbour.

"The city should get some kind of fire protection ready in case they need it," I said. Stanley was right about that.

"They had a fire out of control a fortnight ago. The city was full of smoke. Remember, Amy?"

I nodded. "We had smoke drift over the school yard."

"The men got organized quickly and fought it off."

"How did it start?"

"The brush fires south of town in the C.P.R. land leapt over the dirt barricade. The C.P.R. put in a couple of men and a Chinese to watch the fires so we shouldn't have any more trouble from those fires."

Robert nodded agreement.

There was a lull in the conversation then Frank said, "Did you get all the information you needed in your telegrams yesterday?"

Robert looked at me quickly and I shook my head.

"I think so. Have you been getting the information you're after?"

Frank looked at Robert in silence. It was obvious they were reluctant to continue.

Blessed are the peacemakers, the bible says. I might as well give it a try. "Robert, you want information about some things that are going on in this town." I turned to Frank "And, Frank, you do also. Why don t you pool your ideas? You might find out you were working on the same thing?"

There. I hadn't given either of them any real information about the other but, surely, they knew it would be better to work together.

Robert answered first, "All right. I'll tell you what I'm after, Frank. I think someone trying is trying to stir up the people in the West to separate from Confederation. I think this person is willing to murder and steal to attain that goal."

"And I think," Frank said, "someone is trying to stop my trade with the Interior of B.C. and with the North West. I want to send sugar and lumber and some molasses into the North West and I've had some trouble trying to do it." He paused. "That Métis who died in the bay...?"

Both Robert and I were alert.

Frank continued. "He worked for me. He was bringing me information on who was trying to stop my trade. I had one quick meeting with him and promised to meet him later in the night, but he was killed before he could report. There's a lot of money involved here. I will be a rich man if I get the trade routes open and a poor one if someone else gets in there first."

I was surprised. I shouldn't be. Money is a great motivator and, from what Frank had told me about the potential of shipping and freight, the man who controlled the routes would be powerful. I wonder if that need for power was behind Maude Porter's customer's ambitions. The man had told her he was going to be some kind of emperor.

"I tried going to the constable. You know the one who's on loan from Victoria?"

We nodded.

"The man's thick in the head."

We nodded again.

"He seemed to think I killed the Métis myself."

"He had his suspicions of Robert too."

Frank looked startled.

Robert shrugged. "Don't ask me why. He doesn't seem to need a reason for anything. I don't think he'd recognize a reason if it was introduced to him."

I smiled. The men were united now in a common complaint.

Robert drummed his fingers on the table. "Could we get any help from the new Vancouver city council?"

I was doubtful. "When you remember how they conducted the vote it does give rise to questions about their ability to organize anything."

Frank looked at me.

"There were 499 men eligible to vote last May in the election. One group of fifty men used the same lease to prove they were property owners and eligible to vote."

"You mean fifty men passed one lease from man to man and voted on it?"

I nodded. "And the management at Hastings Mill sent fifty Chinese employees in from the mill to vote, but the townspeople met them and drove them back. It was a lovely day. You should have been here."

Frank started to smile. "Sounds like the great British Parliamentary system all right."

"There was no voters list and no way to establish whether a man voted twice. It was ridiculous really. I don't think we'd get much help from the law or from the council."

"So," Robert summarized. You're looking for a man who has money, who wants your trade routes and who is unscrupulous and willing to murder to get them."

Frank nodded.

"And I'm looking for a man who is trying to stir up the residents to secede from Confederation and someone who is unscrupulous and willing to murder to achieve that." Robert still wasn't being completely honest. He was looking for a man who might be selling guns and supplies to the Métis and making money out of a rebellion and who was unscrupulous and willing to murder to do so. A man who wanted the rebellion would also want to control the trade routes. They were, no doubt, looking for the same man.

"The only person I've heard of with money is that Mr. Sanders you introduced me to, Frank."

Frank looked thoughtful. "I don't know him well. He was interested in investing in the Vancouver to Kamloops Lake freight route. I thought of setting up a supply depot in Ashcroft and using the railroad to move freight. Do you think he might be the one trying to take over my routes?"

"Or finance an insurrection?" I said. "Remember his talk about the government not being good enough. He's an opposition member, isn't he?" I recalled Maude's ideas about the financier from the east. It might be Mr. Sanders.

"I don't remember," Frank said. "Perhaps he's our man."

We sat in silence for a moment contemplating the problem. I could hear the rustle of the cottonwood trees near the corner of the summer kitchen. There must be a slight breeze to disturb them and set them swishing and sliding against the cedar roofing. A goshawk screamed in a dive over the bay and, far-off on a sailing ship, the hoot of a whistle shrieked and was silent. Then I heard the clop of horses' hooves nearby and the slap of the reins.

The kitchen door flew open, and Lydia appeared drenched from top to toe and very angry. Jack Bullman followed her in. Lydia sat on a chair, struggled with tight laces and buttons, and tugged off her shoes.

I was speechless with surprise.

"You won't get wet," she mimicked angrily. "Just sit in the front like the Indian women do. They never fall out."

"The front of what?" Robert asked softly.

"A canoe," I whispered.

"So, I sit in the front. It's fine until I try to get out at the shore. 'Mind the shore,' he says. Mind the shore? It was still four feet away when I jumped. You could have told me it was still some distance away."

Jack didn't answer and Lydia picked up her boots and placed them on a paper near the stove. "'Mind the shore. Mind the shore,'" she quoted sarcastically.

"You jumped too soon, Lydia."

"Of course, I jumped too soon." She turned on Jack in a fury. "I jumped too soon, and I got soaking wet. It's lucky I didn't drown."

"If you had kept your feet, you would only have gotten your feet wet. You didn't have to fall and get everything wet." He glanced down at her sodden dress.

"And." Lydia's voice was loud now. "In coming gallantly to my rescue, you didn't even get your boots wet. You pushed a paddle at me, and I hauled myself out."

"They're good boots," Jack said with a serious face.

Lydia stared at him. "Good boots," she repeated weakly.

"And it was your own bad judgement in the jump that tripped you up. You wouldn't wait for me to help you."

"Bad judgement," she echoed. She stood in front of Jack and stared at him for a long time.

He gazed at her unruffled and she finally turned away.

"You don't mind," she said sarcastically, "if I excuse myself and change into something dry?"

"Not at all," Jack said. I'll pour you a hot cup of tea."

Lydia swept from the room leaving wet streaks on the wooden floor.

Jack picked up two cups and helped himself from the tea pot at the edge of the stove. "Evening," he said quietly to Frank and Robert as if escorting an angry, voluble, sodden woman was a commonplace activity.

Robert and Frank replied politely. Such was Jack's calm self-assurance no one mentioned Lydia.

CHAPTER ELEVEN

I slipped away early the next morning. Lydia, for once, slept late and I was able to swim, breakfast and collect Stanley for a walk before she rose. I wasn't ready to face a denouncement of Jack Bullman at this early hour.

Stanley and I walked up Hastings Road to Carrall. It smelled musty here for there were many skunk cabbages in the swampy land near the corner. It was the only moist area left in this dry country. With no rain for two months, all the grasses had turned brown and most of the pot- holes dried to cracked mud. Even the leaves of the huge maple tree at Carrall and Hastings Road were mottled brown and yellow from the draught. Dust clung to the railings of the houses; shop keepers swept drifts of dirt from their porches. Mr. Hartney was trying to sweep the dirt from the barrels in front of his store as I walked by. Fine dust sifted over my boots and into the bottom hem of my skirt. Shop keepers and customers alike would be glad of a boardwalk on this street. The dirt ridges on the road were worn to smooth ruts by the horse and vehicle traffic and the whole of Carrall Street was inches deep in dust. Two days of rain would churn everything into mud.

Stanley left me occasionally to visit with friends in the shops along the way but managed to catch me before I reached the bottom end at False Creek. Stanley knew where Sung Wick's family lived in the Chinese community, and I planned to visit them. Frank would not approve, naturally, and Robert would think I was wasting time. Nevertheless, I was curious about the way Sung Wick lived and I wanted to warn his family of the bigotry in Vancouver. I thought they lived too close to the city and too close to violence. We were half-way up Carrall Street when I saw the first black cross on the doorstep of a cigar factory. I thought it curious but passed by without comment. I saw two more black crosses on two shops further south.

"Stanley, just nip in here and ask them what the crosses signify."

He wasn't long. "Those people have Chinese workers. The Knights of Labour came by last night and painted those crosses on the doorsteps. That's supposed to discourage anyone from dealing at that shop."

"Is it?"

"What?"

"Discouraging people?"

"So, the man said."

We walked on in silence. I was angry and frustrated. There didn't seem to be any way I could combat such prejudice. On the other hand, I had some sympathy with men who had expected to find a new country with unlimited work opportunities only to be thwarted by a government that imported cheap labour as competition. What did the Knights of Labour adherents think the Chinese people were going to do? Disappear into the air? Stop eating so they wouldn't need to work? Pretend they didn't live here? I said as much to Stanley.

"Leave," he said.

"The Knights want the Chinese to leave?"

He nodded. "They don't care where they go or what they do as long as they leave."

"If I were a heathen Chinese," I said with some vehemence, "I would not be attracted to the particular brand of Christianity that's practiced around here."

Stanley shrugged. "People are peculiar," was all he said.

There were some pigs rooting for clams at the foot of Carrall Street. The tide was on the ebb and the pigs enjoyed foraging in the mud, grunting and snorting and crushing the clams with their grinding teeth. Currants grew in bushes at the side of the road. If someone didn't pick them soon the pigs would strip the branches. The smell of salt drifted in with a slight morning breeze and mingled with the heavy, sweet smell of the currants. Overall, the musty tang peculiar to pigs added spice to this essence of summer. The air was hazy, and I could barely see the shore on the other side of False Creek. Indians lived in a big camp there. I could make out several canoes on the beach but could not see the village. We turned toward the Chinese settlement.

"Have you had any trouble in this area, Stanley?"

Stanley looked at me sharply. "I don't usually advertise I'm coming here. I've only been here a couple of times with Sung Wick. It's not a good idea to be friendly with the Chinese. Not if I want work."

That was a fact of life in Vancouver.

Stanley stripped off several currants and popped them into his mouth. "Tell me about the tax on the Chinese. What's that all about?"

"You mean the tax the Dominion government put on Immigration?"

"I thought it was a tax on importing."

"It's considered a tax on importing Chinese," I said grimly, "as if the Chinese were a commodity. Anyone who brings Chinese into Canada has to pay $50 a head for each one and he is allowed to carry one Chinese per 50 tons of goods on his ship."

Stanley thought that over for a while. He licked the currant juice from his fingers. "The C.P.R. let 3000 Chinese workers go last September."

"Quite a few of them left on the *Alden Besse* for Hong Kong in October. They had only come over for work and left when there wasn't any more. Many want a new life here." I looked over the small one and two-room cabins that made up the Chinese settlement. "It's going to be a problem, Stanley. Anytime you get a group of immigrants together who have a different language and different customs from the general populace and deny them work and opportunity, you degrade your own society and sow problems for everyone."

"Yeah, well, I'd just as soon not get a history lesson, Teacher. That's what you were going to do, weren't you? Tell me about the French Revolution or something?"

I agreed, yes, I was, and I would spare him. "Are there many families here?" I asked,

"Not very many. Four or five. Most of the Chinese are single men. They have families back in China and they aren't going to live here forever."

I looked west toward the woods and east and north to Hastings Mill. The Chinese were isolated here from white neighbours.

Sung Wick, working on the shore repairing a net, was so startled to see us he dropped his hook onto the shale. He recovered his dignity quickly and bowed. I bowed in return. Stanley waved.

He met us in front of his house, a wooden shack near the shore of False Creek. Vegetables grew luxuriously in the garden on either side of a wooden walk without a weed in sight. Lydia would have been envious.

Sung Wick darted into the house and returned with a diminutive woman he introduced as his mother. I didn't catch her name as it sounded like a musical collection of vowels. I bowed. She put her hands into the sleeves of her dress and bowed. I smiled and she answered me with a smile that crinkled the corners of her eyes then slowly moved over her face, lightening her brow, then the edges of her mouth until she looked younger and more lively. We stood in the sunshine making conversation about the weather and the vegetables. Sung Wick translated back and forth so even commonplace remarks took time to convey.

After a polite five minutes, I expressed my pleasure at meeting her and offered my hand. Sung Wick said something in Chinese; his mother looked startled and then tentatively put her tiny hand in mine.

"Good bye," I said solemnly.

She looked at my lips and then repeated slowly. "Good bye." Her eyes flew up and met mine and we both laughed.

"In Chinese, Sung Wick, what is 'goodbye'?"

He told me and I carefully tried to repeat what he said. Both Sung Wick and his mother smiled. Stanley and I bowed and turned away. Stanley casually said something in Chinese and Sung Wick nodded.

"What did you say?"

"I just said good bye. Didn't you recognize it?"

I shook my head. "No."

"Well, don't fall all over me in admiration. That's about all I can manage in Sung Wick's language. Not everyone here speaks the same kind of Chinese, so even if I learn a little of Sung Wick's language I might not be understood by another Chinaman."

Sung Wick left his mother and joined us on our walk along the beach. We approached an older man mending a net on the shore. Sung Wick stopped. "My father," he said. "You would like to meet my father?"

I nodded. "Yes. Thank you."

"He speaks a little English," Sung Wick said, "a very little."

I nodded again and Sung Wick presented me to the older man. He must have been twenty years older than his wife with fine grey hair in a queue down his back. He was only a few inches taller than his son and wore the dark blue uniform of the Chinese—baggy pants and wide-sleeved tunic.

He straightened and transferred a bone hook from his right hand to his left and then nodded to me. "Good morning," he said.

"Good morning. You are working hard." I spoke politely.

He raised his eyebrows and then looked back at me. "I stay close to the house," he said. I looked straight at him then; polite nothings disappeared from my mind.

"You fear the people here?"

"Yes."

"You think they will attack you?"

"Soon," he said.

"Why don't you leave? Go across the creek?"

"There are white people across the creek too, and Indians. The policeman is here."

I looked at Sung Wick's father in consternation. How could I explain he was risking a lot on the courage of Constable Parkinson and the police chief; that it was unlikely the constable was aware of any danger to the Chinese community and, if he was, it was still unlikely the constable would be any help in an emergency.

"You might be safer in the woods." I pointed to the land across False Creek and to the south. "You would be safer away from here."

"My family is safe with me."

I looked past him to the ocean lapping at the shore and to the small boat riding at anchor only a few yards from the ebbing tide.

"Your boat?"

He nodded.

"It has a sail?"

He looked puzzled.

I pantomimed hauling up a sail and his eyes lit with understanding.

He nodded.

"It is a small boat," I said worriedly.

He smiled. "We are a small family."

If he planned to move his family into the water when danger came near, then he probably could manage to protect them. I offered my hand. "Good luck."

He shook hands and said something to Sung Wick in Chinese. I turned for a translation.

"My father says I am to say goodbye here. It is not good for you to be with me." He paused, "or for me to be with you. He says white men are evil now and I stay home now. No lessons." He shook his head. "I come when it is safe."

I nodded agreement.

Sung Wick's father said something more. "He says his boat has no room for you."

"And I must protect myself by not being seen with you?" I finished the thought for him.

"It makes sense," Stanley said. "Some kind of sense."

I agreed and we left Sung Wick with his father on the shore. We walked back down Carrall Street. This time I noticed more black marks on the doorways. One was on Mr. Hartney's dry goods store. I crossed the black mark and walked up to the counter. "I need some blue ribbon, if you please."

"Certainly." The proprietor brought me a choice of two colors of blue. I spent three cents.

"Miss MacDonald," he said as he handed me my purchase. "Don't be too brave. You have a job to hold and some of the Knights of Labour would be glad to harass you out of work if they thought you were trying to go against them."

"The way they are trying to harass you out of a living?"

"They're doing it too, ma'am. I'm going to have to get rid of Joe Choy. He's worked for me for two years and done real well. Now I'll have to let him go. I won't be able to survive the boycott they're putting on me."

"Don't you think most people will refuse to co-operate with such crude pressure."

"Most people don't think of the Chinese as people at all, Miss MacDonald. So, they don't think the Chinese should be treated as people. Then most people won't cross any kind of sign. They think some authority put it there, so they won't go against authority."

"They don't stop to consider it is a self- proclaimed authority?"

"No," he shook his head," they don't."

"Why don't you give Joe Choy a vacation and take him hack in a few weeks when everything dies down?"

"I might do that. Vancouver's starting off on the wrong foot, Miss MacDonald. Hounding decent people this way."

"You know what you should do, Mr. Hartney?"

He looked up at me as I stopped in his doorway.

"What?"

"You should go out at night and paint a black cross on everyone's doorstep. That way the public wouldn't know who is employing Chinese and who isn't?"

He chuckled. "That's a good idea, Miss."

I smiled and left the store. Stanley had disappeared. It was late in the morning, and he needed to eat before he went to work. While I had been on my morning's walk groups of men had drifted together in doorways, on the street corners and around porch of the Sunnyside Hotel. They gathered in buzzes of conversations. Occasionally, I heard loud voices. I saw Robert at the edge of a group of men, his notebook out and his pencil busy. I slipped around behind the men until I was close to him.

"What's going on?"

He handed me a copy of a printed edict. "Read that."

It was a statement, a manifesto, addressed to "All Chinamen". "Due notice is hereby given warning all Chinamen to move with all their chattels from within the Corporation of the City of Vancouver on or before the fifteenth day of June...failing which all Chinamen found in the city after the above date shall be forcibly expelled therefrom and their goods and household effects shall be consigned to either the Harbour or False Creek as convenience may propose. Furthermore, the authorities of the town are kindly cautioned not to risk their lives in trying to rescue the Mongolians, or giving themselves any unnecessary trouble as the undersigned are in terrible earnest." It was signed, "The Vancouver Vigilance Committee."

I hit the paper with an angry swat. "Who are these people?"

Robert kept his attention on the men standing on the porch of the hotel, but he answered me. "They are principally members of the Knights of Labour. *The Vancouver News* is supporting this stand." He indicated another reporter on the other side of the crowd.

"And you?" Robert's paper was still called The Granville Star.

For once, he was not smiling. He turned briefly and looked at me. "I just report what I see. But I'll tell you something, Amy. There's a lot of local feeling behind this. We're in for some trouble."

"What can you do? What can we do?"

"Don't try to do anything heroic. You wouldn't have support. The only thing to do is to try to warn the Chinese people and get them out of the way of the vigilantes."

"What about our marvelous constable?"

"He, at least, has asked for help from Victoria and I understand Superintendent Roycroft is coming as quickly as he can. Also, the police chief here, Mr. Stewart, is standing behind law and order. He's not interested in having the city run by a group of vigilantes."

"That's not a very big contingent of law and order—two policemen—three if Superintendent Roycroft gets here in time. What are you going to do?"

The men's voices were getting louder. They sounded angry.

"I'm going to report what they do. That's what I'm going to do. You are going home. Don't get any ideas about saving the world. No one would listen to you if you got up there and tried to talk reason. No one listens to reason when they are angry." He gestured toward the men around us with his notebook. "These men know what they are doing is inhumane. They know and they don't care. They wouldn't listen to you if you were Joan of Arc. So go home. I'll ride over later; my horse is tied at the back of the Granville Hotel. I'll come and tell you if things settle down or get worse."

"Robert!" I clutched his arm as he turned away.

"What is it?" He shook off my arm impatiently.

"Can you warn Sung Wick and his family? They should leave now."

Robert nodded. "I'll warn them. In fact, I'd better do that right away." He strode down the street and returned in a few moments.

I hadn't moved very far down Hastings Road.

"I told you to go home. Don't go getting all independent and righteous or even curious. Just go home or I'll pull you up on this horse and take you there."

"Don't you dare!" But he sounded as though he'd do just that, so I started walking quickly in the direction of the teacherage. I slipped by two men who were arguing fiercely.

"I've got an old Spencer—takes time to load it but it's not a bad gun."

"Not good enough," the other said. "Find a Henry or an Enfield. We need better guns."

In one afternoon, the city had changed from a peaceful place of prosperity and opportunity to an ugly, undisciplined camp of savages who were looking for guns. I hoped the Chinese people would stay out of the way of any violence and I hoped Stanley was safely out of harm's way.

CHAPTER TWELVE

Jack Bullman had been to the house and, although Lydia did not report on how they settled their quarrel, she did tell me about the uneasiness felt at Hastings Mill. There were fifty Chinese employees there who were worried about the vigilantes in Vancouver.

"They're staying away from the city," Lydia said, "and close to the mill because they think Mr. Alexander will protect them."

"Will he?"

"I don't know, but I don't think the people of Vancouver will attack Hastings Mill. Their respect for property is greater than their respect for people; I wouldn't venture onto the streets right now if I were Chinese."

Despite our worry, the evening and the night passed without incident. The next morning Frank stopped by on his way to New Westminster and joined us in the parlour. Lydia had been reading aloud from *The Vancouver News*. It reported the Chinese had been awarded a sub-contract to clear the tract of land on the hill west of Vancouver.

"Much indignation was expressed by those who heard the rumour and statements were made that the Mongolians would not be permitted to proceed with the work if they once attempted to make a start."

It sounded like a notice of insurrection. *The Vancouver News* certainly published provocative material.

Frank was concerned. "They don't understand what they are doing," he said. "We need those Chinamen to get the work done here. That piece of land isn't mine, but I want the same kind of clearing done next month. If I have to pay the white men's prices, I won't make any money. People aren't looking ahead, not a year, not even a month. We need some of those Chinamen to run businesses. They have contacts in Hong Kong, and I want to run ships between here and Hong Kong. How much trade am I going to get if I can't set up business arrangements between Vancouver and Hong Kong?" Frank's view of racial tolerance was purely practical; but perhaps more influential because of that.

"What can you do?" I was curious.

"I'm going to talk to the mayor in New Westminster. Maybe he'll be able to shake some sense into MacLean and Alexander and that crew in the city council."

"And if he can't?"

"I'll talk to the Premier in Victoria. He spent a lot of time in San Francisco. He knows the trade situation. "

"Victoria doesn't think anything Vancouver does is right," Lydia said. "Victoria would love to see Vancouver in trouble so it could preen itself on its civilized ways and scorn the barbaric customs this side of the Strait."

"If I had my way, Vancouver would be run from Victoria," Frank said.

"Or San Francisco," I couldn't resist adding.

Frank smiled as he rose. "Well, at least in Victoria, they understand the value of trade and don't look to the C.P.R. as a kind benefactor who will look after them forever."

"The C.P.R. will be quite a lot of competition for you, won't it, Frank?"

He nodded and paused at the door.

"I have to get my trade routes moving before they do. They're starting to get ships built in Liverpool calling them *The Empress of India, The Empress of China.* They are going to pick up a lot of trade between China and Vancouver if I don't get my slice of it first. I have to finance a ship soon."

"It means so much to you?"

"It's my whole future. I have everything staked on this China trade. I have to have the money in three months and the ship ready by late autumn. My trade has to start soon after the railroad gets here and it will be here this summer. I'm in a hurry."

"And right now?"

"Right now, I'm off to New Westminster to make arrangements for that shipment of molasses to Battleford through Regina and to see what I can do to keep the Chinamen working."

I wished him luck and returned to the kitchen. Lydia and I packed our salmonberry preserves into the cool cupboard at the far end of the summer kitchen. We had jars of pickles and chutney and some strawberry preserves put away. They looked homey and reassuring somehow as if whatever happened in the future we would, at least, eat well.

Vancouver is a wonderful place to obtain food. There are so many fish here we only need to walk to the nearest creek and scoop up trout. The smelts come in with the tide so abundantly several times a year we can imprison them by the basketful. They are a strange and wonderful sight, churning the waters at night, shooting through the inky sea, flashing with incandescent phosphorous, their tails rattling a peculiar cadence. We don't eat smelts, considering them too oily, but many people capture them and spread them on their gardens to enrich the soil. That is so smelly a process I have forbidden Lydia to try it. The seaweed raked in from the ocean shores is good enough, and not as offensive. Fruit trees do well here and berries. Our small garden produces peas and potatoes and onions enough for our winter supplies. Lydia employs a child from school to hoe and weed, so we expect to have a good crop this summer and autumn. We use the dirty dish water to keep them growing. With this longer summer holiday, I would be able to help Lydia with more of the household chores and would spend some time improving my wardrobe. Even this far from the centres of fashion, I was determined I would not be a dowd.

I took a basket and started down Hastings Road to Hartney's Drygoods Store on Carrall Street. I had a notion to construct a walking suit for the summer picnics and outings we hoped to take. Since I was not teaching, I had the leisure to cut and pin and take the pains needed for a well-fitted dress. I would also cross that black cross painted on Mr. Hartney's doorway.

I walked up Hastings Road and approached the corner of Carrall and Water when I noticed a group of about eight men gathered under the maple tree. This wasn't really unusual. The maple tree was the central gathering place much like Hyde Corner in London. Everyone expresses their opinion here. The Sunnyside Hotel is adjacent and convenient for stoking flagging enthusiasms with locally brewed beer.

I was curious and diverted to Water Street but crossed on the opposite side of the road. The men were talking in low voices with the occasional comment in a rapid and critical tone. It wasn't until I met Robert outside the Courthouse, I realized the men were discussing the arrival of three hundred Chinese from Victoria.

"The Chinese are coming to clear the C.P.R. land?" I got that much from the mutterings and occasional loud comment.

"The boat's on its way. It should be here soon." Robert scratched the back of his head with his pencil. "Should be able to see it dock any minute; it's in the harbour. I hope Superintendent Roycroft is with the Chinese. I think there's going to be a lot of trouble. We don't need more Chinese. Some of those already here don't have work."

"Do the men here have guns?"

"Right now, you mean? Carrying them?

I nodded.

"Haven't seen any."

I felt my shoulders relax a little. "Where is the land they're going to clear?"

"Up there." He pointed west. "MacDougal has the contract."

We turned and looked through the haze of smoke from the ever-burning slash piles to the forest on the west of Cambie Street.

"C.P.R. land?"

Robert nodded.

"350 of the 6,000 acres the government gave them?"

Again, Robert nodded. "And MacDougal is being paid $150 an acre to clear it. He's paying his Chinese Thyee $90 an acre to supply the workers to do the work and the Thyee is paying his workers whatever he wants."

I worked out the sum in my head. "MacDougal's making $21,000 on that one job?" That's what had attracted Frank to the scheme. I remembered the figures. My arithmetic skills must be getting better.

"I could own and run newspapers all across the continent for that kind of money."

"I could support Lydia and Stanley and myself for the rest of our lives with that kind of money."

We turned back to the inlet and looked between the buildings of Water Street to the harbour. The *Princess Louise* was docking at the city wharf. Ropes secured her to the small floating dock and a narrow gangway slid from the ship to the wharf. In less than ten minutes a steady stream of Chinese workers disembarked. I could see them plodding down the gangplank and up the wharf, all dressed the same, all about the same small size, looking like identical beads strung on a string from the ship up the wharf to the foot of Carrall Street. There were a few white men on the street watching but no organized crowd and no guns. The Chinese filed past us, down Water Street and up the rough trail to the bluff. Morton used to have a house up on the bluff overlooking the inlet and that was to be the centre of the clearing activity. The Superintendent from Victoria stood across the street from us on the boardwalk, his arms folded across his chest watching the Chinese, and watching us.

Robert had been writing notes as the Chinese men slipped past us and now turned his attention to the men gathering at the Sunnyside Hotel. There were about fifty and as we looked a man detached himself from the group and started up Water Street. He held a placard hastily constructed and painted, 'The Chinese have came. Mass meeting in City Hall tonight."

The grammatical error irritated my mind before the sinister aspects of the message penetrated my understanding.

The superintendent turned up the trail after the Chinese. Robert headed toward the Sunnyside Hotel.

"What are they going to do?" I clutched his arm.

"God knows." He pulled himself free, flipped a page in his notebook and started toward the maple tree and the men gathered beneath it.

The superintendent must exert some deterrent effect on the men of Vancouver. Most of them were reasonable men who had been brought up to respect law and order. Surely, they would try to deal with this threat to their working lives with politics and not violence. I convinced myself this must be the plan and spent the rest of the day in town doing my shopping and visiting with friends. I was returning home in the late afternoon by Carrall Street. This time the number of men gathered around the hotel was well over a hundred. I hesitated at Carrall and Cordova thinking I might have to detour around such a crowd. The afternoon sun slanted between the buildings holding motes of dust suspended in light. The men's boots had stirred up the street dirt until the combination of smoke and dust clogged my nostrils and irritated my throat. I heard the horses' hooves thudding on the dirt road before Robert reined in beside me.

"Go home," he said.

"This is becoming repetitive," I complained. 'You told me to go home last night."

He dismounted. "Look, Amy. I really think you should keep away from that crowd. They are in a nasty mood and, as much as they all respect you individually, a crowd can lose its conscience and turn a little crazy."

I didn't believe the group of men in front of me, some of whom I knew slightly, and some who were my neighbours and church-going friends, would be anything but reasonable to me.

We stood for a moment in the twilight, Robert holding the reins of his horse and me patting Bess's neck pleased with my easy day and a little excited by the mood of the city.

Suddenly a horse and rider pulled up to the edge of the crowd. They'd come from Water Street and the horse stamped and snorted; the man waved his hat and shouted, "There's 300 Chinamen at the MacDougal camp on Morton's bluff. Are we going to sit here and let those yellow dogs take our jobs?"

There was a moment of silence and then the crowd roared in unison, "No!"

"Then let's get to the City Hall and do something about it!" The horseman urged his mount up the street. Some of the crowd followed the rider and the rest surged as one man toward us.

"Quick!" Robert said. "Up on Bess here." He threw me up astride on the saddle without regard for my skirts or my dignity, slapped the reins into my hands and said, "Get out of here."

I held the horse steady for a moment. "What about you?"

"I have to follow the crowd anyway. Get out of here!" He was shouting now and smacked Bess' side with his hand.

She started. I turned her quickly and cantered ahead of the men, nipped right on Cordova Street and then right again down Abbot, then back on Water Street.

I had heard about the weekly meetings of the Knights of Labour. They had been anti-Chinese for a year now. I hadn't thought they would be able to stir up so many people to support them. The little bay mare moved quickly toward my house, but I managed to hold her for a moment while I peered between the buildings up Columbia Street to the City Hall on Powell. There seemed to be many men around it and a lot of movement in the crowd. Men were speaking but I was too far from them to hear clearly. The roar of the crowd giving unanimous support was ominous. The same stimulus that had precipitated Robert into giving me his horse, and me into touching the horse into a canter made me look for safety. I squeezed my knees against Bess' sides and headed home.

I wondered how I would feel if I were a white woman in China feeling the same inside yet looking odd to others. This whole situation was unfair. The union men would never get Van Horne to stop using Chinese labour. The last pronouncement he made in May was he would not build the New Westminster Railroad extension without Chinese labour. The men hadn't a hope of getting the Dominion government to support anything that opposed Cornelius Van Horne. So, were the men going to rebel? Or riot in the streets? I reined the horse into the yard, dismounted without grace and tied the little mare to the rail in front of the house.

Jack Bullman was eating in the kitchen while Lydia worked at the stove. I said hello, left them and went to my room upstairs where I could look back down Hastings Road at the city. I could not see any of the men, but I could hear distant shouts and an occasional roar from the crowd. Then I saw sparks in the darkening sky and then flame. What had they set alight? How could they have been so foolish as to set fire to anything in this dry country? The flames shot high into the air and then fell back until I saw nothing but smoke for several minutes. After twenty minutes the smoke either stopped or had blended into the existing smoky air and the increasing dark until I couldn't see it anymore. Perhaps they set one of the small Chinese shacks on Cambie Street afire.

I could stay in my room no longer. I had been pacing back and forth in front of the window anxiously wondering what the men were doing, worrying about the city, the people and Stanley out there in it all. I rummaged through Stanley's clothes until I found a pair of old trousers and a shirt, coat, and cap that more or less fit me and disguised me as a young man. I let myself out the front door without telling Lydia. If she thought I was safe in my room, she'd be happier. I patted the little mare and swung astride. It was much more comfortable in Stanley's clothes than in my own.

We slipped quietly out of the yard and west up Hastings Road to Water Street. I was cautious here, prepared to slip behind a building or wheel the horse back. I could hear the shouts of men, the stomp and shuffle of feet, and the slap of reins of a horse near the City Hall on Powell. There were more than two hundred men now periodically shouting together as if they were a great power. I held Bess back in the space between the buildings. Robert was no doubt right. The men would not give me any respect this night, especially if they found me dressed as a boy. On the other hand, I didn't think they had any other objective in mind but the Chinese. The Chinese in this city didn't ride horseback.

A great roar of enthusiasm rose out of the upper floor of the City Hall and men poured down the stairs to join their friends on the street. There were one or two lanterns held aloft by men who led the way down Powell Street, down Water to the trail to Morton's bluff. I followed, well back. The men entered the half-cleared brush trail to the MacDougal camp. I was astounded at the speed they made in that mess of slash and rough ground. I held Bess back and carefully helped her pick her way through rising ground, over tree stumps and down ravines. The men were calling to each other and singing so I could estimate how far ahead of me they were. I had just dismounted and led Bess over a particularly bad combination of fallen tree trunks and slash when I heard voices behind me. I pushed through the slash off the trail and pulled Bess with me. We waited. The voices came closer and one of the men held a lantern up high. It was Superintendent Roycroft, the man who had come with the Chinese this morning. I knew him by reputation; tough, but fair, people said; a provincial policeman empowered by Victoria to act over our local police. Chief John Stewart puffed behind the Superintendent.

Both men were scratched by the bushes on the trail. The pace of their pursuit forcing them into jagged sticks and torn tree trunks. They paused for a moment, labouring for breath, the lantern light glittering in their eyes. Then they ran on.

I mounted again and followed.

There was a clump of cedar on the cliff edge about a hundred yards from the camp. I made my way to it and stayed hidden by shadows but able to see clearly.

The rioters were still singing "John Brown's Body" as they surrounded the camp. By now the ranks were about 300. Some were rough workers from the pineries and some respectable businessmen from the streets of Vancouver. The Chinese huddled on the roofs of the cabins and Chief Stewart stood in front of them with Superintendent Roycroft in front of the chief. The rioters had ripped tents and constructed a huge fire in the middle of the camp. They piled the belongings of the Chinese on the fire feeding a flame that rose into the dark sky lighting the scene with a medieval menace. The men faced the police and the Chinese.

I heard yells from some victims who had run from the rioters. I couldn't see them. but I could hear them scream as they jumped over the bluff and into the water. I heard the bodies falling like a handful of pebbles into a pond. Plonk! Plonk. Plonk. A cold sweat beaded my face. My hands trembled. Those men. They might die. The rioters returned to the fire and gathered behind their leaders facing the police.

"Cease in the name of the Queen." The Superintendent's voice fell into a momentary silence. "Cease in the name of the Queen and return to your homes."

The men stood quietly. The singing stopped.

A voice called from the crowd. "Who says the Chinamen must go?"

A tremendous roar of assent rose in the air. Bess stamped her foot with fear as over two hundred voices boomed into the night. The Chinese were terrified. The white men were animals and the Chinese trapped. The Superintendent stood straight and waited.

The answering "Aye" subsided and the night was again quiet.

"Who says the police must go home?" This time the assent was not as vigorous.

The crowd started down the slope toward the police and the Chinese. The men hesitated in front of the cabin. They stood still for several long moments. The Superintendent waited. If they wanted the Chinese, they were going to have to attack the law. That was too much for the crowd and slowly they backed away and began to leave.

I hadn't realized how tight my muscles were nor how still I had been sitting until I expelled a long breath and slumped in the saddle.

I touched Bess's neck with the rein. She was anxious to move away, and I was anxious to get back into town before the men. We moved as quickly as possible down the trail. I turned right when we reached Cambie and trotted Bess down Dupont to Carrall and down Carrall to False Creek. I swung off the horse at the beach and looked for Sung Wick's house. I couldn't remember which one it was. I almost cried in frustration for I could see the glow of the lantern lights coming closer and I dared not be caught here.

I threw my dignity away and screamed, "Sung Wick! Sung Wick, you must leave!"

The still air seemed heavy. There was no movement from the buildings in front of me. No doors opened and no one came out into the night. Then quietly, so quietly, I wondered if I had I had really heard it, a voice whispered across the water behind me, "It is well."

I whirled around; the reins of the horse still my hand and strained to peer into the dark of the inland bay.

"Sung Wick?" I whispered now.

"It is well, Teacher. Thank you. Go now."

I took a deep breath of relief, flung myself up on the saddle, and dashed for the trees at the edge of the clearing. I crashed into the thicket just as lanterns illuminated the beach.

I froze with fear, afraid the men in this mood might discover me and visit their mob madness on me. Bess stood still, and I sat like a statue on her.

The men found a group of five Chinese in that small settlement. Five men who had tried to hide in their homes. The big white man who had first hauled the Chinese into the light picked up two and slammed his fist into their faces. No one helped him but no one stopped him either. He beat the men, then left them on the beach. He was huge and they were small. There was no contest. I saw a couple of shadows slip out the back of the crowd and swim into the bay. But there were still three Chinese huddled in a group.

"We'll take them to the docks and put them on the boat to Victoria," a speaker yelled his intentions. "Come on let's march them down Carrall Street and put them on the boat. We don't want them here. Let Victoria look after them. We don't want them in Vancouver."

A few" ayes" responded to this.

One shack was a little isolated from the rest and the nearest man with a torch set it alight. I backed my horse further into the thicket as the tinder dry pine instantly caught and flames rose into the sky. There was some cheering and shouting and men started looting the other shacks pulling out beds and books and chairs and throwing them on the fire. They found no more Chinese at home, so they contented themselves with breaking windows and dragging their feet through the gardens. I was angry now. Fear had gone and anger welled up inside me like hot venom. I sat on Bess holding her reins tight so she wouldn't move and seething with the strictures of my abilities and position. These men were ruining my society, behaving like savages, treating decent people as if they were insects. I had no power, no power at all, to stop them. It would help no one if I were to try. Robert was right about that.

I looked at the crowd. Some of them carried lanterns and some torches so I could see many of their faces. Robert should be there taking notes for publication. He would probably be at the edge of the crowd. I looked intently and forgot to keep a tight hold of Bess. She moved forward out of the trees in a sudden movement. I tightened my knees and drew the reins to the right moving quickly toward the new road. I didn't turn to see if I had been noticed. It was still dark and all anyone would see was a young boy on a horse. I wove through the stumps and round the piles of sticks on the C.P.R. right of way picking my way back to Hastings Road and the teacherage. I had seen Robert just before Bess moved. He had been standing well back of the crowd, writing. I don't know if he looked up. He might not have recognized me.

Then a clear thought made me sit straight in the saddle. He would surely recognize his own horse.

I tied Bess to the rail and removed the saddle. It was a light English Calvary Saddle and easy for me to manage, I rubbed her with a cloth Stanley had by the rail and brought her a pail of water.

Lydia caught me as I put the pail in front of the horse.

"What are you doing in those clothes?"

"I wanted to see what was going on." I felt suddenly as if I was ten years old again. I knew I had been foolish to ride out there.

"You wouldn't have a shred of reputation left if anyone saw you in that get-up."

"Then go to bed and stop looking at me," I snapped.

She shut her mouth with a click.

I was instantly contrite. "Lydia, I'm sorry. You must have been worried about me when you found I'd gone,"

She nodded.

"Well, I'm all right and no one saw me." Except Robert, I said to myself.

"Far be it from me to interfere with your life." Lydia was offended, as well she might be, and retreated into sarcasm. "Now you have actually condescended to come home I might as well go to bed. Where's your brother?"

"He's not home?" I was alarmed.

"Now it's your turn to worry."

I took her arm. "Was he home for supper?"

She nodded. "Yes. He said he wanted to go back and do some more work at the warehouse."

"All right. Thanks."

She shrugged and shut the front door with a definite slam. She'd be hard to live with for a few days, but she never stays angry for long—and I had given her some reason.

Bess lifted her head and nuzzled my hand "I don't think we have any oats."

I found a tin of oatmeal in the kitchen and brought a bowlful out to her. I leaned my head against her neck and patted it, looking past her at the city now lying dark on the curve of the bay. A few lanterns were alight in houses beyond the shops, but it was quiet now. Was such a barbaric city worth preserving? Should I stay here? Was Frank right? Was San Francisco a better, more cultured place to live? But they hated the Chinese there too. Did they poison a man because he was Métis? Or beat a man because he was different? Perhaps I should go back to Ontario. I felt nausea well up to my throat and my forehead grow cold and damp as I remembered the scene on the beach. In this mood, I would have taken the next boat back home.

CHAPTER THIRTEEN

I heard Stanley return about four a.m. Lydia called out and he answered. His footsteps thumped on the stairs.

I grabbed my candle, lit it, and hurried onto the landing to meet him. "What happened to you?"

His face and hands were black with soot; his shirt torn in several places and charred through on the sleeves. Even his trousers had ragged holes where embers must have burned unheeded. The whites of his eyes were bright against the soot on his face, but he looked tired: eyelids dropping, and shoulders slumped. "I had to fight the fire down at Cambie Street. Some stupid fools set fire to a Chinaman shack there. You know how close that is to the hotel?"

I nodded and reached to hold him by the elbow, helping him up the last two stairs.

"Everyone who worked at the hotel hauled buckets of water and a lot of men who were afraid the fire would spread just joined the line and helped. It took ages to put it out. We just kept hauling water from the sea and handing it up man to man to man, throwing it on the fire. The shack did burn to the ground, but no other buildings caught any sparks."

"It wasn't close by any other building, was it?"

"Close enough," Stanley said. He yawned and straightened. "I don't know what got into the mob. First thing I knew, a crowd came down the street yelling they were going to save British Columbia for the white man." He grinned a little. "I hope Chief Chip-amkaay didn't hear them. He's got quite a camp across the creek, and he could wipe us out if he wanted to."

"We're lucky his people are civilized."

"They're not as wild as the white men, anyway." Stanley absentmindedly scratched his arm. "I don't know what those fools did after they left Cambie Street. I was too busy to follow them. I hope Sung Wick got away."

"He did."

Stanley turned slowly and looked at me.

"Now how would you know? Even you wouldn't have. . ." His voice trailed away.

I didn't answer and he stared at me for a moment. "Whose horse is that out front?"

"Robert's."

"Where's Robert?"

"Covering the events for his newspaper. I hope he's all right." There was a silence.

Then, "I borrowed your pants," I said.

"Uh huh. Does Robert know you were out there tonight?"

"Don't tell him, for heaven's sake" He might know, but I wasn't going to offer information.

"Don't worry. I'm not telling anyone. I take it Lydia doesn't know you were gone."

"That's where you're wrong. She does know."

Stanley grinned. "Sis, you're as bad as I am. What'd you see?"

I followed him into his bedroom and stood by his bed while he took off his boots and socks. He listened to me, nodding his head occasionally and gave me a satisfied grunt when I told him about Sung Wick's family.

"So, no one was murdered."

"I don't think so. Some of the Chinese were beaten but I didn't see anyone killed; unless they were killed jumping off the bluff.

"They might be all right if they landed in the water, and if they could swim."

He turned back the bed covers.

"Stanley MacDonald! You are not going to bed without washing that dirt from your face and hands and changing your clothes!" I stopped being his friend and became his elder sister.

He paused with one hand on the bed sheet, his teeth white against his black face. "You wouldn't respond to a little blackmail, would you? I won't tell anyone where you've been if I don't have to wash?"

I was startled for a moment, then laughed. "No, I won't. Go wash."

He protested but took my candle, lumbered down-stairs, to the back kitchen and then returned.

"You don't look sleepy," he said.

"I'm not. Good night."

He yawned and retired to his room.

I blew out the candle and sat in the dark by my window looking out over the city. Tall pines obscured some of my view, but I could see the outline of the bay as it curved under the pilings at Water Street. The lights in the Regina Hotel on Cordova Street seemed to hang like stars above the rest of the houses. There were a few lantern lights winking from the centre of town but, as it was almost morning, the lamp-lighter had snuffed the street- lights and the city was in darkness. I almost missed Robert when he came for his horse. I had been watching the road but didn't see him until I caught a glimpse of the white collar above his suit jacket. I was still dressed so I scurried down the stairs and let myself out the front door.

"Robert," I called anxiously and hurried toward him. "Are you all right?"

He finished buckling the saddle and waited for me to come closer. He had the reins of the mare in his hand when I reached him, and I grabbed the stirrup to prevent him from mounting until I had talked to him.

"All right?" he said. "Of course, I'm all right. What about you? Did you have a nice ride?"

Suddenly, I was pinned against the horse. Robert had a hand on either side of the saddle, and I backed up against Bess and stared into the eyes of a very angry man.

"I lend you my horse so you can go safely home and stay away from the rioting. The next thing I see is my horse heading into the trees at False Creek. What the hell were you doing down there?" He grabbed my shoulders and shook me. My teeth clicked together, and my head bobbed like a rag doll's. I was about to fetch him a sharp crack across his face when Bess shifted and pressed me closer to Robert. He dropped his hands and stepped back and continued to abuse me, but verbally now. "You, stupid fearless, mindless, ignorant wench. Don't you know what men can do in a mob? Haven't you ever read any history? What difference would it make to the mob that you are a respectable schoolteacher? You wouldn't have had a chance out there. Not a chance."

I put my hand on his shoulder and looked at him. I had never seen so much emotion on anyone's face, and I didn't know what to do or say.

"Robert, I had to warn Sung Wick. You said you'd do that, but I had your horse, and I knew you wouldn't be able to get over there. I had to warn him."

"And if that mob had known you were warning the Chinese, they would have treated you like a Chinaman."

A long shudder ran over his body. He put his head down on his arm and rested it against the horse. I slipped my hand up to his shoulder in a gesture of comfort and put my head on his chest. He turned his face into my hair, and I could hear him mutter, "Oh God! If that isn't just like you. You had to warn Sung Wick."

He lifted his head, held me tightly by my shoulders and stared at me.

"The Chinese jumped into Coal Harbour at Morton's Bluff rather than face that crowd. Did you know that? They were wild there tonight. They might have killed all the Chinese and MacDougal too."

"But Roycroft stopped them. No one died there tonight—unless those who jumped were hurt?"

Robert stared at me in disbelief. 'No," he said mechanically. "They weren't hurt." He moved his body even closer, and his hands tightened painfully on my shoulders. "So, you were there as well," he said quietly. "You put yourself right into the middle of that mess." His hands slipped up behind me and held my head. I could feel the muscles of his arms tight as wires and his body rigid with anger. I felt my own muscles tense as I stiffened to meet whatever madness was coming. It was a savage kiss. I tried to jerk away from him, but for all his short stature Robert was strong. I hit at his shoulders with my fists. Bess moved away from me, and Robert pressed my back with one hand until my body was tight against him. I felt his lips move into my mouth and suddenly the cruelty went out of the kiss and his lips were soft, his hands gentle.

I didn't move. I was so surprised and confused I lay in his arms as he moved his mouth and his tongue softly over mine, his hands gently over my back. My rigid body relaxed, and I found a pleasure in this soft exploration I had not yet experienced. When I had time to think about this, I would be very angry. But right now, it didn't seem real. I felt as though stood apart from myself looking on, not thinking, just existing. When he drew his lips away and rubbed my cheek with his, I found I could not stand without his support. I wasn't not sure if this was because I had been assaulted by his anger or bemused by his gentleness. I wasn't really sure of any emotion.

"Oh." was all I could find to say. I took a deep breath and stepped away. "I'm all right, I think. At least I was until you came."

I babbled a little because I couldn't reason clearly. "I don't think anyone else knew it was me on the horse."

"Oh, good." Robert said with a quiet sarcasm. "I'm so pleased your reputation is intact." He swung himself up on the mare and turned her toward town. "Then you can bloody well go to bed now and stay there. Good night."

"All right." I said. "Good night." I had felt abused and rejected. Suddenly, I was angry. "I didn't tell you to worry about me," I yelled after him.

He swung the horse back and came to within five feet of me. "You haven't got the judgement of a-six-year-old. How you ever teach school is beyond me. The third form students should be teaching you."

"You....you....No one gave you any right to come around here and insult me."

"It's time someone did. Anyone who hasn't got more sense than to pull a stunt like you did tonight needs a keeper."

"I have a keeper. Lydia's good enough for me!" I shouted at him and then realized I had just admitted I needed supervision. I gulped, trying hard to think of how I could extract myself from such a foolish admission.

Robert chuckled. "Be magnanimous, Amy. Let me have the last word tonight."

"Oh, go home," I said crossly. "I'm sorry I worried you."

He moved the horse closer until he was only a few inches from me. "I'm sorry too," he said. "Did I frighten you?"

I thought back on the last few minutes. "No," I said honestly. I licked my tongue over the small cut in my lip. We stared at each other for a few moments. Then I grinned. "It was an interesting evening. Thanks for the horse."

"The horse?" he said blankly. "Oh, hell." He dug his heels into the poor mare's side and trotted out of the yard.

CHAPTER FOURTEEN

I thought I'd sleep late into the morning but in that half-reality between sleep and consciousness I heard shouting. At first, I struggled with confused remnants of last night's riot, Felicity screaming in delirium and all the children in my school crying for help. As I became more cognitive I realized the noise was real and coming from the city. I flew to the window, but I couldn't see the Sunnyside Hotel. Trees and the curve of the bay hid it from me but assuredly that hotel was at the centre of the noise. I splashed my face with cold water and hastily buttoned my dark walking suit. I hooked the bottom portion of my half boots and, ignoring the sharp muscle pain in my legs that was a reminder of last night's unaccustomed horse-back ride, I rushed down the stairs.

Stanley was ahead of me and had just disappeared down the road.

Lydia hurried through the hall to the front door. "Where are you going?"

"Only far enough to see what's going on."

"Don't go without your basket. It doesn't look decent."

I paused and stared at her. She threw me the market basket from its hook near the kitchen door and I caught it in a reflex action. A sudden muscle twinge stabbed my shoulder. I should ride more often or not at all. The basket might make me look more respectable, but it was awkward to carry. I left it outside beside the road and hurried toward the city.

Men were gathering at the Sunnyside Hotel. This time I stayed well back.

Under the maple tree beside the hotel were six or seven empty wagons and drays. Men held the horses and mules. Some men stood on the hotel porch quaffing their free "eye-opener." Some were laughing, jostling, and shouting to each other across the street. Everywhere there was dirt: thick, choking street dust, drifting over boots, and settling against the wagon wheels. I stopped, shaded my eyes from the sun and watched.

Several men climbed into the wagons and the entourage proceeded up Carrall Street and down Dupont. I hurried after them, careful to keep back of the last wagon. Still, I was in time to see the procession stop on Dupont, some men staying with the horses and wagons and some entering the shops of the Chinese.

"Got another one," a man yelled gleefully "Here tie his pigtail to those two."

They handed a small Chinese roughly through the crowd, shoving him until he stumbled and lurched against the men only to be pushed to the ground. Someone grabbed him by his hair and threw him against the wagon. Another white man pulled his black plait tight and tied him to the two Chinese standing under guard. The Chinese said nothing. One fell and the other two were jerked toward the ground with him. They helped their comrade up and huddled together. I couldn't think of anything I could do that might help. I was afraid the men would notice me, and I would be served some of the barbaric treatment by the mob. I felt cold and nauseous, but I couldn't leave. I slipped into a doorway where the morning sun had not yet reached and where I could still see the street.

An old Chinese man waited for the mob in front of his shop, his hands folded into his faded blue tunic. He looked patient and unafraid. The sun lit the yellow-white of his long hair; his eyes were half closed; his features still. The men stopped in front of him.

"Out of the way, old man," a stocky white man said.

The Chinese nodded, looked over the crowd and said, "Mr. Tyler, please."

The crowd waited and a man in a dark coat came forward. "What can l do for you, Hong Soy?"

"I would like to negotiate some terms."

The man waved the crowd back into a semi-circle about four feet from the two businessmen.

The Oriental and the white businessmen conferred there in the street, their heads bent toward one another almost touching, the old Chinese swaying every so often in a rhythmic movement. The white man gesturing with his hands and shaking his head, then nodding. Mr. Tyler turned to the crowd.

"I've made a deal with Hong Soy."

The crowd murmured but listened for the terms.

"He'll see that all the Chinamen on the street are rounded up and into wagons, if we let him leave one Chinaman in each business."

The crowd objected and Mr. Tyler had to outline the advantages of the plan.

"That way, gentlemen (the euphemism struck me as singularly inappropriate) the Chinamen will be sure their businesses carry on and they won't be hurt. If no one's hurt, then Victoria won't send in the troops."

There was some head nodding. Victoria's supremacy over the politics and practices of Vancouver was resented daily.

"And we don't really care about a few Chinamen anyway. It's the hundreds of workers we don't want here. The shopkeepers are all right. Someone's got to do the laundry, hey?"

The men murmured among themselves for a few minutes. The old man Hong Soy stood immobile as if he awaited a grocery order with no concern or anxiety showing in his face.

"All right. All right. Let's have those Chinamen." The crowd accepted the terms and Hong Soy moved slowly into his shop.

I stayed in my deep doorway watching the Chinese file from the apartments over the shops and from behind the buildings. They shuffled in a line to the wagons and took their places like barrels of shop goods ready for shipment. The *Princess Louise* had already left our city's wharf, so the wagons started down the road to New Westminster and the waiting ship there. This time Vancouver was sending a consignment of Chinese to Victoria. I swallowed the bile rising in my throat and thought fiercely of what I'd like to do to those vulgar, brutal men: ship them to a desert in the far reaches of Australia; stack them up like cord wood on a wagon to hell. I was livid.

The last wagon disappeared around the corner for Westminster Road before I left my hiding place in the doorway and marched down Carrall and back out Hastings Mill Road.

I picked up my basket as I passed my home and continued to stamp my way up Hastings Road toward the mill. I noticed the haze already forming over the water on the inlet. The sailing ships were anchored peacefully in the still bay waiting for lumber. The forest was quiet. Few birds called. The whine from the saw, ever present but habitually ignored, grew louder as I left the trees. An eagle settled onto the top branch of a tall pine and gazed over the water waiting for salmon. When I reached a slight rise of land I looked back toward the city. I took a deep breath and let it out slowly. It looked peaceful. That was ironic.

I saw a dog cart turn up Hastings Mill Road and come my way. Maude. As she approached, I could see her black hat with the feather bobbing at the side. The sun was bright on the back of the horse, glinting a warm brown. I recognized our Saturday horse from the livery stable. Maud 's held a whip in her hand and looked competent and, as she came closer, worried.

She drove past me and called, "I'll see you at the bend in the road."

Dear Maude. So circumspect. I kept my pace at its normal rate and arrived at the blackberry bushes around the corner just as Maude tied the horse to the willow tree.

"How are you this morning?" I inquired politely.

"Annoyed."

She untied her hat, shook the dust from it and replaced it.

"What's the matter? Were you up last night?"

"I was up," Maude said, "but I stayed in the hotel. I didn't see anything but a lot of milling around and a fire. It's the kind of affair I have sense enough to stay well away from."

I nodded agreement. I would not tell Maude I lacked her sense.

"Now, what concerns me. . ." She took my arm and steered me down the path behind the blackberry bushes. ". . . is the fact those men were yelling for guns last night."

The hairs shivered on my arms, and my hands grew cold. I hadn't realized it was a common idea. "Guns?"

"I heard several men shout, 'If we had some decent guns, we could clean out all the Chinamen in the country!'"

"Oh, no." We had arrived at the shore and the calm water of the bay. "We're going to have an insurrection if that kind of talk keeps up—a rebellion, a war right here."

"Yes," Maude said emphatically. "And I have most of my money saved for my bakery. I have no intention of baking bread in the middle of a rebellion. You know who loses when the men shoot each other?"

I waited. I know a rhetorical question when I hear one.

"Not only those who are killed. We all lose. Who looks after the children and the women? Too bad if a few of us accidentally get killed in the name of justice. Who takes up the development of the country while the men are shooting each other? The whole thing is a silly waste of time." Maude slapped her gloves against her hands and scowled,

If she hadn't been so serious, she would have been amusing. She looked on the men of Vancouver as children who needed direction and discipline. Perhaps she was right. I wasn't sure my own inclination to smile wasn't a nervous reaction to this new threat. Maude had a knowledge of men I didn't, and she was very worried. If they could get guns perhaps, we would be in the middle of a war. I tried to remember where I had put the shotgun after hunting with Stanley.

"I don't think war is ever really advantageous," I agreed. "Just exactly what is bothering you today?"

"I am concerned Mr. M. P. Sanders is bringing money into this area to supply guns to these men."

I thought of Superintendent Roycroft's performance. "Then the police would come in battalions and squash any insurrection."

"They would if there was only one rebellion in the country. If the Métis rebel in the North West and the Americans rebel in Vancouver and the Indians rebel in the Cariboo, where do you think the police are going to get their men? The Provincial Police don't have many. The Royal North West have 200 men stationed at Battleford, 100 at Prince Albert, 100 in Edmonton and 50 at Fort Qu'appelle. By the time the Dominion government sent troops out here we could be part of the United States of America."

Maude had either spent the night collecting information or thinking about what she already knew.

"That would have to be masterminded. Someone would have to be in charge of starting the rebellions. They would have to arrange rebellions all over the country at the same time and arrange supplies of both food and ammunition to arrive in time to feed and outfit the rebels." I didn't think it was possible.

"Mr. Sanders from Ottawa could do that."

I pondered what Maude had said for a few minutes.

It could be she was friendlier with Robert than I had supposed and was repeating Robert's fears, for she had some of the same misgivings he had expressed. Would the people here rebel? There were many people in Vancouver who had shown a preference for American association. Frank had—but I didn't think Frank was interested in a lawless rebellion.

"Maude, people already have guns. Don't you think they would have used them last night if they'd really wanted to?"

"Some people have guns. But the guns are old ones that usually need to be loaded slowly. Not very many people have the new repeater rifles. A mob needs a strong leader to really do harm."

I remembered the men of last night and this morning and disagreed with Maude. Those men could cause a lot of harm without a leader. Perhaps to overthrow a government, they would need better organization.

"If you think Vancouver is ripe for rebellion," I said slowly, "what can we do about it? I mean, what can you and I do about it?"

Maude turned and looked at me. "Now that's an honest question. Here I am dithering about what might happen, and you hone right to the centre of the problem. I don't know what we can do about it."

"Could you look at Mr. Sander's pockets some time?" I wasn't sure going through a customer's pockets was possible.

"No," Maude said shortly. "That's against my principles. I do not snoop."

"Oh." I felt I had insulted her. The rules of her profession were outside my education. "Sorry, but if this is war, couldn't you spy a little?"

Maude smiled "No, I couldn't, Amy. I feel badly enough repeating some of the things Mr. Sanders told me. I really couldn't search his pockets."

"All right." I didn't understand Maude's scruples. but I didn't understand her way of life very well. "You could tell Robert of our worries, but I suppose he's thought of them all himself."

I was not approaching Robert on any score. I was still disconcerted by our meeting of last night and not sure of myself.

"Oh, yes. Mr. Carr knows everyone is ready to explode around here. I don't know if the police know that."

"Superintendent Roycroft is here now. Surely, he must understand situations like this. He lived through the Riel Rebellion last year. He ought to be able to diffuse this violence. It's ugly, isn't it?"

We stood in silence looking over the still water of the inlet. I recalled the savagery of the men last night, the injustice of it all and remembered how far we were from British troops and the might behind law and order. A mob like last night's could sweep through Vancouver, into my home, kill me, Stanley, Lydia. We had no protection. Neither did Maude. She turned to me. I noticed the tiny lines at the edges of her eyes, spreading along the creases from her nose to her mouth. She wasn't a young woman, perhaps forty.

"I have waited a long time," she said quietly, "to stop my evening work. I want a respectable, quiet city to live in when I change my profession. Vancouver seemed the ideal place. It's young, tolerant of my kind, and growing fast, so I could lose myself in a new population who wouldn't remember me from a few years back. If this city becomes the centre of a revolution, I will have no chance to start a quiet bakery shop. No chance at all."

Her face hardened and her eyes looked away and over to the mountains across the inlet. "I will not give it all up now."

I comforted her as best I could on the walk back to the dog cart, but, truly, there was little we could do. We had no power in this city; and no hope of getting any. On my way to the teacherage I thought about Maude's dream of a new beginning. In a way she was like the Chinese people moving to Vancouver to find a new life, new work and hoping for acceptance in a new country.

Jack Bullman was working on the cloak room, and I stopped to admire the new lumber and skeleton addition to the school. He walked home with me and joined us for tea mid-morning just as Frank arrived in his phaeton. Lydia glanced quickly at Frank and brought a tray of biscuits and tea into the parlour. Jack joined us there. I couldn't help but think Lydia would never have served Jack in her parlour in Ontario. Here, in Vancouver social classes tended to blur into each other and a man was accepted for what he did and how he behaved—most of the time anyway. It was different in Victoria where it still mattered what family you were born into. Perhaps Frank was right. Perhaps we should separate from Vancouver Island. But not with a rebellion.

"Were you here last night, Frank?" I asked him. I wanted to know if he'd seen anything I'd missed.

He helped himself to Lydia's oatmeal biscuits and smiled his thanks at her.

"No, I was in New Westminster. I have a shipment going up to Kamloops Lake this week to connect with the C.P.R. and I wanted to make sure all the paper-work was ready and the space saved for my load. I heard a few of the boys got worked up about the Chinamen. Anyone hurt?"

I was silent. Frank would be disturbed if he thought I had been anywhere near that riot, and he would never understand the curiosity that enticed me there. Besides, it was a silly thing to have done and I wasn't going to admit to it if I didn't have to. Lydia would not tell him, so it was left to Jack to answer.

"A couple of the Chinamen were beaten, I heard. No one died."

Frank nodded. "Any extra police in?"

Jack sipped his tea deliberately and waited for a few moments before he answered. "The Superintendent from Victoria is here, and I understand about thirty-five provincial constables are arriving today."

This was the first I'd heard of it. Maude would be pleased. No doubt she'd be glad of the extra protection. She'd probably earn extra money too.

"What are they going to do?" I was worried. They could precipitate a riot if they acted aggressively.

"I heard they were going to guard the Chinese for a while. The mayor is pretty upset because he thinks we can handle our own problems here."

"And where was the mayor last night? He's one of the men who signed the eviction notice given to all Chinese. He can't really consider himself impartial." I let my disgust show.

Frank looked amused. "He's not impartial. He's representing the voters. I think he probably is doing an honest job of representing most of the voters. You just don't happen to agree with him."

"That's true." I bit my lip then released it quickly. The bruise was still tender from last night. I didn't tell Frank what I thought of the average voter in this city.

He continued. "I'm concerned about the riots because as much as some people don't want the Chinese in this town, other people do. We need them. I sympathize with those men who don't want Orientals in this city, but I don't want the Chinamen out of here until September. Then I can help transport them back to China where I'm sure they'd be happier."

I was annoyed. "Really, Frank! They are people, you know. Not just a commodity that can be shifted around to suit the economy!"

"So?" he objected. "I'm fair. I pay what they ask, and I don't abuse anyone. But their presence here is a matter of dollars and cents to me. I'd be foolish to deny that."

That was truthfully the way he thought about them. I gave up.

I walked to the door with him. "What do you think will happen in the city now?"

"About the Chinamen?"

I nodded.

"Nothing. The police will calm everyone down."

"Do you think Mr. Sanders instigated all this unrest?"

Frank looked at me sharply "Do you think someone did?"

"Perhaps."

Frank freed his reins and walked to the buggy. He looked thoughtful. "Maybe I should try and interest Mr. Sanders in a debenture with my company."

I looked blank. My knowledge of finances was elementary.

Frank explained. "If I could get Mr. Sanders to pay me several thousand dollars for redeemable debentures, then I could use his money in my freight business and that would tie up the money so he couldn't use it to finance a rebellion."

I grabbed Frank's arm as he went to swing into the buggy. "That's brilliant, Frank! You are really clever. Of course! You could use his money for legitimate purposes, and he wouldn't be able to use it for nefarious ones."

Then an obvious objection hit me. "But if he plans to use it for financing an insurrection, why would he be interested in your debentures?"

Frank chuckled. "He's probably interested in making money. I could make my debenture offer seem so good he'd think he would be tying up his money for a short time only and making a good profit. I'll think about it, Amy. Could be I'll be able to hogtie this character before he causes trouble. I could talk to him about the tea/silk trade. I stand to make a lot of money that way and anyone in with me stands to make money."

"You still think you'll get enough money together to buy a ship?"

"Yes. This supply contract I have now with some financing from my bank in San Francisco should do it."

"Not here?"

Frank snorted. "No, there isn't any support for me here. Luckily, I'm well known in the States. Don't worry. I'll buy my ship."

I believed him.

"If the American banks finance the development of the west, won't we naturally gravitate to the United States?"

"Is that so bad?"

"Victoria would never assimilate."

Frank laughed.

"Victoria will stay a British Colony sitting by itself in splendid isolation forever."

"I suppose Victoria will remain forever English when England has disappeared."

"Victoria won't grow," Frank predicted. "Vancouver will grow. Trade will make the difference here. Victoria, although she has businessmen who understand trade, is too conservative to progress."

"You're on your way to New Westminster?" I stepped back to allow Frank room to mount the phaeton.

"Yes. I'll pick up those barrels of molasses I told you about, heading to Battleford. I need to make sure everything is ready for the shipment. It's a difficult route but I want to get established as a trader. Another shipment came in yesterday by ship."

"Do you have any extra molasses? Lydia was looking for some."

Frank lowered the reins and leaned toward me. "I should have thought and bought you some."

"Not at all. I could have ordered it."

"I'll let you know when the next shipment comes in." He smiled a little shyly. "I suppose all this talk of trade is boring to you."

"No," I said honestly. "I think it's inventive and imaginative. Besides," I smiled, "I approve of trading molasses."

"Well, I appreciate being able to talk about it with an intelligent female."

We were still smiling at each other, basking in each other's approval, when a horse and rider trotted into the yard. It was Stanley on a big, white gelding. He slid off the horse's bare back and stood holding the reins.

"Do you like him? I bought him today."

I knew Stanley had been saving his money, but he hadn't confided in me what he planned to spend it on.

"Very impressive," I said.

"Heavy," Frank said. "Are you planning on packing with him?"

"I thought I might get up a city delivery service," Stanley said eyeing Frank. "I thought I might get some custom from you."

"Certainly. I could probably use your services. Don't get too big though. I don't want any freighting competition."

Stanley laughed. "Not much danger of that yet."

I noticed he said "yet." My little brother was definitely growing up.

"Well, I'll send a little business your way. I sometimes need parts of my orders delivered in the town."

"I'll have to do it after hours when I'm through at the hotel." Stanley was anxious to make that clear.

Frank agreed with those arrangements. "Did you get my barrels loaded today?"

"Should finish them this afternoon. They came off the ship from San Francisco and are going north to Kamloops Lake?"

"That's right and then on to Battleford."

"They should be all loaded on the wagon today. They're sure heavy."

"Molasses," Frank said shortly. Then smiled at me. "And all promised, I'm sorry."

"That's all right," I said. "The next time you get a shipment of molasses save some for Lydia."

He nodded, snapped the reins on his horses and moved out of the yard.

Stanley spent the next ten minutes telling me the advantages of owning one's own horse and the particular advantages of this horse. I nodded and appreciated Stanley's acumen with one part of my mind, but most of my thinking was taken up with Frank's marvelous plan to diffuse Mr. Sander's efforts at rebellion. I could hardly wait to tell Maude. I wasn't going to tell Robert. Robert's help would not be necessary. Frank would stop this rioting and prevent Mr. Sanders from supplying guns.

I had great faith in Frank but the first thing I did after I entered the house was load the Remington and place it behind the kitchen door.

CHAPTER FIFTEEN

I spent the afternoon at the school-house tidying my papers and putting away supplies. Children had spilled chalk behind the back table, and someone had stuffed crusts of bread between cracks in the wall boards. Perhaps it was the mice, but seventy children think of some peculiar ways to alleviate periodic bouts of boredom. I walked home in time to join Lydia and Stanley for supper. Stanley ate quickly.

"I think I'll saddle up Homer and ride back to the hotel. Frank wants those barrels ready to ship in the morning and I could do some work tonight."

"Homer?"

"My horse. That's his name."

"A bit elegant for a pack horse, isn't it?" Lydia said dryly.

"I thought he might take me on a lot of journeys and make my fortune," Stanley said with the serious intent look he assumes when he's trying to keep Lydia and me under control.

"Homer, the creator of Ulysses?"

"That's right."

"Is he a Greek horse?" Lydia teased, "This big white horse with the grandiose name."

"Well," Stanley admitted, "he may not have gotten that far in the world, but he's been around some. He's probably about eight years old. If he stays strong for another ten years, I'll get a lot of work out of him and make some money. It will take a couple of months, maybe a month and a half, to earn the money I paid for him. He's dependable and sort of solid, easy-going. A nice horse."

I smiled at Stanley. He would be another Frank Hartman, wheeling and dealing with freight and sales. Perhaps he'd look after Lydia and me in our old age.

"Frank did say he wanted those barrels loaded first thing in the morning." I agreed.

"He'd like it if I had them ready. He's a good source of income for me. He can give me a lot of jobs."

While I knew Stanley was an enthusiastic entrepreneur, he hadn't yet been willing to work into the night. "Can you manage the loading by yourself?"

"Homer and I can do it. The barrels are on the back deck of the hotel about three feet off the ground. I'll back the wagons to the edge of the deck and roll the barrels into the wagons. I guess I'll find out how well Homer works with me."

I realized then Stanley was anxious to test his horse and he'd rather do that in the privacy of the evening than in public view on a busy day.

"We'll look for you about eleven," I said as he grabbed a scone for sustenance on his way out.

He was late. It was closer to twelve when I heard Stanley's footsteps on the stairs.

"How did Homer work?"

Stanley's tired eyes brightened as he paused by my door. "He works good. I have a little trouble getting him to back up, but he stands still while the wagon bounces around when I'm loading and that's really good. I think I'm going to be able to do all right with him."

"Where did you put him?"

"I hobbled him and tied him to a stake in the ground. I guess I'll have to build a shed for him. Do you think the mill owners will care?"

Hastings Mill owned the teacherage and the property.

"No. I'll tell them I want to stable a horse and they'll probably supply me with the lumber for the shed. They've been very good to us."

"Kind of handy having Jack Bullman sparking Lydia."

"Don't let her hear you say that. It may be true, but Lydia would steam if we mentioned it; at least, I think she would."

Stanley didn't answer, just stood quietly at my door looking down at his boots.

"Well," I was tired and ready for my own bed. "I'm glad your Homer is working out well. Good night?"

"Amy," Stanley said slowly.

I turned back.

"Amy, didn't Frank say those barrels were full of molasses?"

I nodded.

"Well, that's what I thought. One barrel leaked a little and I tried to give Homer a taste of it—of the molasses. You know Uncle Jock used to feed his horses bran and molasses in the winter?"

I nodded again. I wasn't truly interested, but I was polite.

"So, I scraped some off and tried to give it to Homer. He wouldn't eat it, so I thought I'd lick it off my fingers myself."

"And?" I prompted impatient for Stanley to finish his story.

"And it tasted terrible. It wasn't molasses. It was grease."

"Grease? Kitchen grease? Like bacon grease?"

"No. No." Now Stanley was impatient. "Axle grease. Wheel grease, gun grease."

We were silent. Stanley had my attention now. A refrain like a song whirled through my head. "Not molasses—gun grease. Not molasses—gun grease." I took a deep breath. "Stanley if you were shipping guns how would you pack them?"

"In barrels, in grease," Stanley said unhappily.

"Where are those barrels going?" But I knew where they were going.

"To New Westminster and on to Kamloops Lake, Regina and Battleford, North West Territories."

"Oh, my God." It sounded worse when he said it aloud. I had visions of a Métis regiment huddled in a coolie on the prairies waiting for their supply of guns. "We may be wrong. What else can be packed in grease?"

"Machine parts." Stanley said helpfully. "Grease; I mean the whole barrel could be full of grease."

I stood there uncertainly for a moment then said, "All right. Let's find out. Could Homer carry double?"

Stanley seemed to shift away his weariness.' "Sure. I think so. You'd better borrow some of my clothes again."

"I'm glad Lydia sleeps downstairs."

"Yes. It's better if she doesn't know what we're doing."

While I agreed with him, I wondered how often he applied that very philosophy to me.

"We need an iron bar to pry the barrel open and some way of fixing it again."

"I have an iron bar at the hotel. We'll have to try to fit the staves back together again. That might be a problem."

Homer was phlegmatic about carrying double. We rode through the dark night trying to keep to the grass and soft paths so we wouldn't be heard. I don't know what we were expecting, a sudden demand to stop, a shot, a knife? We crept through the city, a city that last night had been so dangerous. Were men still excited by the violence of last night? I glanced around us but could see only the outlines of buildings in the thick night. Robert would probably fly at me if he knew I was out here again. Since Robert hadn't been near me all day, perhaps he didn't care. That thought didn't give me the satisfaction I'd expected, but I refused to think any more on it right now.

"Halt! Who is it?"

The challenge almost startled me into sliding off Homer's back. I gripped Stanley's waist. He pulled back on the reins and stopped.

"Hello, Constable Parkinson. It's Stanley MacDonald again and a friend. I needed a little help loading some of those barrels I was working on earlier tonight. I'm just about finished."

I concentrated on taking deep breaths to steady my fluttering pulse. Constable Parkinson was no danger to anyone.

"That's all right then. I'm keeping an eye on the activities of the men tonight; I don't want to prevent you from working. It's always good to see a young man, two young men'" he said as we moved past him, "working hard."

Sanctimonious prattlehead. I blessed the darkness and his gullibility as I slipped past him unidentified.

The hotel and the shed beside it were very dark. I couldn't see the barrels or the wagon until Stanley walked behind a stack of lumber, found a lantern, and brought it back illuminating the area around us. The barrels were standing upright in the wagon ready for delivery. Boxes and bales of goods were stacked on the wide deck. Shadows elongated and receded in the flickering lantern light. I hoped we were alone for the deep shadows could conceal a contingent of the Métis army for all I knew. That was silly. No one had reported any Métis in town; we were alone. The deck and the shed were behind the hotel so no one could see us unless they came in from the street.

"You hold the lantern, Sis," Stanley said, "and I'll pry into the leaking barrel. It's already had some damage, so it won't be too noticeable if we don't I get it back together exactly as it was. At least I hope it won't be noticeable."

I nodded, then realized he couldn't see my head. "Good idea. I'll keep a lookout for strangers."

Stanley's head came up quickly, the lantern light reflecting gold lights off his hair. "If you see anyone, just tell me. Leave the lantern here and fade back to Homer. No talking, no heroics —just get away."

He sounded like Robert, but he made sense. "Agreed, but we might be dealing in wheel parts."

"I hope so." Stanley worked quickly on the lid of the barrel. He pried up the brass hoop and eased off the wooden lid.

I raised the lantern, and we looked down at the dark smooth viscoid surface.

"It looks like molasses," I said.

Stanley leaned over and sniffed. "Smells like grease."

I put my hands on the sticky substance and wiggled my fingers down about two inches. I touched something hard and pointed. "Hold the lantern, Stanley."

He took it from me, and I used two hands to gently pull out a long metal barrel and the attached wooden stock. It slipped into the lamplight like a straight, black snake.

"Rifles," Stanley said.

I put the rifle on the barrel beside me. "All right," I said briskly, "put the lid back. I'll hold the lantern and you work as quickly as you can. Put that lid back so it looks as though no one's been in it."

"I'll try." Stanley slid the wooden lid into place and inched the brass hoop over it. He grunted and struggled but finally pronounced himself satisfied.

"Get some dirt from the ground and I'll smear that over it so the grease on the lid doesn't look fresh," he instructed.

I left the lantern on the barrel, jumped down and passed up a handful of dirt. My hands were filthy, and I wiped some grease off on Stanley's trousers.

"That's good," Stanley said. "Now, bring that rifle and let's get away."

I was anxious but trying hard not to panic. The shadows looked more menacing now I knew there was an enemy out there somewhere. Stanley blew out the lantern, crept back into the deep shadows and left it on the hotel deck. We slipped quietly back to Homer. Stanley handed me the rifle, mounted, took it from me while I mounted and then returned it to me. We moved as quietly as possible out of the hotel yard and down Water Street toward home. Homer's feet sounded like drums on the plank road, thumping out notice of our presence. I breathed a little easier when his feet struck the soft dirt of Hastings Mill Road.

I still expected to feel a knife in my back at any moment. I would have liked to have another escort. Even Robert. He would have disapproved of my attire and my activities, but he would have defended me against the villains of the night. I felt like the worst kind of sister getting Stanley into a dangerous situation like this. *Wait a minute, Amy. This isn't your fault.*

We hobbled Homer again and staked him to a peg on some grass. Stanley fetched a bucket of water, and then we moved as quickly as we could into the front hall and up the stairs to my room.

Stanley lit the candle. I put the rifle on the floor, and we sat cross-legged, one on either side of it, staring.

I let out a long sigh.

"It's a new Winchester." Stanley picked up the rifle and examined it closely. "It's got 'Browning, Ogden, Utah' stamped on the stock, but it's a Winchester, Model .86 and a repeater. See?" He showed me the inscription, *Manufactured by the Winchester Repeating Arms Co. New Haven, Conn. U.S.A.* He wiped grease from the stock with a shoe rag and carefully extracted grease from the trigger and hammer, then wiped the long barrel smooth. "See that lever action. That's new. This is one of those new fast repeater lever action rifles. They take that heavy Government .45-70 shells."

"What are you talking about?"

"I've heard about these guns. That Mormon, John Moses Browning, is a wizard at design. He designs for Colt and Winchester. This gun must have come from the factory. What's the serial number?" He held the gun close to the light and squinted at the tiny numbers pressed in the iron.

"*Number 1544.* One of the first to come out. These guns must have been ordered before they were made to get here so fast. Someone has good contacts at the suppliers or at the factory."

He shifted the gun from hand to hand estimating its weight and maneuverability. "They take heavy ammunition, so they're good for big game hunting like moose and buffalo!"

"And people," I said thinking of the Chinese.

"And people," Stanley agreed. "The Royal North West police had the carbine Winchester '76 last year in the Riel Rebellion. Same company made them as this one. Those guns they used last year took .45-75 ammunition, a short bottleneck cartridge that's more powerful than the old .44-40s. They had special rear sites on those guns too."

"Are you telling me one of the reasons the police managed to quell the rebellion last year was because they had better arms than the Métis?"

Stanley nodded. "Stands to reason."

"And are you telling me that this gun here, this Winchester — what is it?"

"I think it's a Winchester.86."

"This Winchester .86 is a better gun than the one the police have?"

Stanley shrugged and put the stock of the gun to his shoulder. He sighted down the barrel and then put the gun back on the floor. "It's as good, anyway—better design, less black powder in the ammo, but more power. The ammunition would be easy to get too. There's lots of Government .45-70s around."

"How do you know so much?"

"Men talk about guns a lot at the hotel. Besides, I'm interested."

We sat in silence, watching the candlelight gleam off the wooden stock and glint on the metal barrel.

"How many barrels were there on that wagon?"

"Twelve."

"How many guns in a barrel?"

"I don't know. Maybe 15?"

"180 guns," I said. "That's a lot of guns." All of them capable of shooting people. "Why wasn't someone guarding those guns?"

"I suppose only one person knows they're guns. Everyone else thinks they are a load of molasses. The police are patrolling tonight. Anyone wandering would be stopped, as we were."

"And Frank?"

Stanley looked startled. "I suppose he thinks he has a contract for molasses."

I faced facts. "Do you think he might he running the guns?" Did Frank want money so badly he would sell guns to rebels, cause murder and terror? I couldn't reconcile that much selfish greed with his kindness, his intelligence, and his concern for me, but the guns were in Frank's molasses barrels.

Stanley rubbed the cleaning rag along the barrel of the rifle. He thought for a few moments then said, "Frank is sure he can make a lot of money running a trade route from Vancouver into the North West. He thinks he can compete with the eastern suppliers. I think he's right and he will get rich doing that. He might start a freighting empire. So, I don't think he'd risk losing his chance at the routes just so he can run a few guns. He wants those freight routes."

I nodded and thought of Frank's plans to entice Mr. Sanders into the freight business. Suppose Mr. Sanders was using Frank. Frank thought he was getting a good trade in staples going and Mr. Sanders, by buying in, was getting schedules and contacts, and substituting guns. That seemed more reasonable than thinking Frank was running the guns.

It was two o'clock in the morning. I was tired and afraid I wasn't thinking properly. "Shall we tell Frank?"

"And stop the shipment?"

I nodded.

"I don't think so," Stanley said. "Let Frank send those guns. They're supposed to go to Battleford. Let the police in Battleford or Regina pick them up after they've been delivered. That way they get the rebels and the guns, and that way Frank gets paid for his molasses. If we tell Frank now and he tells the police, then the police will confiscate the barrels and Frank will never get paid."

Frank and Stanley had a lot in common. The whole purpose of this shipment was to make money, so naturally Frank should have a chance to make money. I stretched my arms. At least the ride worked the stiffness from my muscles. I wiggled my shoulders, took a deep breath, and stared at the rifle.

"How do we get the police to confiscate the guns at the other end before they do some damage?"

"If we try to telegraph the police, they wouldn't pay any attention to us."

I agreed. "Women and young men don't rate very high on the police list of credible citizens,"

"So, let's get Robert to do it."

I was instantly antagonistic. "Why not Frank?"

"Frank might want to know how I found out and even though he'd stop the shipment and all that, he wouldn't thank me for snooping in his freight and keeping him from collecting his money. He might not give me any more work."

Business! I should have known. "All right, we won't tell Frank. You can tell Robert."

Stanley agreed.

We put the contraband rifle under my bed. Stanley, at my insistence, crept downstairs for a pitcher of water and some vinegar and we finally cleaned the grease off our hands and went to bed.

CHAPTER SIXTEEN

I lay awake for hours after Stanley left, conscious of the new rifle under my bed and worrying about the importance of it all. A wagon load of new rifles could make the difference between dissatisfaction with the government and a rebellion. Was Robert the right person to stop the shipment? Would he be persuasive enough to convince the Royal North West Mounted Police there were guns in the barrels? He could take our sample. I was encouraged by the thought. Robert could show this rifle to Superintendent Roycroft of the Provincial Police. Surely then the superintendent would listen to Robert. Once the superintendent had seen the rifle, he'd realize there must be a shipment somewhere. I had to wonder if Robert would want to stop the rebellion? A rebellion was real news. Would Robert be so interested in getting a good news story he'd neglect to inform the authorities and then be on hand to cover the resulting story?

I was ashamed of my lack of faith in Robert, but I stubbornly forced my brain to consider all possibilities.

I was tempted to tell Frank. Frank could convince the police they must act. Frank had contacts in Battleford and could wire someone to stop the shipment.

I had to consider Stanley's future too and he was sure his own budding freight business would suffer if we told Frank. I turned restlessly, worried I would make the wrong decision and allow Stanley to make the wrong decision. Would another Riel Rebellion take place using the guns I had failed stop?

I was fiercely angry at my impotent position in society. Why wouldn't men listen to women? No one would credit my information if I did offer it. I couldn't admit to prowling around Vancouver after midnight without branding myself a loose woman. Then I wouldn't have employment because teachers didn't do that kind of thing. My stomach cramped into knots as I followed patterns of thought into a morass of uncertain apprehension.

I must have drifted into some kind of sleep because I missed the predawn lightening of the sky, and it was already morning when I woke. Stanley was gone when I came down for breakfast. He would be looking for Robert, so I suppose the decision was now out of my hands.

Lydia was preoccupied. There were more flowers in the kitchen. She would have to make up her mind about Jack Bullman one of these days.

I walked into town for the exercise, to satisfy my curiosity and to get the mail. I was still on Hastings Mill Road when I saw Frank driving the wagon of barrels toward the New Road to New Westminster. I waved. He nodded and called a good morning but didn't stop. I caught Stanley unloading goods at the Granville Hotel. He told me Frank was taking the barrels to New Westminster himself to meet the trains going north.

"He'll take the New Road to Westminster. Should take him an hour or two."

And one hundred and seventy-nine guns are going east.

"Did you tell Robert?"

Stanley nodded and shouldered a bag of flour. "He'll look after it. He wanted to know what you were doing, out at night again and if I couldn't manage somehow to shackle you to the bed post." He grinned.

I raised my eyebrows. It sounded like Robert.

Stanley moved toward the supply shed. "I told him he might try shackling you to himself?"

I ran after Stanley. "You didn't!" Then, because I couldn't help myself, "What did he say?"

"He said he'd just as soon be shackled to a wasp. At least they sleep at night."

I should have been indignant, but I felt the corners of my mouth twitch and I laughed. "Poor Robert. What's he going to do?"

Stanley unloaded the flour sack on the hotel deck and returned to the wagon. I walked back and forth with him.

"He's going to talk to Superintendent Roycroft and he wants the gun."

"All right. I suppose I can give it to him. When does he want it?"

Stanley shook his head. "He can't really walk into our house and up into your bedroom with you. He won't get in without seeing Lydia. I'll go with him at noon, nip up and get it for him."

"Don't be silly. I can get it and meet him in the yard. Lydia can't see the front yard from the kitchen."

"I've already promised to meet him."

I was annoyed at being left out and promised myself I'd be there to watch Robert collect the gun, but I missed him.

I was distracted by the ship that arrived in Coal Harbour that morning. Thirty-five provincial policemen disembarked to keep the peace between the whites and the Chinese, wished on Vancouver by the provincial government in Victoria. I heard murmurings under the maple tree on Carrall Street.

"They've suspended the city charter and they're going to run our city from Victoria."

There was discontent and some mutterings, but no one was willing to actually resist the police. It was practical to terrorize the Chinese who were unarmed and meek, but not practical to antagonize the police; at least, not today.

The troops marched to the Carter House where they were to be billeted. The city became quiet and orderly. The groups of men disappeared from under the maple tree and business went on as usual. My admiration for Superintendent Roycroft increased. Just the presence of these policemen might be enough to restrict violence. I had hopes he would be able to quell the coming uprising in the North West—if Robert told him. The thought came to me suddenly and stopped me abruptly on the plank walk. Mrs. Johnson bumped into me, and I apologized and exchanged pleasantries with one part of my mind while the other was busy with the thought of Robert promising to inform the police and neglecting to do so.

Don't be silly, Amy, why wouldn't he tell the police?

Because an uprising would make a great newspaper story. Would Robert's love of a story prevent him from doing his duty? Oh, blast! I wish I could get rid of that thought. I wish I had told someone else about the rifle. Frank, for one. He wouldn't be back until tomorrow and by then the rifles would be on their way to Battleford. If I had all the problems under my eye, as they were in a classroom, then I could control them. In the real world of Vancouver and the peculiar world of adult behavior I had little control over anyone. It was frustrating.

I stopped at the salmonberry patch on Hastings Road and picked some of the red berries and ate them. I'd been there five minutes before I noticed the dog cart parked under the trees on the path to the bay. I walked over to it and saw Maude sitting on a stump, her parasol at her feet and her bonnet low over her face.

"Hello." I was restless and glad of her company. "What are you doing down this way?"

I moved closer and found a clean stump for myself.

"I came this way hoping to see you," Maude said and lifted her face toward me.

I was shocked. A purple half-moon drooped under her bloodshot left eye. A dried scratch traveled down her left cheek to her mouth where puffy lips oozed a clear fluid. She dabbed at her mouth with a white handkerchief.

"Oh, Maude!" I jumped to my feet and moved to her, putting one hand on her shoulder. "Dear heavens! What happened?"

She straightened her back and lifted her chin. "I had a rough customer last night. I should be able to tell who is likely to do this sort of thing, but I find I still make the occasional mistake."

"Are you all right?" It was a perfectly inane question, but I couldn't seem to express my sympathy any better.

She shrugged. "I will get over it. In a week or so the swelling will go down and in a couple of weeks my eye will be normal."

She did not want soft words and sympathetic hand-patting.

I was angry—suddenly, very angry.

"I hope he trips on his own feet and falls down a well."

Maude started a lopsided smile and that effort in the midst of the contusions and injuries made me furiously angry.

"And I hope he pricks his finger and gets blood poisoning, and the poison takes over his body and fills him with infection until he dies in his own stink. I hope his innards rot within him and I hope he goes blind and deaf and his brain stays alert so that he can suffer!"

Maude leaned over and held my arm. "It's a hazard of my trade, Amy. Don't distress yourself."

"No one should treat any human like that!"

"Many do though." She paused and then said quietly. "You must suffer when the little tots come to school after their parents beat them."

I nodded. "Yes, I hate that. Some parents, I guess, many parents, think it is good to beat children."

"Save your sympathy for them, Amy. I'm all right. In any case, I'll soon have enough money to open my bakery. Then I will not be vulnerable."

"I hope your money is in a safe place." There is no bank in Vancouver, and I didn't suppose Maude travelled to New Westminster very often.

"It is," she said briefly. "I came to give you some more information."

Maude thought of helping Robert and Frank and me when she was hurt and aching. I felt humble and at the same time ignorant. What was life like for people like her when they were unprotected? Did she have no rights at all?

"Mr. Sanders is too interested in the freighting business, too interested in Frank Hartman's schedules and supply lines."

I was angry again. "Was it he who . . ."

She touched her face. "Don't worry about this, Amy. What Mr. Sanders is in his private life is nothing to you. Besides, he thinks of himself as a gentleman and," she added, "maybe he is."

She hadn't really answered my question, but I knew she would not tell me who had beaten her. I might as well leave the subject. "But perhaps Mr. Sanders isn't honest."

"He might not be honest," Maude agreed. "He was with the Dubrant, the Métis, the night he died."

I sat back down on the stump. "He was? Where?"

"At the Terminus Saloon. There were many people there that night, Mr. Hartman, Mr. Carr among them."

"They never mentioned it."

Maude shrugged. "I wasn't there myself, but I've heard since that the Métis drank in there for an hour or two."

Frank and Robert had been with the men.

"How can we tell if anyone of them had an assignation with him?" I suppose anyone could have bought the man a drink. Anyone in that crowded saloon could have slipped poison into the drink.

"I don't know." Maude lifted her parasol. "I thought it might be an important piece of information, but I don't know if it is. I also thought I'd like to see a decent human being for a while."

I blinked back the tears that had suddenly risen in my eyes. Sympathy was not what Maude needed. Ordinary conversation with ordinary people was what she requested.

I thanked her for coming. She backed the dog cart onto the road and took it slowly back to town. I hoped she'd get her bakery soon.

The problem of the Métis was not getting any clearer. Neither Frank nor Robert had told me of seeing the man at the saloon that night. Where did Mr. Sanders did he fit into this? Frank thought he could control Mr. Sanders. Perhaps Mr. Sanders was using Frank. For a little investment Mr. Sanders got Frank's routes and schedules. Robert should tell Superintendent Roycroft about Mr. Sanders. Robert should come around and see me. I had things to tell him, and he ought to come around so I could talk to him. Was Robert ashamed of the way he'd acted the last time we were together? I walked slowly down Hastings Mill Road thinking about my problems and absentmindedly eating salmonberries.

I remembered the way Robert had begun that kiss last night, but I also remembered the way he'd finished it. Robert had been very angry and then he had been very gentle. Of course, he wasn't supposed to kiss me at all. So, he might well be ashamed of the whole event. On the other hand, perhaps he was afraid I'd want marriage. Of course, any decent man would offer marriage after a kiss like that. Well, I didn't want marriage to him. If I didn't want marriage, especially marriage to Robert, then what difference did it make if he offered it? Simpler if he didn't, but so irritating all the same.

I grinned at myself. I wanted him and I didn't want him. Why didn't I restrict my romantic interests to Frank? I would have an interesting life with Frank—sedate and respectable. He was dependable, reasonable, and treated me as though I was a lady. That's a better basis for marriage than this scrabbling, quarrelsome relationship I have with Robert. It will take Frank a year or two to think about proposing marriage and that would leave me plenty of time to decide. At the moment, being single suited me very well.

CHAPTER SEVENTEEN

The arrival of the thirty-five uniformed constables from Victoria caused dissention in the city.

"The mayor's crazy!" Stanley crammed two pieces of bread with bacon drippings into his mouth and reached for the milk. "He said he could run Vancouver without any blanket-blank Victoria pushing him. I guess Victoria is mad at the way Vancouver threw out the Chinese, so the legislature passed a bill early this morning, 'For the preservation of peace in Vancouver' and sent the constables."

"Why is the mayor angry? I mean, he must have anticipated something like this when he allowed mob rule Wednesday night."

Lydia expects a politician to think of the future. I didn't think Mayor Maclean had any sensible thoughts the night the mob ran through the streets.

"The bill said the municipal authorities were in sympathy with the agitators and were not to be trusted. Victoria didn't think Vancouver would keep the peace or even to keep a fair court. They sent their own magistrate, a Judge Vowell." Stanley certainly picked up a lot of information.

"Are we supposed to be living under a kind of military rule now?"

He nodded and scraped out the last of the mustard pickles from the jar. "Vancouver is going to have to pay for housing the troops too."

I laughed. "Now that really will upset the city council."

"They're hopping mad," Stanley agreed. "But there isn't much they can do about it. Thirty-five constables will keep order all right.

That Roycroft could probably do it by himself." Stanley managed to find the last piece of cheese in the cupboard and brought it back to the table. "I'm getting some extra work because the troops need their goods hauled from the boat and they pay me to move it. I worked all morning on that. Should finish by supper time. I'm going to earn Homer's purchase price right away."

"Where are you going to keep all this money?"

Stanley looked thoughtful. He smoothed his sandy hair back on his head in the mistaken belief it stayed flat. Bits of hair sprang up as he took his hand away making him look like an endearing hedgehog. "Do you think you could ask Mr. Alexander to stash it in the safe at the mill? I won't have time to get over there."

I nodded and accepted the role of the leisured woman of the house, eager to run errands for the hard-working male. "I might take a walk over there this afternoon to see how Jack's coming on with the cloak room. I'll ask Mr. Alexander then. He's a councilman; is he upset by the troops?"

Stanley shrugged. "Maybe. He doesn't want the Chinese to go. He needs them in his mill. Maybe he's glad to see the troops. It's not something I'm going to ask him though."

I spent a few hours helping Lydia with the housework. I needed to reinstate myself in her good graces. She was speaking to me— but only just—and I knew a few hours together working on the house would smooth the remaining jagged feelings left from my outburst the other night.

So, I dusted and shook quilts and polished silver for two hours. Then, having done my penance, I washed my face and hands and headed east on Hastings Road to the mill.

There was still smoke in the air. Men were clearing brush south of the town and hundreds of small fires burned around the city. My eyes smarted occasionally when a particularly thick cloud of smoke blew around me. I walked up the plank boardwalk past the school and entered the mill office.

Dust was on the windows and the floor but the piles of green ledger books and cream-coloured stationery on the desk were in sufficient use to establish a dust-free island in the centre of the room. Mr. Alexander was not available. He was in the city, a neat, efficient looking clerk told me. Could he help?

I explained Stanley's problem and the clerk arranged a method of deposit and receipts that would ensure Stanley's money was well looked after. I thanked him.

He assured me it was not the practice of the mill to bank the money of the Vancouver residents, but they would be happy to be of service to the brother of the teacher.

I was duly grateful and left the man to his work.

The smoke seemed less thick now as I walked back to the school. Jack had boarded in the cloak room and built low seats around the interior walls, the same around the exterior. I sat in the afternoon sun with my back against the west wall looking toward the city. Mr. Alexander's big two storey house cut off some of my view. He had lovely shade trees in his front yard and some scrub vine maple in the back. I could see the roof of the Sunnyside Hotel and beyond it the chimneys of the Granville Hotel. The new Regina Hotel wasn't visible because the ground dipped and rose, blocking it. Behind me, the mill saws whined their steady complaint and the slap and thump of lumber being piled in the mill yard added a steady bass resonance. I could hear men calling occasionally to the horses as they pulled loads to the wharf. Two small tugs whistled instructions to each other, scooting round the bay, nosing logs into tidy booms. Seven sailing vessels waited for lumber. On the wharves piles of lumber were ready for loading as well as a pile of long thick spars destined for Britain and the ship building trade.

I wiggled my feet inside my boots and looked up the path toward the Grant cottage. I might as well find out how the rest of the family were doing and perhaps get some news of how the measles had affected other children. I was afraid to find out, but I ought to be prepared if there were going to be any more deaths.

"It's too soon to say, Teacher," Mrs. Grant moved the dinner dishes from the table and brushed the crumbs into her apron and then dropped them into the wood box. "Joey seems better but those measles can stay three weeks and it's only been one week since our little Felicity died. I think Joey's better," she said again. "The doctor doesn't come here anymore."

The doctor didn't come because the children were not seriously sick. The relief I felt was enormous. "And what about other families?"

"It's hit the Davidsons; they're sick but no one's died there. That Indian family living near the trees lost two children. The doctor said the Indians get hit hard because they don't have any way of fighting it yet."

"Which children died?" I had four Indian children in my class.

"Ruth!" Mrs. Grant called out the back door and Ruth, barefooted and pale responded with a, "Yes, Mum?"

"What little Indians died with the measles?"

Ruth looked down at the doorstep, then lifted her eyes to mine. "Theodore," she said, "and Isaac,"

We exchanged a swift glance of mutual bereavement. Theodore had been a student in the infants' class—anxious to learn and full of flashing good humour. Isaac, his older brother had been Ruth's age—quiet, even sullen, and uncomfortable with English.

"I'm sorry," I said inadequately. "When did this happen?"

"A couple of days ago. Is that right, Ruth?"

She nodded, her eyes downcast. She waited a moment and then slipped out the back door.

I drank a cup of tea with Mrs. Grant. She talked about her children and displayed the white bows she had saved from Felicity's funeral, her rough hands smoothing the satin. She spoke of the kindness of her neighbours and showed me in many ways she had accepted Felicity's death. I marveled at her. She had clearly loved Felicity very much, yet she was resigned to her death. I could not have let my daughter go without anger and bitterness. I was having trouble reconciling the deaths of my pupils. I would be inconsolable if my child had died.

I finished my tea and left. Ruth was washing towels in a tub set on an old stump in the back yard. She was scrubbing over a wash board and didn't stop when I came up to her. She worried me. She seemed thinner and paler without the sparkle I had known in the past.

"Are you all right, Ruth?" She kept her eyes down but nodded. "Ruth," 'I said with emphasis.

She looked up and met my eyes.

"Are you getting enough to eat?"

Her eyes shifted away toward the water of the bay and then back. "Enough."

"Ruth Grant," I said in a peremptory tone. "You must eat. It will not help anyone if we lose you too. That would be wasteful and extremely selfish of you. I want you to look after yourself." I felt like a fraud giving that kind of advice. I hadn't lost my sister and my friends. But I was alarmed by Ruth's passive demeanor and pale complexion. "I count on you to help me next year and I don't want you unhealthy and weak because you are thinking of your own feelings all the time. Now please see you're in shape for the new school term."

She looked straight at me, wondering, her hands still on the washboard. "I'll try."

"Good," I said briskly. I had planned to walk away full of efficient good humour, but Ruth was still looking at me and I found I couldn't turn away from those sad, brown eyes. I squatted down on the ground.

Ruth stood there, the soap dripping from her hands, still staring at me. I opened my arms, and she flew into them. I hugged her close and rocked her back and forth.

"You miss her so much."

Then she started to cry—great wracking sobs as if her whole body convulsed. She buried her head in my shoulder, but I heard her.

"She was so little, and she was so good. Why would God take her, Miss? Why Felicity?"

"It's not fair?" I suggested.

"It's not fair" Ruth wailed the age-old cry.

"No, it isn't," I agreed.

"It isn't?" Ruth stopped her wild crying and thought about what I had said. 'You don't think it's fair, Miss? What about God?"

"I think Felicity's death was an accident," I said firmly. "She certainly didn't deserve to die. Not at all. It was an accident—just like a man falling off a log boom. An accident."

"It wasn't her fault then?" Ruth said.

Dear heavens. This poor child had been thinking Felicity had invited retribution from an angry God.

Ruth sniffed energetically for a few seconds and wiped her eyes. "She'll have Theodore to play with now, won't she, Miss?" Ruth stepped back to her laundry tub and picked up the soap. 'She always liked Theodore."

"Yes, that's right." I rashly committed myself to the Methodist doctrine of universality and completely ignored the High Church's teaching on baptism of the heathen.

"She'd like that."

Ruth was much calmer now. I said my goodbyes and left her a little comforted. I must come back in a week and ensure she was getting more to eat. Once out of sight of Ruth, my shoulders sagged. Little Theodore. Such a darling little child. I suppose his mother missed Isaac as much as Theodore, but Theodore was my favorite.

I walked by the fence past Mr. Caufield's cottage and collected yellow daisies from the field by the road. At the end of the rows of homes, I turned south. I knew Theodore's family lived back there somewhere and, if I asked my way, I'd find them. I did not want to visit. I didn't know what to say. I'd never met his family. Perhaps they didn't speak English. The father must speak some English if he worked in the mill, but the mother might not know any English words at all. Which didn't make the least bit of difference because I had to go anyway.

I inquired of a pupil I met the way to Theodore's house and was directed to a low two-room cabin near the trees. A dog snarled at me but was restrained by a rope tying him to the fence. No one answered my knock and for a few minutes I thought I would be able to lay the flowers on the sill and leave. Mrs. Scow eventually opened the door. She was young, no more than my age, and quite lovely. She reminded me of a spring trillium I'd seen in the forest—a solitary beauty. Her eyes were almost black, her hair long and dark. She had high cheek bones and clear smooth skin.

"I am the teacher," I said proffering the flowers. "Do you speak English?"

"A little." She took the flowers hesitantly and looked at me. I gestured at the flowers. "For Theodore and Isaac."

Her eyes suddenly darkened more, and she stepped outside and pulled the door shut behind her. She sank to the steps, the flowers clutched in her hand and stared out over the path toward the mill. I didn't want to leave, nor did I want to stand above her. So, I lowered myself to the doorstep.

"I'm sorry," I said.

"We took them home," she said slowly and quietly.

"Home?"

She waved toward the south. "To Snauq."

Oh no! I thought to myself. I hope they were dead when she took them home. Otherwise, there will be measles at Snauq. Adults too. "They are there now?"

She nodded and looked up. "They are...." she groped for the English word and gave up indicating height with her hand.

"High?" I guessed. "Up high?"

She nodded and pantomimed branches and leaves.

"In a tree?" Again, she nodded.

We sat there in silence. I would like to be laid to rest in a tree. That seems to me to be a lovely thought. Why do we bury people in the cold ground? It would be easier to think of your loved one swaying in the air and the sunshine instead lying in the cold and damp of the earth. I had a momentary vision of Isaac and Theodore peering at me from the branches of a tree, Theodore ready for mischief, ready for any kind of play. We sat for about five minutes saying nothing. Then I rose and touched her hand.

"I am sorry." I said.

"You are brave to come to see me."

I blushed. She was brave. She had four children and had lost two of them. She faced a new culture and a foreign environment. She learned a new language and she thought I was brave to risk the tittle-tattling of a few malicious tongues from those who thought Indians were not people. I was embarrassed by her assessment of my courage.

"No," I said shortly. "I am sorry."

"You are good," she said this time.

That I'm certainly not. I wish I could speak her language for I am sure we would have discussed life very deeply then, but her English was too meager to attempt such a philosophical discussion and my Salish was non-existent.

"Goodbye." I touched her hand again and she nodded. I left her there, clutching the flowers, sitting on the doorstep.

"I will never have children. I will never have children. I will never have children," I chanted to myself as I picked my way up the rough path to the plank road.

CHAPTER EIGHTEEN

I walked the plank road to the edge of the mill site and then, less easily, over the wagon road to the west. The sun was still high in the sky, but the light diffused in the smoke-filled air creating an unreal atmosphere of oppression. I could see the trees near the teacherage and the patch of pines along the road ahead but, in some areas, the landscape was obliterated by hanging clouds of smoke, especially in the western part of the city. I would be glad when the men had finished all their clearing operations.

I heard the slap of the reins, the thud of horse's hooves and the creak and banging of the wooden wagon before Frank moved up beside me from the old Westminster Road. He pulled the team to a rest, wiped the perspiration from his forehead with the back of his sleeve, and invited me aboard. I was disturbed to see the barrels still standing upright in the wagon. "I thought you were going to deliver this load'?' Frank nodded. "I thought so too, but when I got it to New Westminster I had a message there telling me the train was three days late leaving the east and won't be connecting with Kamloops Lake until Tuesday. My muleskinner didn't come down the Canyon and I couldn't transfer my load."

"Oh, oh." That was a complication. The guns are back in town. "How annoying." It was a weak comment, but the best I could do.

"Yes," Frank's frustration was similar to mine. "I had to haul them back here today and then I'll have to haul them back again on Sunday. I'll telephone on Sunday to make sure the train left on time. New Westminster can phone Port Moody for me and check.

I wish I'd done that today, but I don't like using the telephone in George Black's butcher shop."

"Why ever not?" I have never even touched a telephone in my life, but I was fascinated by the one in the butcher shop. I'd love to try it.

"Because everyone in the country hears what you say. That's no way to do business."

"Why didn't you unload the barrels in New Westminster? Or leave the wagon there?"

Frank didn't seem to resent the questions. He couldn't know he was hauling guns.

"I didn't have anywhere to leave them. I could have stayed and watched the wagon. Or I could have paid to have the barrels stored, but I needed the wagon and the team to get back to Vancouver and it seemed easier to leave everything on the wagon and bring the whole shipment back than to unload today and reload on Sunday."

"How maddening."

"It was," Frank said briefly.

I glanced back at the full wagon as I mounted and settled my skirts beside Frank. One hundred and seventy-nine repeater rifles. It was ridiculous to be sedately sitting in front of one hundred and seventy-nine repeater rifles. I stared ahead.

"You must feel as though you've wasted your whole day," I sympathized.

Frank shook the reins, and the team began to pull. "I do, but it gave me an idea of the importance of the telephone system. You know, the Burrard Inlet and Westminster Telephone Company is just beginning. I could buy into it now at a nominal amount. In five years, I bet I could get my money back and a good profit too. We'd need to expand, though. Get a line, not just from Port Moody to New Westminster to Vancouver, but from Port Moody to Vancouver and get more people in Vancouver to have their own telephone. Mr. Alexander should have one at the mill. The real estate firms should each have one."

Frank mused his way through a profit-making idea while I considered the problem of the guns in the wagon behind me.

If Frank knew he was taking guns into the city, he would not be sitting here calmly discussing business. The city was under military rule. There were three hundred men ripe for insurrection smarting from the injustices of the provincial occupation order. They would be formidable if armed. Would Frank be tempted to sell the rifles if he knew he had them? I controlled a shudder. I had a child's urge to possess enough magic to instantly banish the rifles from the wagon. I glanced back. They were there all right—twelve solid barrels full of guns. The only safeguard was no one, except the Superintendent, Stanley, Robert, and me knew the guns were here—and one other person, of course. One other person. The one who imported them. That was far too many people to keep a secret for long.

We swung down the road winding under the trees, into the open, then rolled over the bridge that spanned the tidal waters. At high tide, the waters of False Creek moved in to meet the waters of Burrard Inlet at Columbia Street. The smell of skunk cabbage was strong, and I've always felt this was an unhealthy place to tarry. A miasma seemed to hang over this area and gave me thoughts of consumption, typhoid, and other specters of death. We moved away from the bridge and were soon at the gate to my house. We sat for a moment discussing the city and the military rule.

"They won't stay long," Frank opined. "The people of Vancouver will be too busy building and doing business to worry about the Chinamen."

"The Mayor seems to have allowed the citizens to carry the law in their own hands."

"You can't blame Mayor MacLean too much." Frank defended the mayor. "He's supposed to abide by the majority rule."

I must have looked quite cynical for Frank smiled.

"He's not such a bad fellow. I knew him in Battleford last year."

Didn't Frank tell me he hadn't been in Battleford last year? Perhaps not. I couldn't remember. "What did he do there?"

"He was a purchasing agent for the government during the Riel Rebellion. I sold supplies to him. He was fair enough. I think he'll do all right as mayor. The men were pushing him Wednesday night. He couldn't do much else but what they wanted."

"I spend a lot of time teaching children that what everyone wants isn't necessarily what they should do. If everyone steals, they ought not to steal. If everyone lies, they ought not to lie. If everyone treats a fellow human being with cruelty, they ought not to follow suit."

"All right," Frank said good humouredly, and patted my arm. "Don't worry about it. I'm sure it's all under control now."

I felt anger stir within me. My opinions obviously were not important to Frank. I caught my lip in my teeth and held my temper. Frank certainly did well not to quarrel with me. He was considerate and pleasant. I should hold onto my temper.

"Why all the smoke today, Frank?" I did my best and changed the subject.

"They're burning slash west of the town."

"There seems to be more than the usual amount."

"That's partly because the air is so still and the smoke hangs around town, and partly because they are trying to get rid of ten to twenty feet of dry slash that was left when they knocked down that forty acres behind Cordova Street."

"How did they get all those big trees down so quickly? One day they were standing and only a few days later they were flat."

Frank was in no hurry now. He looped the reins around his hand while I climbed down from the wagon. The team stood quietly, their heads drooping. It had been a long day for them.

"They do what they call 'back cutting.' They notch many trees one way so they will fall in a certain direction. Then they cut completely through at the edge of the wood lot. When the first row of trees falls it takes with it all the notched trees."

"Like a stack of dominoes?"

"Just like that. The first row knocks out the ones behind it and so on. It makes a tremendous rumbling noise. Didn't you hear it?"

"I may have and thought it was thunder."

"It sounds something like that. They can take out ten to twenty acres at once that way."

"So, they get them down. And then?"

"Then they haul away the big trees—skid them to the water—and leave all the slash and debris."

"And later burn the slash and debris."

"Right. That's what's going on now. It will clear the way for pasture land and development. Should be quite a nice area behind Cordova there?

"And you own it?"

He laughed. "No, not that piece. I don't have the money I need yet for big enterprises. But I will this time next month."

"I hope you do, Frank."

I waved to him as he started toward the city. The barrels bumped and swayed but stayed in the wagon. I hated to see them return to Vancouver.

After dinner just as the twilight deepened to dark, I headed for the ocean. My swimming had improved, and I was braver about getting my face wet. There was no smoke right over the water. It seemed to hover about three feet above and gave me a head room of clean air. Lydia disapproved, of course, but she didn't try our new-won peace by audibly criticizing and contented herself with a sniff as I slipped out the back door.

Stanley had been home for supper. I told him about the barrels returning to town and he promised to pass the information on to Robert. I splashed in the bay, now able to move out over my head without fear I would drown.

The twilight stretched shadows one into another until daylight disappeared. The cedars hung tall over this bay, bringing darkness early. I was now only a dark blob in an inky pool. I determinedly practiced the awkward circular motions I had devised to keep myself afloat. I would not think of the unfortunate Métis who had died here. Nor would I think of the exasperating man who kissed me one day and ignored me the next. With a good deal of effort, I disciplined my mind and succeeded reasonably well.

I spent most of my time in that ocean pool speculating on the smuggler of the guns. I reviewed the men I knew in town and tried to fit them into a smuggling scheme. Everyone was a businessman and an entrepreneur, even Stanley. Everyone wanted to make money. To instigate a revolution perhaps one needed an entrepreneurial spirit as well as a political cause. My mind kept returning to Mr. Sanders and Mayor MacLean. Someone had commissioned that load of rifles. The police were here; the guns were here. I felt as though I was at the beginning of a battle; the participants were ready; all that was needed was someone to signal the beginning of a war.

CHAPTER NINETEEN

Stanley had all his money on the kitchen table the next morning: piles of dollars, some short bits, some long bits, a small pile of gold nuggets, gold coins and a few pennies.

"How much, Midas?" I asked.

"One hundred and sixty dollars,"

"One hundred and sixty dollars will buy you a lot in town, pay for Homer and leave some for yourself."

"I didn't know I had so much. I kept putting it away in a sock under my bed. This last week I must have made almost as much as I did the year before. Business is really getting better."

He counted out two dollars and handed it to Lydia. "For food."

Lydia was embarrassed. 'You don't eat that much, child."

It was a blatant lie. Stanley easily ate twice as much as Lydia and I together.

"I'm making money. I pay board," Stanley said.

Lydia caught my eye. I nodded. She had to take the money or insult Stanley's manhood. I knew the money would find its way back to Stanley in a present of some kind—a new blanket for Homer, new clothes, or shoes or some such thing for Stanley. Last week Stanley was a school-boy who earned a little money as a helper at the hotels. This week he was a man with a horse and a business. Lydia was finding it hard to adjust to the change.

She took the money. "What are you going to do with the rest?"

Stanley stuffed all his riches into a leather sack. 'I'm going to take it over to the mill this morning and put it into the safe." He swung his cache toward me. "Can I have one of those deposit slips you got?"

"May I," I corrected, taking one grammatical error at a time. I went to the dining room and fished out the slips from the cupboard drawer. I helped Stanley fill it out, counting the different kinds of money and entering each in its proper place.

"What are you doing the rest of the day?"

"Hauling beef and supplies to the Carter House. They're busy now with those troops billeted there."

"I hear the troops were being charged twenty-four cents a pound for beef. A shocking charge." Lydia scrubbed at the sink with a wet cloth. "People raise their prices because they don't like the troops and think they'll drive them out with exorbitant costs."

"Won't do them any good," Stanley said. "The city has to pay for keeping them here."

Vancouver's spite would rebound on the city's coffers.

I walked out to admire Homer as Stanley mounted, then stayed in the yard enjoying the eastern sun on my face and the warmth of the morning. I was still there, warm, and almost languid when Robert arrived on his mare.

"Europa waiting for Zeus," he said wickedly as he tied the mare to the rail.

"More likely Artemis waiting for Otus."

He stood close to me and took my hand. 'Truly? Do you hate me?"

His words hung in the air. I had a sudden feeling of happiness. I stifled it. It would not do for me to care for Robert. I would stay independent as long as possible.

"Oh, go away, Robert." I stepped back, and he laughed.

"Do you have any news?" I asked. He was far too confident. My voice revealed my annoyance.

"I've contacted the Royal North West Mounted in Battleford. They'll be waiting for the train at Regina."

"Dandy. The train will be three days late, perhaps even three weeks late." I repeated what Frank had told me.

"I'll telegram the change of plans. The North West police will wait."

"At least you got someone to listen." I had almost convinced myself no one would believe us.

"Oh, they listened all right. I showed Roycroft the rifle and that caught his attention. He believes someone is running guns through Vancouver, but he doesn't want to catch them."

"He doesn't what?"

"He doesn't want to catch them here," Robert corrected his statement. "He'd prefer to have the guns confiscated in the North West. If he had to confiscate the guns here it would only complicate his problems with the anti-Chinese rioters. He doesn't want any kind of arms in the city; a revolution here would be hard to suppress."

I remembered the scene on Morton's bluff when the men had been prepared to battle without guns. "It could be dangerous. I don't want the guns here either."

"And those are repeating rifles. One man could kill many people. A mob would kill hundreds."

We were silent for a moment. "Are you sure Frank is safer if he doesn't know?"

"Don't you tell him," Robert admonished in his usual peremptory voice. "You'll put him in a bad position if you tell him. He'll be bound to turn the guns over to Roycroft and Roycroft doesn't want them,"

"All right. Then the only people who know about the guns besides you and me and Stanley, are the superintendent and the person who is smuggling the guns, and who, presumably, wants the guns in Battleford, not Vancouver."

"Right."

The morning had been clear but now the haze thickened, and the smoke drifted this way from the clearing fires past Cordova Street. I patted the mare.

"Did you find out anything more about the man who was killed here?"

Robert nodded. "Roycroft had some communication from Battleford. Apparently, the Métis was a messenger from the North

West Mounted police to the provincial police. Not all the Métis want to rebel; some of them work with the police. He was supposed to alert the provincial police there had been new guns seen in the North West and to ask for help in trying to locate the supply. A letter came after the man died. The N.W. Mounted planned to leave the Métis in Vancouver hoping someone would contact him about guns. They sent spies to several cities trying to trace the source of the guns."

"Do you think the man found the source?"

"Must have. No reason to kill him otherwise."

I suddenly remembered Maude's information. "You were in the Terminus Saloon with the Métis the night he died. So was Frank. You didn't tell me that."

"Should I have?"

"Well, of course, you should have. What did you see?"

"Not a thing. I noticed a stranger. Talked to him for a while trying to get some news of the North West for Wednesday's copy, bought him a drink and left him. His English wasn't very good."

"Bought him a drink!"

"I didn't poison him, Amy. Stop imaging things. You have such a flattering idea of my capabilities."

"But you could have poisoned him."

"Anyone could. Some of the liquor they serve there could have poisoned him without help from anyone else."

"But why?"

"He must have approached someone or done something suspicious, so the gun runner knew he was a danger."

"The North West Mounted Police must have been grateful for the information you sent."

"Their answering telegram indicated that, while it was appreciated, it was no big surprise."

I thought about the difficulties of communicating with the authorities in this large country. "You were in New Westminster yesterday to telegram?"

He nodded.

"What do they think in New Westminster of our military take-over?"

"They think we asked for it. They say the military are here to 'civilize' Vancouver."

I laughed. "That will annoy the C.P.R. and the local aristocracy."

"New Westminster sees us as a community of rough barbarians without culture or future. The sooner we're stamped on the better."

"Smug, aren't they? You'd think they were from Victoria."

"Oh, Victoria thinks even worse things about us," Robert said. "And Vancouver people are working up a fine fury against Victorians. It might be even stronger than the original anti-Chinese feelings."

"I'm inclined to agree with Victorians right now. The troops will keep order, won't they?"

"They'll keep order."

"I wish those guns would move out of town."

"Roycroft has someone watching the wagon."

"Not Corporal Parkinson I hope?"

"God, no. One of his own men from Victoria."

"And Frank's going to keep his eye on it too. It's valuable cargo, after all, even if he thinks it's just molasses. And, I suppose, Stanley?"

Robert nodded. "Not much gets past Stanley; but he's busy." He put the reins over the mare's head, mounted and turned toward town. "We'll all watch. Good afternoon, Amy." He doffed his cap.

I felt depressed as I watched Robert ride away. I'd like to keep him as a friend, and I wasn't even sure how to do that. I hadn't told him I was pleased to see him. I hadn't smiled at him. All I'd done was accuse him of murdering the Métis.

CHAPTER TWENTY

I told Lydia I was going into town to check for mail. What I needed was a walk to soothe my restless spirits. I felt as though something was about to happen. Something *ought* to happen, and I didn't want to wait at the teacherage for it. I had a basket over my arm, so I looked purposeful as I made my way briskly toward Carrall Street. The smoke thickened here, but relief came with the occasional breeze.

There were few men in the streets. The corner of Carrall and Water Street sported only four under the maple tree. The presence of the troops must have a sobering effect on the citizens already. Or, perhaps, the men were resting from their previous activities.

I stopped at Mr. Hartley's dry goods store, noticing the black cross had been removed from the doorstep and the step scrubbed almost white.

"Warm day, Miss MacDonald."

"Indeed, yes. We haven't had rain for almost two months, have we? Is that normal for this country?"

"The Indians tell me this is an unusual summer. They look for rain any time now," he said.

"I confess I'll be glad of it." I fingered some of the ribbons and decided on several fasteners for the new walking suit I planned to make.

"It's quiet here today." I inquired, finally coming to the real reason for my visit. I was a little ashamed of my curiosity but not so ashamed I neglected to try to elicit information.

"It is now."

"Were any of the Chinese around here hurt yesterday?"

""No. Although Hoy Sung's son was hit around the head a little. He's all right."

"So, the vigilantes got what they wanted, did they?" I tried to keep the disgust from my voice.

"For now, Miss Macdonald. For now," Mr. Hartley said dryly. 'The Chinese have patience. They'll be back."

I paid for my purchases and continued up the street, nodding to several acquaintances and searching as discreetly as I could without gawking for any trace of the Chinese. There wasn't one in sight, not a pigtail, not a blue suit, and no singing sound of conversation anywhere. I hoped Sung Wick and his family found a safe place to stay. I turned the corner at False Creek and viewed the Chinese settlement.

It was very quiet in the afternoon sunlight. The smoke drifted north of this spot, leaving the air fresh and clear. I could see the Indian village of Snauq across the water on the south side of False Creek. A few canoes were drawn up on the beach.

Around me all was still. There was no one in any of the gardens in the Chinese settlement or, as far as I could see, in any of the houses. There were smashed fences and scattered tools, cabins with empty windows, chimney bricks lying on the ground next to broken buckets and Sung Wick's damaged gate. It hung on one hinge, half-open, and responded with a reluctant squeak when I pushed. The garden was trampled, onion stalks broken, new pea vines crushed into the dirt, tall Chinese lettuce tipped and some uprooted and flung against the fence. I studied the garden critically for a moment, put down my basket, knelt on the walk and went to work. I heaped soil over exposed roots and trimmed broken stems and leaves. I scrapped the rich loam into hills around the pea vines and piled all the wilted and dead vegetables at the back of the yard. I was encouraged by each live plant I found and spent an hour straightening and relocating salvageable seedlings. Some vegetables were beyond help but many were worth reclaiming, until finally I achieved some semblance of order and productivity. I found an abandoned bucket without a hole, located the well and the hand pump, made six trips to the garden and watered the vegetables.

Finished, I washed the dirt from my hands at the pump, picked more dirt from underneath my fingernails and laughed at myself. Sung Wick and his family would be back, and when they returned, they would probably do a better job of salvaging the garden than I had, but I felt better for making to effort. I stood back and stared at the house and only then noticed the broken glass from the windows had been carefully removed. I walked back to the house and opened the front door. Inside the floor had been swept and the room tidied. Someone had been here, perhaps Sung Wick's family, perhaps one of the Chinese men from the businesses on Cordova. I shut the door and walked back down the path and through the broken front gate. I left the gate as it had been. The house should look abandoned and neglected to any passerby.

I was glad I was wearing my dark blue skirt. The dried bits of soil brushed off easily and I still maintained a somewhat presentable appearance as I walked back down Carrall. I was just clean enough to stop at the Sunnyside Hotel for tea. It was late by this time, about four-thirty, and Lydia would be looking for me soon. I saw Stanley, working in the yard up the street loading and unloading supplies at the Granville Hotel. The hotels were certainly keeping him busy, and he had said something about more business unloading freight at the Terminus Saloon. Occasionally, he took jobs at the Deighton Hotel, but it was not as busy as it was reputed to have been when Gassy Jack operated it. He had been dead some ten years now and Mr. Chase had little need for Stanley's services.

I sat near the window and sipped my tea watching the street and trying to gauge the mood of the town. There were more men on the street now and several troopers from Victoria. I was able to look at them from the window without attracting attention to myself.

The blue uniforms were impressive: brass buttons down the

front, dark breeches. and jacket. The Stetson hat looked like a cavalry officer's cap. I suppose they were a mounted patrol most of the time. They didn't look very old, scarcely older than Stanley, but very eager and anxious to appear professional. I saw no firearms on any of the policemen. Two troopers walked past the hotel, and I could hear their spurs jingling before I saw the flash at the heels of the tall shiny boots. They were smartly turned out. I hoped they were efficient also.

While I objected to military rule, it was preferable to the vigilante attempts to keep order that had plagued San Francisco thirty years ago and threatened us at this time. I didn't want to live with mob rule or assassinations in the name of order. I infinitely preferred the impartial application of British justice with all its vagaries and inadequacies.

The men on the streets were keeping their distance from the troops and all seemed quiet.

I heard the rustle of silk and turned my head in time to see Maude, elegant in a deep red gown, move toward the inside stairs leading to the upper hotel rooms. Frank had her arm and was talking to her. It seems Maude knew everyone! I looked away but not in time to avoid Frank's eyes. I studiously looked out the window for a moment until I heard the chair at my table scrape and turned to see Frank smiling at me.

"May I join you?" I nodded but couldn't help a swift glance toward the stairs. Maude had gone.

Frank's eyes followed my glance.

"She was in trouble," he said. "She's had a rough time lately." He seemed embarrassed. "I feel sorry for her."

I caught his eye, amused he felt defensive and warming to him because of his compassion for Maude. She had been treated badly. It was kind of Frank to be concerned. He probably thought I suspected him of making an appointment with her. Perhaps he had been.

I nodded for lack of something to say and bit my tongue before I burst out with: *What were you really talking about?*

It would be ridiculous for me to ask a friend what his connections with a town prostitute were. Frank would be highly embarrassed by such a question and Robert, I almost gulped aloud at the impropriety of it, Robert would probably tell me.

I felt the blush creep up my throat and hurriedly looked out the window again. "Do you think the police will stay long?"

Frank leaned toward the glass. "Possibly a week. Vancouver city council can't afford to feed them and house them for long."

I smiled. "I don't suppose they counted on getting the bill for maintaining thirty-five policemen."

"It might serve to keep order in the future. Insurrection costs money."

We chatted about the new city plans for street lighting. Vancouver would bring in the electric carbon lamps similar to Victoria's. That meant we would no longer see our lamplighter drifting down the streets in the evening creating light, one lamp at a time. The new lights would make the streets brighter with less labour and maintenance. Electric lights illuminated the wharf at Moodyville making night loading possible. Frank suggested we'd have electricity in our homes soon.

We talked about the tea trade from the Orient and the increasing merchandising this area could support. Frank, as usual, was interesting and informative about business.

I stood to leave, mentioning Lydia would worry if I tarried any longer.

Frank reached into his jacket and brought out a box tied with pink ribbon. "Would you accept this? It's only a few chocolates from Domingo's."

"Domingo's? Of San Francisco?" Even I had heard of the famous chocolate manufacturer from the Bay City.

Frank nodded. "If you share with Lydia perhaps, she will not be annoyed at me for refusing her molasses."

"Oh, she's not annoyed with you. She thinks you are a solid respectable influence on me. She will be pleased with the chocolate. I've only tasted it two or three times but it's delicious."

He smiled, pleased I had accepted the candy.

I didn't think I'd compromised my soul. In any case, I might consider doing that for Domingo's chocolates. "Would you care to come to dinner after church tomorrow? Lydia could thank you herself then and you know she sets a generous table on Sunday noon."

Frank accepted with thanks. I placed the chocolates in my basket as we left. Frank accompanied me to the Hastings Mill Road. There he tipped his hat and returned to the city.

I couldn't wait until I got home to try the chocolate. I untied the pretty ribbon and opened the box. The chocolates were each about the size of a biscuit, some a rich, dark shade and some a creamy mocha. I broke one and left half of it in the box. Lydia wouldn't mind if I just had a taste. I savoured the first bite of that delicious, delectable, sweet. I rolled it around my mouth draining every smooth nuance of flavour through my tongue. I licked faint traces of it from my lips until the pleasure of it was a memory. I wondered if Frank had delivered some of these chocolates to Maude. I remembered the two of them at the foot of the stairs, Frank holding Maude's arm and leaning over her, talking, perhaps arranging a rendezvous. There would be much I could forgive a man if he brought me chocolates, but perhaps not that.

CHAPTER TWENTY-ONE

I stopped at the kitchen door and set the basket just outside on the wash-stand. I used a small broom to clean the dust from my boots when I heard Jack Bullman's voice.

"I'm a plain man, Lydia, and I want a plain answer."

"I'm needed here," Lydia said. "I told Amy I'd keep house for her and Stanley. There's a lot to do here, cooking and managing the house. I'm my own master." There was silence for a moment. Then, "Amy made a place for me and I'm not moving. I'm quite happy as I am."

"Aye, but I'm not. I'm not going to come and sit in your kitchen for another ten years and never get into the bedroom."

"Jack!" Lydia sounded annoyed. "That's no recommendation!"

There was silence for a second then Jack spoke so quietly I almost missed it.

"Did you no' enjoy it then with your first husband?"

"No," Lydia said shortly.

More silence. I couldn't walk in now!

"I promise you, love; you'll enjoy it with me."

"I understand all men say that."

Jack sounded exasperated and his voice boomed. "Well, Lydia! Either you trust me and marry me, or I must leave. I have prospects in the Cariboo. There is need for good lumbering. The country is opening up and I can make a living there. If I can't love you, I'll leave Vancouver for I'm not wanting to live and work here and see you every day."

"The Cariboo?" Lydia's voice was sharp.

I propped the broom outside the door and listened.

Lydia continued. "That God-forsaken place hundreds of miles from here? Why would you want to go there?"

"I told you. I couldn't stand to see you all the time and never get any closer."

"I won't be pushed into marriage." Lydia sounded peevish.

This was too much for Jack. His voice rose in anger. "No one's pushing you. Marry me and live with me as my wife or stay here, single, and alone with Miss MacDonald and Stanley. Suit yourself, Lydia." His voice grew calmer. "I'd like you to suit yourself."

"You'll not eat properly up there in the wilderness."

"I don't need you to look after me. I've lived forty years without your cooking. I'll eat just fine."

"I'm not necessary to you. Is that it?"

"You're necessary to me, but it isn't your cooking I'm after."

"Oh."

There was quiet for a moment. Then Lydia said, "Do you mean you love me?"

"Oh, aye. What in God's name do you think I've been saying?"

"I don't know. I've not had any experience with the finer feelings."

Jacks' voice was low as if he was trying to put forth an argument Lydia would believe."

"You're full of the finer feelings—courage and honesty. I'd just like to teach you about some others. You don't have to return my feelings. I know you don't feel the same about me. I'm not expecting that."

"What kind of a woman do you think I am? That I could give up my independence and live with a man I didn't care for? When I married Alistair, I was young and living at home. I, at least, thought I cared for him."

It was Jack's turn to be silent. Then, "There's no hope for me?" he asked quietly.

"I didn't say that." Lydia's voice was full of exasperation, and I heard a pot bang on the counter.

"Lydia." Jack's voice was stern. "Stop fidgeting around and look at me! Would you speak plain? No shilly-shallying. Will you marry me or no?"

"All right. All right," Another pot hit the counter. "I'll marry you." There was absolute silence for about thirty seconds. I stood paralyzed.

Then I heard Lydia say in a softer voice. "Jack, truly, I'm scared to death. Will it be all right?"

Jack tone bubbled with relief and good humour. "It will be all right. It will be grand."

"Put me down, you oaf. Put me down. Ah, Jack."

I rattled the doorknob as I opened the door wider and gave them time to present a decorous appearance. Lydia was flushed and Jack looked as though the smile on his face would be permanent.

"Is Stanley in yet?" Lydia asked bemusedly, one hand straightening her hair, the other tugging at her apron.

"I'll look," I said and walked through the kitchen to the hall.

"Stanley!" I yelled up the stairs.

He came from his room, and I enlisted his help to carry the supper dishes to the dining room table. I didn't tell him about Lydia and Jack. After all, I wasn't supposed to have heard them and wouldn't admit I had.

We ate our meal in comparative silence: Stanley preoccupied with weariness and the serious business of obtaining sustenance, Lydia and Jack presumably preoccupied with their new-found accord, and I anxious not to betray what I'd heard.

Lydia cleared off the dishes and brought in a cobbler pudding. She said casually as she dished it into bowls, "Jack and I have decided to get married, so I thought you might like to know."

I, just as casually, accepted the bowls of pudding and passed them to Stanley and Jack. "That's nice. When's the wedding?"

Stanley's jaw dropped open and Lydia automatically said, "Don't chew with your mouth open, Stanley?

He shut it with a snap, hurriedly swallowed his food and said, "You're what?"

Jack leaned toward him. "Getting married," he said. "Won't affect you much. You can continue to live here. I'll just move in."

"Oh," Stanley blinked, looked at Lydia, at me, then he straightened. "Congratulations." He offered Jack his hand. Jack beamed and shook hands with Stanley.

"Uh, best wishes, Aunt Lydia." Stanley offered his hand to Lydia.

I have never seen Lydia so flustered. She stood, looked uncertain and then accepted Stanley's hand and continued to stare at him. He smiled and finally, she smiled back.

"Thank you." At last, she sat back in her chair.

"Yes," I nodded at Jack and then Lydia, "my very best wishes to you both. When is the wedding date?"

"We haven't decided yet," Lydia said.

"But it might as well be this summer," Jack said quickly, "so we can all settle in here before school starts in the autumn."

Lydia blinked but then nodded. "I suppose so."

"Why don't you come over to the mill tomorrow and see if there is anything you might want to add to the house from my things?"

Jack was not waiting long. Lydia had said "yes" and he seemed to be determined to marry her before she could change her mind.

"Could you visit Jack's place after lunch? I've invited Frank to dinner. Is that all right?" I looked at Lydia.

Lydia, the householder, nodded briskly. "Certainly. I have a joint ready for tomorrow so we might as well stay and eat it. I'll go with you tomorrow after dinner, Jack."

"We'll do the dishes tomorrow as an engagement present." Stanley said.

Lydia's eyebrows rose. "Thank you," she said in surprise.

"I'll bring the democrat tomorrow," Jack offered. "So you won't have to walk and in case there is anything we want to transport back here. I have a very good book-case and some fine chairs you might like to have in the parlour."

"So, we will all continue to live here?" Stanley wanted things clear.

Lydia nodded. "I think so. You and Amy still need someone in the house, and we are close to the mill so Jack won't be inconvenienced." She looked at me.

I nodded acceptance. Then smiled. "It's sounds wonderful, Lydia."

She flushed and was quiet.

Stanley went to bed after supper, and I found a book to read in the parlour leaving the engaged couple alone in the kitchen.

Jack left about nine and Lydia came in and sat across from me on the straight-backed Jacobean chair she'd brought from Ontario.

"Are you sure this is what you want?" I asked the traditional question.

"Yes, yes," Lydia said.

"And you're sure you want us to stay here?"

"That too," Lydia assured me.

"Lydia, what about in a year or two when the babies start coming? You'll want your own home without Stanley and me then. We should start looking for a home of our own."

"There won't be any babies, Amy. The doctor told me years ago I wouldn't have any babies."

I looked at her blankly.

"It has something to do with my having had mumps when I was fifteen."

"I thought it was only men who were affected by that."

"Apparently not. At least, that's what the doctor told me. I never did conceive with Alistair."

I thought that over then ventured. "You know, Lydia, that could be quite a relief. Almost an advantage in marriage."

Lydia smiled and smoothed her brown hair back into its bun. "Yes, childbirth is frightening and some children a great trouble."

I nodded. Then Lydia let her head fall forward a little, her fingers playing with the trim of her shawl. 'The only trouble is," she said quietly, "I find myself wanting to see a brace of little Jacks."

I reached out impulsively and took her hand. "I'm sorry, Lydia."

She nodded and looked up. Her eyes were dry. "I never felt this way about Alistair, and it comes as a surprise I have such feelings." She smiled slightly. "I would like to see little boys with Jack's stocky frame and bright eyes." She took a deep breath. "But it can't be helped and I'm sure I have enough to do with you and Stanley."

I released her hand. "And are you sure it's Jack you want?"

"Oh, yes," Lydia said without hesitation. "That's certain. He's. . . kind and good fun. I can quarrel with him!"

Then I believed she had made the right choice.

"I wish you very happy."

"Thank you." She rose briskly and walked to the door. "Do you think you could get Frank to bring me some of that sweet sugar from San Francisco? I'll make the wedding cake."

"Frank expects another cargo on the *Parthia* next week. He says he's getting another shipment of molasses too. I'll ask him for sweet sugar."

I wondered if the next shipment of molasses would contain guns. I must ask Robert to find that out. Heavens! What if this supply of guns was just the beginning of a massive shipment of arms? The new railroad could speed supplies to the North West in a matter of days. The gun runner might have set up a continuing supply of ammunition and guns; this load might be only the first. Perhaps it wasn't the first. I hadn't considered that before. The Mounted Police said they had seen a few new rifles. What if more were stored around Battleford unknown to the police? I must get Robert to check that out. Dear heavens! If guns could be supplied as easily as molasses, we were going to have a civil war. The police weren't going to be much help. The police in the North West were going to wait for the train—even if it took a month. We could be swimming in guns by that time. I had to talk to Robert.

"What's the matter?" Lydia spoke sharply breaking into my abstraction.

"Nothing. Oh, the sweet sugar. Yes, I'll ask him. Oh!" I said again. "I forgot the chocolate."

I rose hurriedly and ran for the box. It was still in my basket.

Lydia was pleased and thought she might keep some of the chocolate to decorate the wedding cake. Thoughts of the wedding cake turned us to speculation on the wedding itself.

"Perhaps August 21st?" I suggested.

Lydia agreed and, pending Jack's approval, the wedding plans began. We spent a busy hour with paper and pen compiling a list of the food we would need for a collation here at the teacherage after the ceremony. Everyone who knew Lydia and Jack would come so we needed to provide for about two hundred. Later, before bed, I sat by the window, the tedious tasks of unbuttoning my skirt, blouse, petticoat, and chemise accomplished. The dark city of Vancouver curved against the faintly lit waters of Coal Harbour. I could see a few coal oil lanterns lighting Water Street and reflecting off the high tide that lapped at the pilings of the Sunnyside Hotel and George Black's butcher shop. It was a quiet night. warm and soft.

I hoped Lydia would be happy. It was one thing to not want children, like me. It was another to want them and be unable to have any. Lydia would never speak of it again and never, even by inference, let me see she mourned her loss. I spent a few minutes that night fiercely praying for her happiness.

CHAPTER TWENTY-TWO

I decided to dress with some care today. This was an outing, after all, and Frank appreciated sartorial elegance. Not that I wanted to look like Maude, but I could be a little more dashing than usual. I chose light cotton pantaloons with pink ribbons and hand-tatted lace. No one would see them, but they were elegant, and I knew they were fashionable. The chemise was a little heavier and trimmed with the same ribbon. My dress was a pale blue with a curved draping effect in the front of the skirt—very flattering, dropping to just above my ankles with a short flounce at the bottom. I really couldn't bring myself to wear one of the large bustles that are back in fashion and settled for a small wire cage fitted over my hips, a very small crinolette compared to many I've seen, that lifted the skirt up in the back. I wish the bodice didn't fit quite so tightly. This was my Sunday best; I could be a little uncomfortable for one day.

My hair would not behave. There wasn't much I could do but curl it into fat ringlets, anchor it with twenty-three hairpins and pray it stayed there.

Stanley didn't go to church with us. He had been tired the night before and was sleeping when we left the house. Rather than risk censorious tongues I assured Father Clinton after the service that Stanley looked forward to attending evensong. Evensong meant Stanley not only got more rest on Sunday mornings, but he socialized with the young people who preferred the evening service. Lydia and I accepted a ride from Frank back to the teacherage and arrived to find Stanley adding wood to Lydia's box in the summer kitchen.

The joint had been cooked the night before and reheated. Lydia served greens with raw oysters she had obtained yesterday. Her pickled beets and pickled eggs added a sharp flavour to the meal and her girdle cakes were delicious. We finished the meal with gooseberry tart and strong tea.

Frank and Jack discussed lumbering and the future of the mast and spar industry that occupied so much of the Hastings Mill inventory. Stanley was interested in the conversation and asked intelligent questions. Lydia was a little quiet, but she had been busy assembling the meal and also, I imagine, busy in her own head with plans and ideas for her future.

Jack and Lydia excused themselves after the tea pot had been drained and rode off in the democrat toward the mill. Lydia wanted to have a good look at Jack's furniture before she transferred any of it here.

Stanley was good on his offer to do the dishes and, after helping him store the remaining food, I tied on a very smart blue hat that sat high on the back of my head and accompanied Frank in his gig.

It was another warm, sunny day. The water in the inlet glinted silver. Birds dived and pirouetted like black dots far out in the bay, skimming the water and then rising. I saw an eagle floating in the air currents high above the trees, drifting, waiting. I squinted against the sun and then lost sight of it against the blue of the mountains on the north shore. There were several ships lying close to the floating cannery, *Spratt's Ark*, and beside it, the anchored hulk of the *Robert Kerr*. The *Robert Dunsmuir* sat placidly on the deep waters of Coal Harbour. Many sailing ships, bare-masted against the western sky, gathered near the wharves at Hastings Mill.

The horse walked sedately up Hastings Mill Road and down the planks and dirt of Water Street. We nodded to several friends and talked pleasantly of Frank's trip this evening. He planned to stay overnight in New Westminster and return to Vancouver tomorrow. I wish I had some reason to go with him as I would love to shop in a bigger centre and see some of the interesting sights of the city. Accompanying Frank on an overnight journey was unthinkable, at least, if I wanted to have any friends and any employment when I returned. So, I smiled and nodded and wished I had more freedom to move from place to place. We planned to leave the horse and gig at the end of the road and the start of the path to the Reserve. Frank had made arrangements to meet a party of six for a walk around the Reserve and perhaps a game of croquet.

I hadn't forgotten my worries over the smuggled guns, but I was lulled by the warm day, the satisfying meal, and the pleasant company; I was not alert. When Frank stopped the gig in front of the Granville Hotel, I only smiled my inquiry.

"I want to check on my barrels," he said. "I won't be a minute."

He tied the horse to the hitching rail and disappeared around the corner of the hotel. I sat up straight. Why so much concern for molasses? Had the superintendent told Frank about the guns? I glanced down the street looking for the trooper who was supposed to be guarding the consignment. He sat on the verandah of the hotel, his head back against the wall, sound asleep. Or at least, he looked to be sound asleep. He might be feigning it. There weren't many people on this section of Water Street, but I caught a glimpse of a man in the shadowy doorway of a shack on the corner at Cambie. I was tense when Frank returned.

He wasn't checking molasses. He couldn't be. He'd never be this concerned over an ordinary shipment of molasses. Robert, and Stanley and the superintendent and me—that was too many people to keep a secret. I knew it would leak out eventually. What was Frank going to do?

He smiled. "Everything's okay."

He picked up the reins and shook them over the horse's back. We drew up to Cambie Street and I turned quickly catching sight of Mr. Sanders, his hand up in a salute, leaning against the doorjamb, smoking. I turned and saw Frank respond with a brief wave. It looked like a signal given and received.

Pictures flashed into my mind of Frank bending over Maude, concerned about her, taking time to talk to Stanley, offering Lydia chocolates, treating me with solicitude. I could not believe he knowingly transported guns. Yet he was in some sort of collusion with Mr. Sanders.

"So, he knows about the guns too? Is there anyone who doesn't?"

Frank checked the pace of the horse with one hand and gripped my wrist with the other.

"What do you know about guns?"

My eyes flew to his and we stared at each other. If he didn't know I knew about the guns, then he didn't get his information from our group. He had the information because he had always had the information.

"You've always known about the guns, haven't you Frank? You brought them here." Maude had said the gun runner had to be someone who had political ideals and monstrous greed. Sanders had the politics; Frank had the greed. "You're running guns. That's treason." It still seemed like an intellectual problem to me, an arithmetic question that had a solid correct solution somewhere.

Frank kept his hand tight on my wrist and jerked the gig to a standstill. He spoke across me to the lounger in the doorway. "Get in."

Mr. Sanders tossed his glowing cigar to the dirt and jumped to the step of the buggy. There was no room for him to sit so he stood and secured himself with both hands on the edge. We continued toward the trail to the Moody Reserve moving very slowly.

"Good afternoon, Miss." His lips drew back in an automatic smile exposing his rabbit-like teeth, yellow with brown stains. He was dressed immaculately as he had before, good dark suit, watch and gold chain, white shirt, loose black tie, the image of a gentleman.

I looked up at his eyes, the same small, black, eyes I'd seen before. I had the same feeling of revulsion. He made me think of snakes, lizards, and life under the rocks.

"Miss MacDonald knows about the guns."

Mr. Sanders looked at Frank's grip on my wrist and quickly imprisoned my other arm.

I pulled away from him. Frank looked down. "Get your hands off her!"

Mr. Sanders obeyed, and I tried to control my sudden anger and think. Frank wasn't lost to all compassion.

"Look, Amy. I'm making money. I told you I needed it."

We ignored Mr. Sanders.

"You killed the Métis."

"He wasn't a white man. I've never killed a white man."

I felt my forehead go cold and nausea rise in my stomach.

"Are you going to kill me now?" I asked the question sarcastically but realized in the ensuing silence he was considering it. He might have to kill me. It was then I finally had sense enough to be afraid.

"No!" he said emphatically, his hand still restraining me. "I'll hide you until the shipment's gone. I'll send you to my father's place in San Francisco. Sanders, you can take her. You can stay with her on the boat and turn her over to my father. If you touch her, I'll kill you."

"All right. All right, but if I had a free hand for a while, she'd be a lot meeker."

Frank glared at him.

"All right. Take it easy. Why do I have to take her?"

"Because I don't need you here. I have your money in the freight lines now and you're no use to me. You'll be all right in San Francisco. You can come back when the fighting is over."

"Naturally, I'll be back. The new government is going to need a leader. I am the only one who has the vision."

I looked at Mr. Sanders for a moment, momentarily fascinated by such belief in the divine right to rule.

Frank frowned, concentrating, the entrepreneur busy with plans. "Sanders will hold you in San Francisco, Amy, until the revolution is over. You're best out of it anyway. Then we'll be married."

I laughed, a high, shrill, almost hysterical laugh. "Oh, lovely," I said when I could. "What a marvelous basis for marriage. Abduction, escorted by a brutal maniac and imprisonment. Then marriage to a murderer. I can hardly wait." I looked straight into his eyes. Frank the handsome one, Frank the ambitious, Frank the rapacious. I ignored Mr. Sanders. He bounced on his perch beside us.

We had left the planked street behind, and the horse's hooves fell with soft thuds on the narrowing path. The air was very still. Smoke from the many fires hung, as usual, over the city and over the tangle of brush and drying slash in front of us. I wondered if Frank and his "friend" would try to abduct me here. Or would they try to kill me? Not right now, I didn't think. There were too many strollers who used this trail; too many people had seen them with me. Unless Frank lost all reason. Would a murderer necessarily be reasonable? He must know I would not stay with him. He might persuade himself for a while he could manage me, but he must know I would run when I could. So, he would need to kill me. When was he going to do it? Perhaps later, in the woods at Moody Reserve.

Suddenly the horse threw up his head and trumpeted a wild cry. Frank pulled tight on the reins and half stood to see what could be on the path ahead. Mr. Sanders gripped the edge of the gig so tightly I could see the skin stretched across his knuckles. A sudden wind whipped the ties of my hat across my face, and, for a moment, I couldn't see. I grabbed them holding them down. The wind was strong and increasing. I had never experienced such a wild gust. I had the confused and theatrical idea Zeus would scream from the sky and denounce Frank.

"What is it?" Mr. Sanders shrieked in my ear.

"I don't know!" Frank shouted. He was still standing. "I can't see anything. I don't like that wind. I'll turn and go back to town." The wind tore at my blue hat and whistled through the light material of my dress. Frank had both hands on the reins now and I gripped the side of the gig. My skirt billowed and I had to hold it to keep it from rising over my legs. The horse plunged against the traces, but Frank managed to turn him. I smelled the acrid pitch and bark that had been part of our lives here for months—and smoke. I was so used to it that it was only now I realized it was thick and strong filling my nose and making my eyes smart. Frank urged the horse to a fast trot. The wind was now almost behind us coming from the southwest. I glanced that way and saw a solid wall of flame licking high in the air like a terrifying scene from Paradise Lost.

"Frank! Fire! "

"My God!" Mr. Sander's terror was equal to my own.

Frank turned, then flicked the horse's back with the reins. We shot toward Water Street, rocking and pitching over the rough road. Somehow, Mr. Sanders hung on.

We had to slow our pace when we passed the shacks at Cambie Street for the townspeople were alert and fleeing the city toward Hastings Mill, running in front of us, beside us and blocking the street. Frank checked the horse.

I glanced back at the fire. It towered above, masses of flames reaching toward us. I felt the heat on my arms and back. When we approached the Granville Hotel Frank slowed even more and started to turn into the alley. I grabbed his arm, looking back at the flames.

"What are you doing?"

"I have to get my wagon."

"Don't be silly, Frank! Look at the fire."

"You're crazy, Hartman!"

"I have to get that wagon load. My whole future depends on delivering those supplies: my ship, my routes. Let go of my arm!"

There, sitting in the gig with people screaming and running by us, with the flames bearing down, I looked at his eyes and understood the insane depth of the greed that drove him,

"It's so important?" I said.

"It's a gold mine," he said simply. "A gold mine."

"I'm getting out." Mr. Sanders braced himself for a jump. Frank's arm shot across me and twisted the front of Sander's shirt tight at the neck. "You're in this with me. You'll help me save those barrels."

Frank jerked the reins and urged the horse toward the back of the hotel.

Frank was fully occupied with Sanders and the reins. I pushed myself up from the seat, jumped, hit the ground, and rolled. I glanced back at Frank. He had forced the horse and gig into the alley, Sanders now sitting beside him, intent on rescuing his guns.

I ran toward Carrall Street. The heat from the fire pushed me on. The wind, still strong and combined with the heat, pushed me toward the end of Water Street. I spared one thought for Frank. I hoped he'd give up the wagon, free the horse and race the fire.

Every breath I took seared my throat and chest. I could not think about it. I could only race to safety. People flew into the street in a wild attempt to save themselves. A man in his Sunday pants, suspenders and no shirt shot past me, his bare feet slapping on the boards. A mother clutching her infant burst from George Black's house. I saw the police Chief Stewart unlocking the door of the jail. We were running like field mice in front of a grass fire.

My crinolette bounced from side to side tearing at the thin material of my dress. I clutched my skirts well over my knees and took as big a stride as I could. There was a great heat on my back, and I was afraid to turn around and look. I tried to think and not just panic following the people in front of me. Where was the safest place'? The water? If I turned and ran between the buildings and into the inlet I might be hurt jumping off the pilings. The water was twelve feet below and, if the tide was out, there would not be any water. I continued to run with the crowd.

My chest hurt and I breathed shallow gasps of the hot air. There was no sky above me now. Everything was black with smoke. If I didn't burn to death I would suffocate. I coughed and stumbled but kept moving with the flow of the crowd.

CHAPTER TWENTY-THREE

Sparks flew. Bits of wood and twigs flamed in the air and dropped around me setting fires to the buildings on both sides of Water Street. People on the sidewalk jumped onto the street as the fire raced along the wooden boards faster than they could run. A woman struggling with children ran into the street and collided with me. We stopped momentarily and she thrust an infant into my arms then grabbed the toddler from the ground.

"Please." She looked into my face. "Please, Teacher. Take the baby." She coughed and lifted the older child into her arms.

I clutched the baby close to me with one hand, pulled up my skirts with the other and ran on.

"Amy!" I heard my name shouted above the roar of the wind and the flames. I glanced up but kept running. I was at Carrall Street now and the buildings to the south were on fire.

"Amy! Run to the wharf!" This time the shout was right beside me and I looked up to see Robert. The whites of his eyes were bright against his black face, his red beard dark with soot. He looked like a wild kind of a leprechaun. He grabbed my shoulders and turned me toward the water.

We sped down the hill to the wharf with hundreds of others. Once I put the baby's face close to my ear. It was crying. I tucked it back down to my breast and ran on. I cursed the foolish crinolette and tight skirt that hampered my movements. By now, my skirt ripped away from my waist in some places, but the material still wrapped around my legs and frustrated running.

Robert pushed me ahead of him to the farthest end of the city wharf. It was hot here too, but the wharf was not yet burning. We crowded to the very end. The water drenched the low-lying boards as the wind pushed the waves high and up onto the planks. My chest heaved with as I tried to breathe the thin, dry air. The baby was still crying, so I knew it was alive. I let the wind whip my tattered skirts around my legs, wrapped both arms around the infant and rocked him. He soothed and was quiet.

Robert and I turned and looked back at the city. The flames reached so far into the heavens we could see only fire and clouds of smoke. Hell must be like this: power, destruction, inevitable annihilation. I looked away, out into Coal Harbour to the hulk, *The Robert Kerr*. It had been moored near Deadman's Island and now dragged its anchor, travelling with the wind across the bay toward Hastings Mill. That same wind tore at our clothes and sent a stinging spray over the wharf.

The flames were flying ahead of this fierce wind and coming this way. There would be no safety on the wharf. The fire would be here in moments. The heat was intense.

'Take off your skirt!"

I stared at Robert. He reached over and ripped my skirt, breaking the button at the waist and tearing the seam.

"Step out of it!"

I was glad to do so and managed to unbutton the wire cage of the crinolette and let it drop. I kicked it over the edge of the wharf and into the water.

"Give me the baby. Take off your shoes."

I didn't think. I just obeyed.

I struggled with the buttons and managed to get one shoe off before Robert said,

"Into the water, Amy. Now!"

I looked at him once and then slid over the side and into the water. I had the ridiculous thought I was glad I wore my best pantaloons.

Robert and the baby were beside me.

I grabbed a short log that had been floating nearby and a wide plank.

"Put the baby on the plank, Robert."

"I'll wet the blanket first."

Robert dipped the blanket with the baby in it into the water. The child howled with discomfort. Robert placed him on the plank.

"Now kick," he said. "We have to get out of here."

The wind had passed us traveling northeast. The swells of the waves moved us east, they and away from the fire. I was grateful.

"Duck your head and keep your hair wet."

I realized then my bonnet had burned off my head. Only the ties and the neck piece were left. I ducked and never gave a thought to how I felt about going under water. My shoe was heavy and cumbersome, but I was glad I had at least one foot free and no heavy dress material to weigh me down.

We kicked and pushed our log and plank into the waters of the bay. At the surface of the water the air was fresh and free from smoke. I raised myself up once to try to see ahead and felt the heat from the flames on my hair. I stayed low after that.

Gradually, we pulled away from danger and started to look for some kind of raft. Robert spotted one first, a wharf that had broken loose and floated in the middle of the bay. Several dozen people were boarding it: some were swimmers, some refugees from smaller rafts, boards, and logs.

We made for that, our little passenger again protesting.

I was grateful beyond measure that I was not afraid to swim out in the bay. I would not allow myself to think of those whose fear of water was so great they hadn't been able to leave the wharf.

We clambered aboard the raft. Robert handed me the child, and I did what I could to comfort it. I thought Robert looked peculiar: his face streaked with soot, his hair burned and singed so it looked frizzled and patchy. He had no shoes and his trousers, I noticed for the first time, were in tatters.

I smiled. "You look silly."

He grinned at me. "Look at yourself."

I still had on one shoe. My petticoat hung wet and might as well not have been there for all the cover it was. My blouse had holes burned in a few places in front and when I tried to look over my shoulder at my back Robert suggested I didn't need to bother since I wouldn't see much of the blouse.

"Is it burned off?"

"Pretty well."

There were no sleeves left either. I found it amazing this could have happened to me without my being aware of it. I had a burn on my arm but no other real injury. The baby seemed to be fine. I discovered it was a little girl, about six months old, in a pink dress and white bootees. She seemed to be whole and without injury although her blanket had several burned areas on it.

"Take her for a minute," I said. I sat on the floating wharf and removed my other shoe. It was a great relief to be quit of it.

We picked up as many survivors as we could and then started to paddle our way toward an anchored ship not too far from us, the men kicking with their feet and a few trying to steer with planks and poles. Waves occasionally broke and ran over the edges. The raft was submerged at one end. We were anxious to get to a safer vessel. The fire had raced to Hastings Mill and then the wind had dropped as suddenly as it had begun. The fire fell back on itself and suddenly died. There was smoke everywhere and we could not see the city, or what was left of the city.

We approached the ship near the rope netting that hung down over the side. The men secured our wharf to the netting and called up for a ladder to be lowered.

"There's no one here but me. I'm the caretaker," a voice replied.

"Well, caretaker," Robert called with good humour, "find a ladder of some sort and lower it to us."

"I'm not allowed to let anyone on the ship," he answered.

We looked at one another in disbelief. Another wave broke over the raft, pushing us against the ship.

"Watch your hands and feet," Robert advised the men. "You could be smashed against the ship."

He called again. "We need refuge. We're coming aboard."

"No, you can't," the man called down.

We could see him now, an old man, about sixty, following his orders with the stubborn righteousness of a Methodist minister denouncing the devil. "I'm not allowed to let anyone on board. You'll have to go back." The barrel of a gun poked over the edge.

I looked back at the smoldering city and then up at the ship's deck. Rage welled up inside me, and I didn't think. I picked up my shoe and grabbed the netting.

"I'm coming aboard,'" I yelled up at the old man; "And if you get in my way, I'll smash your head in."

I began to climb, my bare feet getting a sure grip in the strong rope net, the buttons of my shoe in my teeth. Hand over hand I swarmed up the sides as if I had apprenticed as a pirate. I was so angry I gave no thought to my bare legs, pantaloons, or sodden petticoat. That man up there was denying us sanctuary. I clambered over the side and saw the man had his shotgun at the ready. When he saw I was a woman he lowered it in surprise. I swung my shoe but didn't need to release it for Robert and several other men dropped to the deck and surrounded the caretaker. He prudently pitched the gun over the side, turned and ran below the decks.

"Let's get him," one of the men said but half-heartedly, without real intent.

There was suddenly no vengeance in anyone. We were alive. We were safe. That was enough.

Overwhelmingly weary, I sat on a coil of rope and closed my eyes. I felt Robert beside me. His arm moved up around my shoulders, giving me immeasurable comfort. I would not think of Frank. Not right now. We sat like that for a few minutes—grateful for life and stubbornly resisting the thought of those who had perished.

"The baby?" I asked.

"Coming," he answered. "You shoved her into the hands of the nearest person, and he has her."

I opened my eyes and saw one of the men carefully lifting the child over the side and passing her to another man. She was crying again. I held out my arms, and he gave her to me. I cradled the little girl, rocked, and crooned to her, trying to comfort her and myself. She quieted, and I nestled her into my shoulder drawing comfort from her warmth and the little movements of her hands and feet. It was over. I sat there on the coil of rope looking out over the bay, watching the ashes drift and settle over Vancouver.

CHAPTER TWENTY-FOUR

Within a half an hour the heavy clouds of smoke moved east, and we could see the wharf at Hastings Mill crowded with people. They had been ready to abandon the wharf for the sailing ships lying in the harbour before the wind dropped and the fire died a hundred and fifty yards from the wharf. I hoped Stanley was there. If he hadn't start the washing up right away but returned to bed for another sleep, he may not have been aware of the fire until it swept over the house. There was nothing left of the teacherage. I could see the point of land where the house had been. There was no house, just a broken frame sending up trails of smoke. Everything was gone. All my clothes, my books, all my mother's jewellery, and keepsakes. I didn't feel any regret for those things yet. It was just a way of keeping my mind busy so I wouldn't think about what might have happened to Stanley. If he had been in the kitchen doing the dishes he would have taken to the water. Stanley could swim.

I watched the people on the mill wharf move slowly back toward their homes. Nothing had been burned at the mill site. That meant Lydia and Jack were all right—if they had stayed at the mill site.

I continued to sit on the coil of rope rocking the baby. I could see several dugout canoes moving delicately through the debris, picking up survivors and carefully maneuvering two dugouts one on either side of the swimmer so that they hauled the sodden survivor without tipping the canoes. The native people had responded very quickly. Robert joined the men at the ship's rail watching the approach of a rowboat coming to evacuate us. We were going to have to climb down to it. I had climbed up the rope netting without a thought of how I was doing it. The descent would be much more difficult. As well, I now was aware of my bedraggled and indecent appearance. There was no help for it, though. I must leave the ship and the only way to do so was over the side.

I queued with the men and allowed Robert to carry the baby. I hoped the child's mother had survived the fire.

I concentrated on placing one hand and one foot securely on the netting before I moved the other. Robert stayed directly below me and shielded me from curious looks. He managed the baby by placing the child inside his coat and buttoning the coat together in front somewhat in the manner of the Indian women.

After I settled myself in the rowboat one of the sailors offered me a blanket.

"Here you are, Missus."

I wore the blanket like a gypsy shawl. Dirty and odiferous as it was, I was grateful for it. Robert gave me the little girl. She was crying again. Perhaps she was hungry.

The child's need pricked my lethargy, and I looked up and around at the men who were with us. I recognized the butcher and several businessmen of the town. There were no other women. If you can't swim, and most women can't, you can't escape into the water. If you went into the water in petticoats and yards of dress material, you'd be weighted down and drown. I wondered how many had. All my group were suffering from some effects of the fire. Most of the men had clothes burned away in some areas. Some seemed to be suffering from burns on their arms. The face of one poor man was swollen and oozing clear fluid from raw burns.

The strong wind had taken most of the billowing clouds of smoke away and left us with the smoldering haze of the ruined city. Ashes were everywhere, but we could now see the damage caused by the fire. There was one building left standing.

"Robert, what is that?" I pointed. The building looked odd, still standing tall amid the smoke and charred ashes of the acres around it. Robert squinted, looking west. Several other men tried to decide what building had escaped the fire.

"It has to be the Sunnyside, the Granville, the Deighton or the Regina. No other building is that big."

"Must be the Regina Hotel," one man said. "It's that far along toward the Morton's Bluff."

Heads nodded.

"Why would it not burn? Everything else did?" To me it seemed either magical or miraculous.

Robert shrugged. "It's only been built two weeks. Maybe the lumber was green and didn't burn as easily as the dry wood. Or maybe the wind shifted in front of it? I don't know."

"Could be that cleared lot in front of it kept the fire away." An older man spoke. His black hair was grizzled with gray where the fire had singed it.

The sailors pulled on the oars, and we moved quickly through the water toward the Hastings Hill wharf. Ready hands steadied the boat when we arrived, and thanksgiving was offered by someone that we were safe.

We climbed out and made our way to the land. Lydia was waiting there. I was so relieved to see her I almost dropped the baby. Lydia was so relieved to see me she never noticed the baby until the little one started crying again.

"What's that?"

"Where's Stanley?" We spoke simultaneously.

Lydia answered me first. "Stanley's all right. He has his horse. They escaped into the water and swam over here to the wharf."

I started to shake with relief and didn't hear all she said. She had to repeat herself.

"I said, Stanley is all right. He's helping the cook load some provisions for the refugees. The Mayor has asked that we all meet at the foot of the Westminster Bridge on the New Road at False Creek. We'll decide what needs to be done then."

"This is a baby," I said unnecessarily. "Someone handed it to me. I think it was Mrs. Tupper. Yes," I repeated surer now as I remembered the wide blue eyes staring at me in the midst of the heat and panic of the fire. "Mrs. Tupper. This must be little Eloise."

Lydia held out her arms and I gratefully handed over the crying child.

"She needs some milk," Lydia said. "Jack!" She turned and moved to where Jack hitched horses to a wagon. "Could you find me some milk from the cook for this child?"

Jack handed the traces to a nearby man and looked at the baby. He reached out a big finger and little Eloise clutched it. Jack frowned, then nodded. "I don't think the cook has any milk, but Mrs. Grant might. I'll ask."

I remembered Ruth's strictures quoted from her mother about the necessity of keeping milk sweet and clean and decided the baby would be well cared for.

I suddenly felt as though my feet would not take another step. I swayed for a moment and then sat down quickly on the ground. The blanket slipped from my shoulders, and I pulled at it weakly. My bones and muscles were fluid and unreliable. I didn't know whether there truly was a haze in the air, or whether my eyes were misting and the sights in front of me wavering because of my weariness.

Someone touched my shoulder. "Drink," I accepted the hot tea gratefully and sipped its sweet warmth. The ground steadied and I took a deep breath, I looked up to thank my benefactor. It was Mrs. Scow.

She smiled and indicated my tatters. "No clothes?"

I looked down at my petticoat. I hadn't realized it too hung in tatters and revealed much more of me than had ever been exposed in public before. I tucked the blanket more closely around me.

"That's true." I thought of the ashes of the teacherage. "I have no clothes at all."

She touched my shoulder again. "Clothes later," she said and left me.

I suppose she was bringing tea to many people and had to leave me, but I was irritated. Clothes may come later but I needed something right now. I couldn't go around in a ripped petticoat and a blanket. Where was Robert when I needed him'?

I craned my neck trying to look through the groups of people talking and moving around the wharf and the mill site. I saw Robert through a break in the crowd talking and nodding his head and listening to a tall speaker who was obviously excited about something. There was something odd in Robert's behaviour and I stared at him for a few minutes before I realized what it was. He wasn't taking notes. He had no pencil and no notebook. I smiled to myself. I was without clothes and Robert was without a pencil.

Lydia had abandoned me for the baby, and I didn't know where to go or what to do next. I was still sitting on the ground covered by the blanket and holding my teacup when Mrs. Scow returned. She held out a dark green walking skirt. It was about six inches too wide in the waist but it was long and would cover me. I thanked her. She slipped the skirt over my head, and I let the blanket down underneath it. When I stood Mrs. Scow held the skirt to my waist and buttoned it. I grabbed it as she took her hands away before it traveled over my hips to my ankles. Mrs. Scow stared at it and then chuckled. I clutched the voluminous material and started to laugh too. We leaned on each other almost choking, as much in emotional relief as in real mirth. Tears welled up in my eyes and I half-cried and half-laughed. Mrs. Scow held my shoulders and smiled and patted me until we were both calmer.

"A piece of string would probably help," I suggested.

"Good." She left me holding the skirt at my waist and returned in a few minutes with a strong piece of parcel string. I looped it through the belt welts and tied it in place. Now, if I didn't trip over the hem, and didn't stumble or step on anything dangerous with my bare feet, I could at least join the rest on the march to the Westminster Bridge. Mrs. Scow patted my shoulder again and slipped through the crowd.

I forgot to ask her whose skirt it was. Obviously, it wasn't hers. She is much smaller than I am. The owner of this skirt was of substantial stature. Mrs. Grant? Perhaps. In any case I would have to wear it for some time. I had no home and no clothes.

When everyone had been refreshed and those who needed medical attention had received it, we started to walk toward the False Creek and the Westminster Bridge. Robert had abandoned me to a good story for the next issue of the *Granville Star* and Lydia had gone to deal with the baby. I joined the procession down Hastings Mill Road toward the New Road to Westminster. I had gone only a few hundred yards, far enough to realize walking bare feet was going to be painful, when Mrs. Scow ran up beside me.

"Here, Teacher," she said and handed me a pair of the leather slippers the Indian people wear instead of shoes or boots. Moccasins.

I sat on a rock and pulled the soft leather shoes onto my feet. Then wrapped the thongs around my ankles to keep the slippers secure. They felt thin, like stockings, but I was grateful for anything. When I started walking on them, I was surprised to find they were not only comfortable but adequate in dulling the sharpness of the stones.

I had resigned myself to the walk and felt more cheerful about it when I heard Stanley call. I had ceased to worry I had lost him after Lydia reported him safe; but I was almost overwhelmed by the feelings that filled me when I saw him astride Homer moving up along the edge of the road. I stepped away from the procession and waited for him.

"Lydia said I'd find you here. Are you all right?"

I smiled so widely at him he must have thought I was demented.

"And you didn't get burned at all?" he continued.

I shook my head.

"Why can't you say something?" He walked the horse up to me and pulled to a stop. "Did you get shocked into being a mute or something?"

I shook my head again and then coughed and cleared my throat. "Uh, I'm all right." I grinned at him. "You look great—all in one piece."

His eyes lit with understanding. "It's great to see you too. Although," he looked down at my dirt and then back up at my frizzled hair and sooty face. "I've seen you looking more handsome."

We stood like that for a minute or two, enjoying the sight of each other, and then Stanley said, "Do you want to ride astride? No one is going to pay much attention to what you do today."

"Today," I said as I stood on a stump and Stanley brought Homer close to me, "no one will recognize me."

I slid onto Homer's back. My long skirt didn't ride up very high on my legs and the moccasins came well up past my ankles, so I was reasonably covered. I gripped Stanley's waist and concentrated on staying on.

"No trotting now, Stanley, or you'll dislodge me."

We walked at a slow pace along the Hastings Mill Road. The fire had come as far is Mr. Alexander's house but had not touched it or any houses past it. West of Mr. Alexander's there was ashes and charred wood.

"How long did the fire last," I asked Stanley.

"I figure about forty-five minutes from the time it hit the edge of town at Dupont and Cambie. It flamed through town from the southwest and took every building except the Regina Hotel."

We stared at the ashes, black stumps and standing trees.

"The maple tree must have been about two feet thick at the base." I tried to see where the tree had been at the corner of Carrall and Water. That had been our meeting centre. Everyone debated and gave speeches and made decisions under that tree. It had seemed a symbol of civilization. There was a black patch on the ground when we passed that spot, only a reminder of the tree.

The sun was fiery red through the haze in the western sky. It was about five in the evening now but darker than usual with the smoke hanging over the land. The wind that had so suddenly whipped the fire to a fatal menace had taken the first great clouds of smoke away, but now the smoldering of the debris increased the haze in the still air.

I realized I was hungry. What were we going to do? All our careful provisions were burned. I had no money except a few dollars in Mrs. Alexander's safe. The rest of the people in this long procession had nothing. We moved up the New Road to New Westminster and, since there were no trees and no buildings, I could see past Carrall Street and out toward the C.P.R. roundhouse clearing where the fire had begun.

The Chinese community on the shores of False Creek was desolate. I hoped Sung Wick had stayed on their boat. Perhaps, as they had made provisions for living away from Vancouver before the fire; they might be more able to survive than the rest of us.

I slid off the horse when we reached the meeting grounds and found a rock wall to sit on. Hundreds of people were already here, including the mayor. He had set up a tent and tried to organize people so they could find their relatives. Sunday afternoon is traditionally a time when families are out, the youngsters with their friends and the parents on a walk or a drive. I hoped there would not be much tragedy even though I knew that was a faint hope.

Suddenly, I remembered something I hadn't thought I'd noticed at the time. When Robert called me as I first reached Carrall Street a man was driving a horse toward Water along Carrall. As I watched, the flame engulfed him and the horse. Although I'd seen it with my eyes, my brain never understood it until how. I shuddered. I hoped I would not remember too many other things. I forced my mind back to the mother who had given me her infant, Mrs. Tupper. I had glanced back after I ran and seen her struggling to run carrying the older child. She hadn't been able to keep up to the people ahead of her and she would not put the child down. There was not much reason to suppose she had lived.

The morgue was set up near the Bridge Hotel and the bodies were being carried there.

I sat on a rock and stared at the people moving around me. Stanley tied Homer to the bridge works and began to search for his friends. I saw Maude. I was so glad to see her I forgot her injunction to ignore her in public and flew from my perch to grab her by the shoulders.

"Maude! You made it!"

We stared at each other in silence for a moment and then I really looked at her and was astounded to see she was made up as carefully as usual. Her hat had no burn marks and she looked to be the only properly dressed woman around.

"Where were you?"

She led me a little away from others. "I was in the Regina Hotel."

Stanley came up and I introduced him without a thought of reputation or contamination.

"In the Regina Hotel?" Stanley was enthralled- "How did you survive?"

"There were several gentlemen there," Maude said.

Dear God, I thought to myself. *How does she do it? Several at once!* I was caught between admiration and pity. Then: *Don't be silly, Amy. They just happened to be in the hotel.*

"They beat the flames as the fire ignited the wood. We managed to put out every fire that started. I don't know how. Luck and providence, I guess. We could hardly believe we'd survived. When we went outside after the fire and saw we were in the only building left standing, well, we just walked back into the bar and helped ourselves to a drink."

"Congratulations," Stanley said.

"I feel lucky," Maude agreed.

"I hear John Boultbee and Mr. Johnson lay down in the earth and buried their faces in the dirt."

"And lived?"

"And lived," Stanley said.

I thought of the ferocity of the fire. "I don't understand why they weren't killed."

We shook our heads, but in the next hour or so we heard many such odd stories. The native people from the village across the water had launched their dugout canoes and rescued many who had run into the water. They were feeding them and looking after them in their village. Mr. Carswell had died in the well where he had hoped to find protection. The fire swept over the well and sucked up the good air. A young man, named Johnson, whom I didn't know, and his mother were found in the same well. Mrs. Tupper had died as well as the child she was trying to save, and Frank, of course. I had given Frank up for dead when he had insisted on going back for the guns. I knew then Frank's greed was such that he would not have left a profitable cargo. They found his remains near his horse surrounded by the brass hoops of the barrels and the iron of the guns.

I would tell Robert and Stanley and Maude about Frank later. They should know he had been running the guns to the Métis. Someone should check into Mr. Sanders too to see if he survived the fire. The provincial police and the Royal North West Mounted needed to know that particular smuggling route from San Francisco would not be supplying the North West with guns now.

I would mourn Frank in my own time, at some other time. Not now. He had betrayed us all. But he had qualities that were quite wonderful, and he had been an exciting person to know. My disappointment in his character was not sufficient that I could rejoice at his death. I could only wish he had chosen to let the guns burn.

"And they say the mayor swore in Jackson Abray as a special constable to rescue the barrels of whiskey someone had sent into the inlet." Stanley picked up that bit of information.

I thought that particular action typical of the city's priorities.

"I hear Waller escaped out of the back of his restaurant but had his hair burned right off his head."

"Is he all right?" I asked Maude.

"Apparently," she shrugged. "He just lost his hair."

"You look good," I said admiringly.

"I'll need my looks." Maude turned toward the west and stared at the remains of the city. 'I kept my money in the Granville Hotel. It's all gone now." She made the statement without pathos and almost without emotion. "

"It would be a good time to start a bakery," I said.

"With what?" This time her voice held irony and bitterness.

"You want to start a bakery?" Stanley said, cheerfully ignoring Maude's tragedy. I don't think Stanley was unaware of Maude's profession. He couldn't have worked around the Granville Hotel as long as he had without understanding the nature of Maude's business.

"I had planned to do so," Maude said quietly, "but I don't have the capital to buy a shop, oven and the equipment I need."

"Well," Stanley said. "Maybe we could do a deal."

Maude and I turned to him.

"I have an idea," Stanley said. "that Vancouver is going to build itself up again. I think it's really going to grow. I've got some money in the Hastings Mill safe and I could finance you a little way. Stake you like miner," he said seriously. "I could go the lot, and a building and an oven, I think. I've got that much. Maybe you could borrow the rest from someone else. You give me fifty percent of the profits for five years and I'll set you up. After that you can buy me out if you like."

Maude stared at him. "Agreed," she said succinctly, "but we'll have to negotiate those terms."

I sat back on my stump and looked out over the crowd. Robert still moved among the people. This time he had a pencil and notebook, no doubt purloined from the mill office. He seemed to be writing down names and facts and only pausing a moment when the wagonload of supplies arrived from New Westminster. The people of New Westminster had responded to our plight with blankets and food. We would be all right for tonight.

Maude and Stanley continued to discuss their business.

Robert came over to me and laid his arm on my shoulder.

"Are you all right?"

I nodded. "Stanley and Maude and I will go back to the mill and stay with friends there. Probably at Jack's place or perhaps friends of Lydia's. Look for us at Jack's later. I suppose you are going to stay and get every last piece of information out of the survivors."

He looked at me sharply. "Naturally."

'I hate to tell you this, Robert, but you don't have a printing press now."

"I'll have one by next week. In fact, the whole town is going rebuild inside of a month, you wait and see."

I smiled. He was probably right. There was little discouraging talk of returning east. Scraps of conversation I heard were much in the line of Stanley's and Maude's—building, reconstructing.

"You'll have clothes, and food and a house and home and me," he said grinning. He had leaned closer, and his face was only inches from mine.

I looked at him steadily for a moment.

His grin started to fade, and I reached up and stroked his cheek. "We'll talk about it, Robert."

He squeezed my hand and then swung back toward the crowd. He had much to do tonight.

We ate some of the food sent by the Knights of Labour from Westminster and then told the mayor we were going back to the mill. We sent Stanley on ahead to warn Lydia we were coming and then Maude and I walked back down Westminster Road.

"I can hardly believe I will be able to start the bakery." Maude was exultant. 'The fire was the end of my first life. Today is the beginning of my next one. I'm going to order one of those new stoves from San Francisco. It has a hot water reservoir on it and a big warming oven." She brightened and walked more quickly as she talked about her plans.

I hated to dampen her spirits, but I didn't want her deluded about the extent of Stanley's wealth.

"He doesn't have a lot of money, you know. Maude. He could perhaps buy the ovens or maybe the lot, but I don't know how much he can do."

"I know, Amy. It doesn't matter. He has me believing I can do it. After all, the rest of the businessmen in town have to borrow money. I don't see why some of that borrowed money shouldn't come my way." She walked in silence for a moment and then said. "Stanley gave me faith, Amy. He seemed to believe I could open a bakery shop. It seemed the most sensible thing in the world when we were talking. I came away from him believing I could do it. Stanley's been very good for me. I'll take the money he can spare and give him a percentage of the profits. Not fifty percent, of course."

"Good. He'll be happy."

We walked on. The darkness mingled with the smoke bringing a warm, early twilight. No one would suffer by being forced to sleep outside at the bridge. I thought about Robert. I remembered him waiting while the fire bore down on him, waiting for me. I remembered him pushing me into the water, helping me onto the raft. I remembered him talking to the men on the ship but looking back every once in a while to smile at me. I wondered what a brace of little Roberts would look like: blue eyes, bright red hair, and shiny faces.

"Maude, all those things you told me the first day we met, about having children and not having children. Could you tell me again?"

She looked at me sharply. "Are you going to take on Mr. Carr?"

"I suppose so."

She nodded. "We'll have a long talk."

The smell of charcoal and resin was strong. Smoke occasionally blew our way stinging our eyes and irritating our throats. We were in no danger. There was nothing left to burn. The embers of the fire grew bright then faded as the slight breeze passed over them. It looked like a fairyland of glowing light and darkness; the darkness hiding the tragedy. Tomorrow the men would look for more bodies to transport to the makeshift morgue at the Bridge Hotel.

Tonight, we walked back to the mill in an odd, magical wasteland of black night and the flickering embers of the afternoon's fire. In spite of the tragedy and horror of the day, in spite of Frank, and the many lives lost, in spite of the sorrows that were to come, I felt an odd kind of contentment as though I had become part of this country. zzzzz